Penguin Books

Ukridge

P. G. Wodehouse was born in 1881, and
educated at Dulwich College. He was in the
Hong Kong and Shanghai Bank for two years
and then got a job on the 'By the Way'
column of the old *Globe*. His first stories were
school stories written for *The Captain*, in one
of which Psmith made his first appearance. He
paid a visit to America in 1904, and another in
1909 when he sold two short stories for $300
apiece, and decided to remain there. Eventually
he sold a serial to the *Saturday Evening Post*,
and for the next twenty-five years almost all
his books appeared first in this magazine. In
1906 he wrote some lyrics to music by Jerome
Kern, and some years later he formed a
partnership with Guy Bolton, which resulted
in a number of shows and straight plays. Mr
Wodehouse worked at plays with George
Grossmith and Ian Hay, and has made some
adaptations. He has written seventy books,
many of which are published in Penguins.

UKRIDGE

P. G. Wodehouse

Penguin Books

Penguin Books Ltd, Harmondsworth,
Middlesex, England
Penguin Books Australia Ltd, Ringwood,
Victoria, Australia

First published by Herbert Jenkins 1924
Published in Penguin Books 1964
Reissued 1973

Made and printed in Great Britain by
C. Nicholls & Company Ltd
Set in Linotype Pilgrim

Contents

Chapter 1

Ukridge's Dog College

'Laddie,' said Stanley Featherstonehaugh Ukridge, that much-enduring man, helping himself to my tobacco and slipping the pouch absently into his pocket, 'listen to me, you son of Belial.'

'What?' I said, retrieving the pouch.

'Do you want to make an enormous fortune?'

'I do.'

'Then write my biography. Bung it down on paper, and we'll split the proceeds. I've been making a pretty close study of your stuff lately, old horse, and it's all wrong. The trouble with you is that you don't plumb the well-springs of human nature and all that. You just think up some rotten yarn about some-dam'-thing-or-other and shove it down. Now, if you tackled my life, you'd have something worth writing about. Pots of money in it, my boy – English serial rights and American serial rights and book rights, and dramatic rights and movie rights – well, you can take it from me that, at a conservative estimate, we should clean up at least fifty thousand pounds apiece.'

'As much as that?'

'Fully that. And listen, laddie, I'll tell you what. You're a good chap and we've been pals for years, so I'll let you have my share of the English serial rights for a hundred pounds down.'

'What makes you think I've got a hundred pounds?'

'Well, then, I'll make it my share of the English *and* American serial rights for fifty.'

'Your collar's come off its stud.'

'How about my complete share of the whole dashed outfit for twenty-five?'

'Not for me, thanks.'

'Then I'll tell you what, old horse,' said Ukridge, inspired. 'Just lend me half a crown to be going on with.'

If the leading incidents of S. F. Ukridge's disreputable career are to be given to the public – and not, as some might suggest, decently hushed up – I suppose I am the man to write them. Ukridge and I have been intimate since the days of school. Together we sported on the green, and when he was expelled no one missed him more than I. An unfortunate business, this expulsion. Ukridge's generous spirit, ever ill-attuned to school rules, caused him eventually to break the solemnest of them all by sneaking out at night to try his skill at the coco-nut-shies of the local village fair; and his foresight in putting on scarlet whiskers and a false nose for the expedition was completely neutralized by the fact that he absent-mindedly wore his school cap throughout the entire proceedings. He left the next morning, regretted by all.

After this there was a hiatus of some years in our friendship. I was at Cambridge, absorbing culture, and Ukridge, as far as I could gather from his rare letters and the reports of mutual acquaintances, flitting about the world like a snipe. Somebody met him in New York, just off a cattle-ship. Somebody else saw him in Buenos Ayres. Somebody, again, spoke sadly of having been pounced on by him at Monte Carlo and touched for a fiver. It was not until I settled down in London that he came back into my life. We met in Piccadilly one day, and resumed our relations where they had been broken off. Old associations are strong, and the fact that he was about my build and so could wear my socks and shirts drew us very close together.

Then he disappeared again, and it was a month or more before I got news of him.

It was George Tupper who brought the news. George was head of the school in my last year, and he has fulfilled exactly the impeccable promise of those early days. He is in the Foreign Office, doing well and much respected. He has an earnest, pulpy heart and takes other people's troubles very seriously. Often he had mourned to me like a father over Ukridge's erratic progress through life, and now, as he spoke, he seemed to be filled with a solemn joy, as over a reformed prodigal.

'Have you heard about Ukridge?' said George Tupper. 'He has settled down at last. Gone to live with an aunt of his who owns one of those big houses on Wimbledon Common. A very rich woman. I am delighted. It will be the making of the old chap.'

I suppose he was right in a way, but to me this tame subsidence into companionship with a rich aunt in Wimbledon seemed somehow an indecent, almost a tragic, end to a colourful career like that of S. F. Ukridge. And when I met the man a week later my heart grew heavier still.

It was in Oxford Street at the hour when women come up from the suburbs to shop; and he was standing among the dogs and commissionaires outside Selfridge's. His arms were full of parcels, his face was set in a mask of wan discomfort, and he was so beautifully dressed that for an instant I did not recognize him. Everything which the Correct Man wears was assembled on his person, from the silk hat to the patent-leather boots; and, as he confided to me in the first minute, he was suffering the tortures of the damned. The boots pinched him, the hat hurt his forehead, and the collar was worse than the hat and boots combined.

'She makes me wear them,' he said, moodily, jerking his head towards the interior of the store and uttering a sharp howl as the movement caused the collar to gouge his neck.

'Still,' I said, trying to turn his mind to happier things, 'you must be having a great time. George Tupper tells me that your aunt is rich. I suppose you're living off the fat of the land.'

'The browsing and sluicing are good,' admitted Ukridge. 'But it's a wearing life, laddie. A wearing life, old horse.'

'Why don't you come and see me sometimes?'

'I'm not allowed out at night.'

'Well, shall I come and see you?'

A look of poignant alarm shot out from under the silk hat.

'Don't dream of it, laddie,' said Ukridge, earnestly. 'Don't dream of it. You're a good chap – my best pal and all that sort of thing – but the fact is, my standing in the home's none too solid even now, and one sight of you would knock my prestige into hash. Aunt Julia would think you worldly.'

'I'm not worldly.'

'Well, you look worldly. You wear a squash hat and a soft collar. If you don't mind my suggesting it, old horse, I think, if I were you, I'd pop off now before she comes out. Good-bye, laddie.'

'Ichabod!' I murmured sadly to myself as I passed on down Oxford Street. 'Ichabod!'

I should have had more faith. I should have known my Ukridge better. I should have realized that a London suburb could no more imprison that great man permanently than Elba did Napoleon.

One afternoon, as I let myself into the house in Ebury Street of which I rented at that time the bedroom and sitting-room on the first floor, I came upon Bowles, my landlord, standing in listening attitude at the foot of the stairs.

'Good afternoon, sir,' said Bowles. 'A gentleman is waiting to see you. I fancy I heard him calling me a moment ago.'

'Who is he?'

'A Mr Ukridge, sir. He –'

A vast voice boomed out from above.

'Bowles, old horse!'

Bowles, like all other proprietors of furnished apartments in the south-western district of London, was an ex-butler, and about him, as about all ex-butlers, there clung like a garment an aura of dignified superiority which had never failed to crush my spirit. He was a man of portly aspect, with a bald head and prominent eyes of a lightish green – eyes that seemed to weigh me dispassionately and find me wanting. 'H'm!' they seemed to say. 'Young – very young. And not at all what I have been accustomed to in the best places.' To hear this dignitary addressed – and in a shout at that – as 'old horse' affected me with much the same sense of imminent chaos as would afflict a devout young curate if he saw his bishop slapped on the back. The shock, therefore, when he responded not merely mildly but with what almost amounted to camaraderie was numbing.

'Sir?' cooed Bowles.

'Bring me six bones and a corkscrew.'

'Very good, sir.'

Bowles retired, and I bounded upstairs and flung open the door of my sitting-room.

'Great Scott!' I said, blankly.

The place was a sea of Pekingese dogs. Later investigation reduced their numbers to six, but in that first moment there seemed to be hundreds. Goggling eyes met mine wherever I looked. The room was a forest of waving tails. With his back against the mantelpiece, smoking placidly, stood Ukridge.

'Hallo, laddie!' he said, with a genial wave of the hand, as if to make me free of the place. 'You're just in time. I've got to dash off and catch a train in a quarter of an hour. Stop it, you mutts!' he bellowed, and the six Pekingese, who had been barking steadily since my arrival, stopped in mid-yap, and were still. Ukridge's personality seemed to exercise a magnetism over the animal kingdom, from ex-butlers to Pekes, which bordered on the uncanny. 'I'm off to Sheep's Cray, in Kent. Taken a cottage there.'

'Are you going to live there?'

'Yes.'

'But what about your aunt?'

'Oh, I've left her. Life is stern and life is earnest, and if I mean to make a fortune I've got to bustle about and not stay cooped up in a place like Wimbledon.'

'Something in that.'

'Besides which, she told me the very sight of me made her sick and she never wanted to see me again.'

I might have guessed, directly I saw him, that some upheaval had taken place. The sumptuous raiment which had made him such a treat to the eye at our last meeting was gone, and he was back in his pre-Wimbledon costume, which was, as the advertisements say, distinctly individual. Over grey flannel trousers, a golf coat, and a brown sweater he wore like a royal robe a bright yellow mackintosh. His collar had broken free from its stud and showed a couple of inches of bare neck. His hair was disordered, and his masterful nose was topped by a pair of steel-rimmed pince-nez cunningly attached to his flapping ears with ginger-beer wire. His whole appearance spelled revolt.

Bowles manifested himself with a plateful of bones.

'That's right. Chuck 'em down on the floor.'

'Very good, sir.'

'I like that fellow,' said Ukridge, as the door closed. 'We had a dashed interesting talk before you came in. Did you know he had a cousin on the music-halls?'

'He hasn't confided in me much.'

'He's promised me an introduction to him later on. May be

useful to be in touch with a man who knows the ropes. You see, laddie, I've hit on the most amazing scheme.' He swept his arm round dramatically, overturning a plaster cast of the Infant Samuel at Prayer. 'All right, all right, you can mend it with glue or something, and anyway, you're probably better without it. Yessir, I've hit on a great scheme. The idea of a thousand years.'

'What's that?'

'I'm going to train dogs.'

'Train dogs?'

'For the music-hall stage. Dog acts, you know. Performing dogs. Pots of money in it. I start in a modest way with these six. When I've taught 'em a few tricks, I sell them to a fellow in the profession for a large sum and buy twelve more. I train those, sell 'em for a large sum, and with the money buy twenty-four more. I train those –'

'Here, wait a minute.' My head was beginning to swim. I had a vision of England paved with Pekingese dogs, all doing tricks. 'How do you know you'll be able to sell them?'

'Of course I shall. The demand's enormous. Supply can't cope with it. At a conservative estimate I should think I ought to scoop in four or five thousand pounds the first year. That, of course, is before the business really starts to expand.'

'I see.'

'When I get going properly, with a dozen assistants under me and an organized establishment, I shall begin to touch the big money. What I'm aiming at is a sort of Dog's College out in the country somewhere. Big place with a lot of ground. Regular classes and a set curriculum. Large staff, each member of it with so many dogs under his care, me looking on and superintending. Why, once the thing starts moving it'll run itself, and all I shall have to do will be to sit back and endorse the cheques. It isn't as if I would have to confine my operations to England. The demand for performing dogs is universal throughout the civilized world. America wants performing dogs. Australia wants performing dogs. Africa could do with a few, I've no doubt. My aim, laddie, is gradually to get a monopoly of the trade. I want everybody who needs a performing dog of any description to come automatically to me. And I'll tell you what, laddie. If you like to put up a bit of capital, I'll let you in on the ground floor.'

'No, thanks.'

'All right. Have it your own way. Only don't forget that there was a fellow who put nine hundred dollars into the Ford Car business when it was starting and he collected a cool forty million. I say, is that clock right? Great Scott! I'll be missing my train. Help me mobilize these dashed animals.'

Five minutes later, accompanied by the six Pekingese and bearing about him a pound of my tobacco, three pairs of my socks, and the remains of a bottle of whisky, Ukridge departed in a taxi-cab for Charing Cross Station to begin his life-work.

Perhaps six weeks passed, six quiet Ukridgeless weeks, and then one morning I received an agitated telegram. Indeed, it was not so much a telegram as a cry of anguish. In every word of it there breathed the tortured spirit of a great man who has battled in vain against overwhelming odds. It was the sort of telegram which Job might have sent off after a lengthy session with Bildad the Shuhite:

Come here immediately, laddie. Life and death matter, old horse. Desperate situation. Don't fail me.

It stirred me like a bugle: I caught the next train.

The White Cottage, Sheep's Cray – destined, presumably, to become in future years an historic spot and a Mecca for dog-loving pilgrims – was a small and battered building standing near the main road to London at some distance from the village. I found it without difficulty, for Ukridge seemed to have achieved a certain celebrity in the neighbourhood; but to effect an entry was a harder task. I rapped for a full minute without result, then shouted; and I was about to conclude that Ukridge was not at home when the door suddenly opened. As I was just giving a final bang at the moment, I entered the house in a manner reminiscent of one of the Ballet Russe practising a new and difficult step.

'Sorry, old horse,' said Ukridge. 'Wouldn't have kept you waiting if I'd known who it was. Thought you were Gooch, the grocer – goods supplied to the value of six pounds three and a penny.'

'I see.'

'He keeps hounding me for his beastly money,' said Ukridge, bitterly, as he led the way into the sitting-room. 'It's a little hard. Upon my Sam it's a little hard. I come down here to in-augurate a vast business and do the natives a bit of good by establishing a growing industry in their midst, and the first thing you know they turn round and bite the hand that was go-ing to feed them. I've been hampered and rattled by these blood-suckers ever since I got here. A little trust, a little sympathy, a little of the good old give-and-take spirit – that was all I asked. And what happened? They wanted a bit on account! Kept bothering me for a bit on account, I'll trouble you, just when I needed all my thoughts and all my energy and every ounce of concentration at my command for my extraordinarily difficult and delicate work. *I* couldn't give them a bit on account. Later on, if they had only exercised reasonable patience, I would no doubt have been in a position to settle their infernal bills fifty times over. But the time was not ripe. I reasoned with the men. I said, "Here am I, a busy man, trying hard to educate six Pek-ingese dogs for music-hall stage, and you come distracting my attention and impairing my efficiency by babbling about a bit on account. It isn't the pull-together spirit," I said. "It isn't the spirit that wins to wealth. These narrow petty-cash ideas can never make for success." But no, they couldn't see it. They started calling here at all hours and waylaying me in the public highways till life became an absolute curse. And now what do you think has happened?'

'What?'

'The dogs.'

'Got distemper?'

'No. Worse. My landlord's pinched them as security for his infernal rent! Sneaked the stock. Tied up the assets. Crippled the business at the very outset. Have you ever in your life heard of anything so dastardly? I know I agreed to pay the damned rent weekly and I'm about six weeks behind, but, my gosh! surely a man with a huge enterprise on his hands isn't supposed to have to worry about these trifles when he's occupied with the most delicate – Well, I put all that to old Nickerson, but a fat lot of good it did. So then I wired to you.'

'Ah!' I said, and there was a brief and pregnant pause.

'I thought,' said Ukridge, meditatively, 'that you might be able to suggest somebody I could touch.'

He spoke in a detached and almost casual way, but his eye was gleaming at me significantly, and I avoided it with a sense of guilt. My finances at the moment were in their customary unsettled condition – rather more so, in fact, than usual, owing to unsatisfactory speculations at Kempton Park on the previous Saturday; and it seemed to me that, if ever there was a time for passing the buck, this was it. I mused tensely. It was an occasion for quick thinking.

'George Tupper!' I cried, on the crest of a brain-wave.

'George Tupper?' echoed Ukridge, radiantly, his gloom melting like a fog before the sun. 'The very man, by Gad! It's a most amazing thing, but I never thought of him. George Tupper, of course! Big-hearted George, the old school-chum. He'll do it like a shot and won't miss the money. These Foreign Office blokes have always got a spare tenner or two tucked away in the old sock. They pinch it out of the public funds. Rush back to town, laddie, with all speed, get hold of Tuppy, lush him up, and bite his ear for twenty quid. Now is the time for all good men to come to the aid of the party.'

I had been convinced that George Tupper would not fail us, nor did he. He parted without a murmur – even with enthusiasm. The consignment was one that might have been made to order for him. As a boy, George used to write sentimental poetry for the school magazine, and now he is the sort of man who is always starting subscription lists and getting up memorials and presentations. He listened to my story with the serious official air which these Foreign Office fellows put on when they are deciding whether to declare war on Switzerland or send a firm note to San Marino, and was reaching for his cheque-book before I had been speaking two minutes. Ukridge's sad case seemed to move him deeply.

'Too bad,' said George. 'So he is training dogs, is he? Well, it seems very unfair that, if he has at last settled down to real work, he should be hampered by financial difficulties at the outset. We ought to do something practical for him. After all, a loan of twenty pounds cannot relieve the situation permanently.'

'I think you're a bit optimistic if you're looking on it as a loan.'

'What Ukridge needs is capital.'

'He thinks that, too. So does Gooch, the grocer.'

'Capital,' repeated George Tupper, firmly, as if he were reasoning with the plenipotentiary of some Great Power. 'Every venture requires capital at first.' He frowned thoughtfully. 'Where can we obtain capital for Ukridge?'

'Rob a bank.'

George Tupper's face cleared.

'I have it!' he said. 'I will go straight over to Wimbledon tonight and approach his aunt.'

'Aren't you forgetting that Ukridge is about as popular with her as a cold welsh rabbit?'

'There may be a temporary estrangement, but if I tell her the facts and impress upon her that Ukridge is really making a genuine effort to earn a living –'

'Well, try it if you like. But she will probably set the parrot on to you.'

'It will have to be done diplomatically, of course. It might be as well if you did not tell Ukridge what I propose to do. I do not wish to arouse hopes which may not be fulfilled.'

A blaze of yellow on the platform of Sheep's Cray Station next morning informed me that Ukridge had come to meet my train. The sun poured down from a cloudless sky, but it took more than sunshine to make Stanley Featherstonehaugh Ukridge discard his mackintosh. He looked like an animated blob of mustard.

When the train rolled in, he was standing in solitary grandeur trying to light his pipe, but as I got out I perceived that he had been joined by a sad-looking man, who, from the rapid and earnest manner in which he talked and the vehemence of his gesticulations, appeared to be ventilating some theme on which he felt deeply. Ukridge was looking warm and harassed, and, as I approached, I could hear his voice booming in reply.

'My dear sir, my dear old horse, do be reasonable, do try to cultivate the big, broad flexible outlook –'

He saw me and broke away – not unwillingly; and, gripping my arm, drew me off along the platform. The sad-looking man followed irresolutely.

'Have you got the stuff, laddie?' inquired Ukridge, in a tense whisper. 'Have you got it?'

'Yes, here it is.'

'Put it back, put it back!' moaned Ukridge in agony, as I felt in my pocket. 'Do you know who that was I was talking to? Gooch, the grocer!'

'Goods supplied to the value of six pounds three and a penny?'

'Absolutely!'

'Well, now's your chance. Fling him a purse of gold. That'll make him look silly.'

'My dear old horse, I can't afford to go about the place squandering my cash simply in order to make grocers look silly. That money is earmarked for Nickerson, my landlord.'

'Oh! I say, I think the six-pounds-three-and-a-penny bird is following us.'

'Then for goodness' sake, laddie, let's get a move on! If that man knew we had twenty quid on us, our lives wouldn't be safe. He'd make one spring.'

He hurried me out of the station and led the way up a shady lane that wound off through the fields, slinking furtively 'like one that on a lonesome road doth walk in fear and dread, and having once looked back walks on and turns no more his head, because he knows a frightful fiend doth close behind him tread'. As a matter of fact, the frightful fiend had given up the pursuit after the first few steps, and a moment later I drew this fact to Ukridge's attention, for it was not the sort of day on which to break walking records unnecessarily.

He halted, relieved, and mopped his spacious brow with a handkerchief which I recognized as having once been my property.

'Thank goodness we've shaken him off,' he said. 'Not a bad chap in his way, I believe – a good husband and father, I'm told, and sings in the church choir. But no vision. That's what he lacks, old horse – vision. He can't understand that all vast industrial enterprises have been built up on a system of liberal and cheerful credit. Won't realize that credit is the life-blood of commerce. Without credit commerce has no elasticity. And if commerce has no elasticity what dam' good is it?'

'I don't know.'

'Nor does anybody else. Well, now that he's gone, you can give me that money. Did old Tuppy cough up cheerfully?'

'Blithely.'

'I knew it,' said Ukridge, deeply moved, 'I knew it. A good fellow. One of the best. I've always liked Tuppy. A man you can rely on. Some day, when I get going on a big scale, he shall have this back a thousandfold. I'm glad you brought small notes.'

'Why?'

'I want to scatter 'em about on the table in front of this Nickerson blighter.'

'Is this where he lives?'

We had come to a red-roofed house, set back from the road amidst trees. Ukridge wielded the knocker forcefully.

'Tell Mr Nickerson,' he said to the maid, 'that Mr Ukridge has called and would like a word.'

About the demeanour of the man who presently entered the room into which we had been shown there was that subtle but well-marked something which stamps your creditor all the world over. Mr Nickerson was a man of medium height, almost completely surrounded by whiskers, and through the shrubbery he gazed at Ukridge with frozen eyes, shooting out waves of deleterious animal magnetism. You could see at a glance that he was not fond of Ukridge. Take him for all in all, Mr Nickerson looked like one of the less amiable prophets of the Old Testament about to interview the captive monarch of the Amalekites.

'Well?' he said, and I have never heard the word spoken in a more forbidding manner.

'I've come about the rent.'

'Ah!' said Mr Nickerson, guardedly.

'To pay it,' said Ukridge.

'To pay it!' ejaculated Mr Nickerson, incredulously.

'Here!' said Ukridge, and with a superb gesture flung money on the table.

I understood now why the massive-minded man had wanted small notes. They made a brave display. There was a light breeze blowing in through the open window, and so musical a rustling did it set up as it played about the heaped-up wealth that Mr Nickerson's austerity seemed to vanish like breath off a razor-blade. For a moment a dazed look came into his eyes and he swayed slightly; then, as he started to gather up the money, he took on the benevolent air of a bishop blessing pilgrims. As far as Mr Nickerson was concerned, the sun was up.

'Why, thank you, Mr Ukridge, I'm sure,' he said. 'Thank you very much. No hard feelings, I trust?'

'Not on my side, old horse,' responded Ukridge, affably. 'Business is business.'

'Exactly.'

'Well, I may as well take those dogs now,' said Ukridge, helping himself to a cigar from a box which he had just discovered on the mantelpiece and putting a couple more in his pocket in the friendliest way. 'The sooner they're back with me, the better. They've lost a day's education as it is.'

'Why, certainly, Mr Ukridge; certainly. They are in the shed at the bottom of the garden. I will get them for you at once.'

He retreated through the door, babbling ingratiatingly.

'Amazing how fond these blokes are of money,' sighed Ukridge. 'It's a thing I don't like to see. Sordid, I call it. That blighter's eyes were gleaming, positively gleaming, laddie, as he scooped up the stuff. Good cigars these,' he added, pocketing three more.

There was a faltering footstep outside, and Mr Nickerson re-entered the room. The man appeared to have something on his mind. A glassy look was in his whisker-bordered eyes, and his mouth, though it was not easy to see it through the jungle, seemed to me to be sagging mournfully. He resembled a minor prophet who has been hit behind the ear with a stuffed eel-skin.

'Mr Ukridge!'

'Hallo?'

'The – the little dogs!'

'Well?'

'The little dogs!'

'What about them?'

'They have gone!'

'Gone?'

'Run away!'

'Run away? How the devil could they run away?'

'There seems to have been a loose board at the back of the shed. The little dogs must have wriggled through. There is no trace of them to be found.'

Ukridge flung up his arms despairingly. He swelled like a captive balloon. His pince-nez rocked on his nose, his mackintosh flapped menacingly, and his collar sprang off its stud. He brought his fist down with a crash on the table.

'Upon my Sam!'

'I am extremely sorry –'

'Upon my Sam!' cried Ukridge. 'It's hard. It's pretty hard. I come down here to inaugurate a great business, which would eventually have brought trade and prosperity to the whole neighbourhood, and I have hardly had time to turn round and attend to the preliminary details of the enterprise when this man comes and sneaks my dogs. And now he tells me with a light laugh –'

'Mr Ukridge, I assure you –'

'Tells me with a light laugh that they've gone. Gone! Gone where? Why, dash it, they may be all over the county. A fat chance I've got of ever seeing them again. Six valuable Pekingese, already educated practically to the stage where they could have been sold at an enormous profit –'

Mr Nickerson was fumbling guiltily, and now he produced from his pocket a crumpled wad of notes, which he thrust agitatedly upon Ukridge, who waved them away with loathing.

'This gentleman,' boomed Ukridge, indicating me with a sweeping gesture, 'happens to be a lawyer. It is extremely lucky that he chanced to come down today to pay me a visit. Have you followed the proceedings closely?'

I said I had followed them very closely.

'Is it your opinion that an action will lie?'

I said it seemed highly probable, and this expert ruling appeared to put the final touch on Mr Nickerson's collapse. Almost tearfully he urged the notes on Ukridge.

'What's this?' said Ukridge, loftily.

'I – I thought, Mr Ukridge, that, if it were agreeable to you, you might consent to take your money back, and – and consider the episode closed.'

Ukridge turned to me with raised eyebrows.

'Ha!' he cried. 'Ha, ha!'

'Ha, ha!' I chorused, dutifully.

'He thinks that he can close the episode by giving me my money back. Isn't that rich?'

'Fruity,' I agreed.

'Those dogs were worth hundreds of pounds, and he thinks he can square me with a rotten twenty. Would you have believed it if you hadn't heard it with your own ears, old horse?'

'Never!'

'I'll tell you what I'll do,' said Ukridge, after thought. 'I'll take this money.' Mr Nickerson thanked him. 'And there are one or two trifling accounts which want settling with some of the local tradesmen. You will square those –'

'Certainly, Mr Ukridge, certainly.'

'And after that – well, I'll have to think it over. If I decide to institute proceedings my lawyer will communicate with you in due course.'

And we left the wretched man, cowering despicably behind his whiskers.

It seemed to me, as we passed down the tree-shaded lane and out into the white glare of the road, that Ukridge was bearing himself in his hour of disaster with a rather admirable fortitude. His stock-in-trade, the life-blood of his enterprise, was scattered all over Kent, probably never to return, and all that he had to show on the other side of the balance-sheet was the cancelling of a few weeks' back rent and the paying-off of Gooch, the grocer, and his friends. It was a situation which might well have crushed the spirit of an ordinary man, but Ukridge seemed by no means dejected. Jaunty, rather. His eyes shone behind their pince-nez and he whistled a rollicking air. When presently he began to sing, I felt that it was time to create a diversion.

'What are you going to do?' I asked.

'Who, me?' said Ukridge, buoyantly. 'Oh, I'm coming back to town on the next train. You don't mind hoofing it to the next station, do you? It's only five miles. It might be a trifle risky to start from Sheep's Cray.'

'Why risky?'

'Because of the dogs, of course.'

'Dogs?'

Ukridge hummed a gay strain.

'Oh, yes. I forgot to tell you about that. I've got 'em.'

'What?'

'Yes. I went out late last night and pinched them out of the shed.' He chuckled amusedly. 'Perfectly simple. Only needed a clear, level head. I borrowed a dead cat and tied a string to it, legged it to old Nickerson's garden after dark, dug a board out of the back of the shed, and shoved my head down and chirruped. The dogs came trickling out, and I hared off, towing old Colonel Cat on his string. Great run while it lasted, laddie. Hounds picked up the scent right away and started off in a bunch at fifty miles an hour. Cat and I doing a steady fifty-five. Thought every minute old Nickerson would hear and start blazing away with a gun, but nothing happened. I led the pack across country for a run of twenty minutes without a check, parked the dogs in my sitting-room, and so to bed. Took it out of me, by gosh! Not so young as I was.'

I was silent for a moment, conscious of a feeling almost of reverence. This man was undoubtedly spacious. There had always been something about Ukridge that dulled the moral sense.

'Well,' I said at length, 'you've certainly got vision.'

'Yes?' said Ukridge, gratified.

'*And* the big, broad, flexible outlook.'

'Got to, laddie, nowadays. The foundation of a successful business career.'

'And what's the next move?'

We were drawing near to the White Cottage. It stood and broiled in the sunlight, and I hoped that there might be something cool to drink inside it. The window of the sitting-room was open, and through it came the yapping of Pekingese.

'Oh, I shall find another cottage somewhere else,' said Ukridge, eyeing his little home with a certain sentimentality. 'That won't be hard. Lots of cottages all over the place. And then I shall buckle down to serious work. You'll be astounded at the progress I've made already. In a minute I'll show you what those dogs can do.'

'They can bark all right.'

'Yes. They seem excited about something. You know, laddie, I've had a great idea. When I saw you at your rooms my scheme was to specialize in performing dogs for the music-halls – what you might call professional dogs. But I've been thinking it over, and now I don't see why I shouldn't go in for developing amateur talent as well. Say you have a dog – Fido, the household pet – and you think it would brighten the home if he could do a few tricks from time to time. Well, you're a busy man you haven't the time to give up to teaching him. So you just tie a label to his collar and ship him off for a month to the Ukridge Dog College, and back he comes, thoroughly educated. No trouble, no worry, easy terms. Upon my Sam, I'm not sure there isn't more money in the amateur branch than in the professional. I don't see why eventually dog owners shouldn't send their dogs to me as a regular thing, just as they send their sons to Eton and Winchester. My golly! this idea's beginning to develop. I'll tell you what – how would it be to issue special collars to all dogs which have graduated from my college? Something distinctive which everybody would recognize. See what I mean? Sort of badge of honour. Fellow with a dog entitled to wear the Ukridge collar would be in a position to look down on the bloke whose dog hadn't got one. Gradually it would get so that anybody in a decent social position would be ashamed to be seen out with a non-Ukridge dog. The thing would become a landslide. Dogs would pour in from all corners of the country. More work than I could handle. Have to start branches. The scheme's colossal. Millions in it, my boy! Millions!' He paused with his fingers on the handle of the front door. 'Of course,' he went on, 'just at present it's no good blinking the fact that I'm hampered and handicapped by lack of funds and can only approach the thing on a small scale. What it amounts to, laddie, is that somehow or other I've got to get capital.'

It seemed the moment to spring the glad news.

'I promised him I wouldn't mention it,' I said, 'for fear it might lead to disappointment, but as a matter of fact George Tupper is trying to raise some capital for you. I left him last night starting out to get it.'

'George Tupper!' – Ukridge's eyes dimmed with a not

unmanly emotion – 'George Tupper! By Gad, that fellow is the salt of the earth. Good, loyal fellow! A true friend. A man you can rely on. Upon my Sam, if there were more fellows about like old Tuppy, there wouldn't be all this modern pessimism and unrest. Did he seem to have any idea where he could raise a bit of capital for me?'

'Yes. He went round to tell your aunt about your coming down here to train those Pekes, and – What's the matter?'

A fearful change had come over Ukridge's jubilant front. His eyes bulged, his jaw sagged. With the addition of a few feet of grey whiskers he would have looked exactly like the recent Mr Nickerson.

'My aunt?' he mumbled, swaying on the door-handle.

'Yes. What's the matter? He thought, if he told her all about it, she might relent and rally round.'

The sigh of a gallant fighter at the end of his strength forced its way up from Ukridge's mackintosh-covered bosom.

'Of all the dashed, infernal, officious, meddling, muddling, fat-headed, interfering asses,' he said, wanly, 'George Tupper is the worst.'

'What do you mean?'

'The man oughtn't to be at large. He's a public menace.'

'But –'

'Those dogs *belong* to my aunt. I pinched them when she chucked me out!'

Inside the cottage the Pekingese were still yapping industriously.

'Upon my Sam,' said Ukridge, 'it's a little hard.'

I think he would have said more, but at this point a voice spoke with a sudden and awful abruptness from the interior of the cottage. It was a woman's voice, a quiet, steely voice, a voice it seemed to me, that suggested cold eyes, a beaky nose, and hair like gun-metal.

'Stanley!'

That was all it said, but it was enough. Ukridge's eye met mine in a wild surmise. He seemed to shrink into his mackintosh like a snail surprised while eating lettuce.

'Stanley!'

'Yes. Aunt Julia?' quavered Ukridge.

'Come here. I wish to speak to you.'

'Yes, Aunt Julia.'

I sidled out into the road. Inside the cottage the yapping of the Pekingese had become quite hysterical. I found myself trotting, and then – though it was a warm day – running quite rapidly. I could have stayed if I had wanted to, but somehow I did not want to. Something seemed to tell me that on this holy domestic scene I should be an intruder.

What it was that gave me that impression I do not know – probably vision or the big, broad, flexible outlook.

Chapter 2

Ukridge's Accident Syndicate

'Half a minute, laddie,' said Ukridge. And, gripping my arm, he brought me to a halt on the outskirts of the little crowd which had collected about the church door.

It was a crowd such as may be seen any morning during the London mating-season outside any of the churches which nestle in the quiet squares between Hyde Park and the King's Road, Chelsea.

It consisted of five women of cooklike aspect, four nurse-maids, half a dozen men of the non-producing class who had torn themselves away for the moment from their normal task of propping up the wall of the Bunch of Grapes public-house on the corner, a costermonger with a barrow of vegetables, divers small boys, eleven dogs, and two or three purposeful-looking young fellows with cameras slung over their shoulders. It was plain that a wedding was in progress – and, arguing from the presence of the camera-men and the line of smart motor-cars along the kerb, a fairly fashionable wedding. What was not plain – to me – was why Ukridge, sternest of bachelors, had desired to add himself to the spectators.

'What,' I inquired, 'is the thought behind this? Why are we interrupting our walk to attend the obsequies of some perfect stranger?'

Ukridge did not reply for a moment. He seemed plunged in thought. Then he uttered a hollow, mirthless laugh – a dreadful sound like the last gargle of a dying moose.

'Perfect stranger, my number eleven foot!' he responded, in his coarse way. 'Do you know who it is who's getting hitched up in there?'

'Who?'

'Teddy Weeks.'

'Teddy Weeks? Teddy Weeks? Good Lord!' I exclaimed. 'Not really?'

And five years rolled away.

It was at Barolini's Italian restaurant in Beak Street that Ukridge evolved his great scheme. Barolini's was a favourite resort of our little group of earnest strugglers in the days when the philanthropic restaurateurs of Soho used to supply four courses and coffee for a shilling and sixpence; and there were present that night, besides Ukridge and myself, the following men-about-town: Teddy Weeks, the actor, fresh from a six-weeks' tour with the Number Three 'Only a Shop-Girl' Company; Victor Beamish, the artist, the man who drew that picture of the O-So-Eesi Piano-Player in the advertisement pages of the *Piccadilly Magazine*; Bertram Fox, author of *Ashes of Remorse*, and other unproduced motion-picture scenarios; and Robert Dunhill, who, being employed at a salary of eighty pounds per annum by the New Asiatic Bank, represented the sober, hard-headed commercial element. As usual, Teddy Weeks had collared the conversation, and was telling us once again how good he was and how hardly treated by a malignant fate.

There is no need to describe Teddy Weeks. Under another and a more euphonious name he has long since made his personal appearance dreadfully familiar to all who read the illustrated weekly papers. He was then, as now, a sickeningly handsome young man, possessing precisely the same melting eyes, mobile mouth, and corrugated hair so esteemed by the theatre-going public today. And yet, at this period of his career he was wasting himself on minor touring companies of the kind which open at Barrow-in-Furness and jump to Bootle for the second half of the week. He attributed this, as Ukridge was so apt to attribute his own difficulties, to lack of capital.

'I have everything,' he said, querulously, emphasizing his remarks with a coffee-spoon. 'Looks, talent, personality, a beautiful speaking voice – everything. All I need is a chance. And I can't get that because I have no clothes fit to wear. These managers are all the same, they never look below the surface, they never bother to find out if a man has genius. All they go by are his clothes. If I could afford to buy a couple of suits from a Cork Street tailor, if I could have my boots made to order by

Moykoff instead of getting them ready-made and second-hand at Moses Brothers', if I could once contrive to own a decent hat, a really good pair of spats, and a gold cigarette-case, all at the same time, I could walk into any manager's office in London and sign up for a West-end production tomorrow.'

It was at this point that Freddie Lunt came in. Freddie, like Robert Dunhill, was a financial magnate in the making and an assiduous frequenter of Barolini's; and it suddenly occurred to us that a considerable time had passed since we had last seen him in the place. We inquired the reason for this aloofness.

'I've been in bed,' said Freddie, 'for over a fortnight.'

The statement incurred Ukridge's stern disapproval. That great man made a practice of never rising before noon, and on one occasion, when a carelessly-thrown match had burned a hole in his only pair of trousers, had gone so far as to remain between the sheets for forty-eight hours; but sloth on so majestic a scale as this shocked him.

'Lazy young devil,' he commented severely. 'Letting the golden hours of youth slip by like that when you ought to have been bustling about and making a name for yourself.'

Freddie protested himself wronged by the imputation.

'I had an accident,' he explained. 'Fell off my bicycle and sprained an ankle.'

'Tough luck,' was our verdict.

'Oh, I don't know,' said Freddie. 'It wasn't bad fun getting a rest. And of course there was the fiver.'

'What fiver?'

'I got a fiver from the *Weekly Cyclist* for getting my ankle sprained.'

'You – *what*?' cried Ukridge, profoundly stirred – as ever – by a tale of easy money. 'Do you mean to sit there and tell me that some dashed paper paid you five quid simply because you sprained your ankle? Pull yourself together, old horse. Things like that don't happen.'

'It's quite true.'

'Can you show me the fiver?'

'No; because if I did you would try to borrow it.'

Ukridge ignored this slur in dignified silence.

'Would they pay a fiver to *anyone* who sprained his ankle?' he asked, sticking to the main point.

'Yes. If he was a subscriber.'

'I knew there was a catch in it,' said Ukridge, moodily.

'Lots of weekly papers are starting this wheeze,' proceeded Freddie. 'You pay a year's subscription and that entitles you to accident insurance.'

We were interested. This was in the days before every daily paper in London was competing madly against its rivals in the matter of insurance and offering princely bribes to the citizens to make a fortune by breaking their necks. Nowadays papers are paying as high as two thousand pounds for a genuine corpse and five pounds a week for a mere dislocated spine; but at that time the idea was new and it had an attractive appeal.

'How many of these rags are doing this?' asked Ukridge. You could tell from the gleam in his eyes that that great brain was whirring like a dynamo. 'As many as ten?'

'Yes, I should think so. Quite ten.'

'Then a fellow who subscribed to them all and then sprained his ankle would get fifty quid?' said Ukridge, reasoning acutely.

'More if the injury was more serious,' said Freddie, the expert. 'They have a regular tariff. So much for a broken arm, so much for a broken leg, and so forth.'

Ukridge's collar leaped off its stud and his pince-nez wobbled drunkenly as he turned to us.

'How much money can you blokes raise?' he demanded.

'What do you want it for?' asked Robert Dunhill, with a banker's caution.

'My dear old horse, can't you see? Why, my gosh, I've got the idea of the century. Upon my Sam, this is the giltest-edged scheme that was ever hatched. We'll get together enough money and take out a year's subscription for every one of these dashed papers.'

'What's the good of that?' said Dunhill, coldly unenthusiastic.

They train bank clerks to stifle emotion, so that they will be able to refuse overdrafts when they become managers. 'The odds are we should none of us have an accident of any kind, and then the money would be chucked away.'

'Good heavens, ass,' snorted Ukridge, 'you don't suppose I'm suggesting that we should leave it to chance, do you? Listen! Here's the scheme. We take out subscriptions for all these papers, then we draw lots, and the fellow who gets the fatal card or whatever it is goes out and breaks his leg and draws the loot, and we split it up between us and live on it in luxury. It ought to run into hundreds of pounds.'

A long silence followed. Then Dunhill spoke again. His was a solid rather than a nimble mind.

'Suppose he couldn't break his leg?'

'My gosh!' cried Ukridge, exasperated. 'Here we are in the twentieth century, with every resource of modern civilization at our disposal, with opportunities for getting our legs broken opening about us on every side – and you ask a silly question like that! Of course he could break his leg. Any ass can break a leg. It's a little hard! We're all infernally broke – personally, unless Freddie can lend me a bit of that fiver till Saturday, I'm going to have a difficult job pulling through. We all need money like the dickens, and yet, when I point out this marvellous scheme for collecting a bit, instead of fawning on me for my ready intelligence you sit and make objections. It isn't the right spirit. It isn't the spirit that wins.'

'If you're as hard up as that,' objected Dunhill, 'how are you going to put in your share of the pool?'

A pained, almost a stunned, look came into Ukridge's eyes. He gazed at Dunhill through his lop-sided pince-nez as one who speculates as to whether his hearing has deceived him.

'Me?' he cried. 'Me? I like that! Upon my Sam, that's rich! Why, damme, if there's any justice in the world, if there's a spark of decency and good feeling in your bally bosoms, I should think you would let me in free for suggesting the idea. It's a little hard! I supply the brains and you want me to cough up cash as well. My gosh, I didn't expect this. This hurts me, by George! If anybody had told me that an old pal would –'

'Oh, all right,' said Robert Dunhill. 'All right, all right, all right. But I'll tell you one thing. If you draw the lot it'll be the happiest day of my life.'

'I shan't,' said Ukridge. 'Something tells me that I shan't.'

Nor did he. When, in a solemn silence broken only by the

sound of a distant waiter quarrelling with the cook down a speaking-tube, we had completed the drawing, the man of destiny was Teddy Weeks.

I suppose that even in the springtime of Youth, when broken limbs seem a lighter matter than they become later in life, it can never be an unmixedly agreeable thing to have to go out into the public highways and try to make an accident happen to one. In such circumstances the reflection that you are thereby benefiting your friends brings but slight balm. To Teddy Weeks it appeared to bring no balm at all. That he was experiencing a certain disinclination to sacrifice himself for the public good became more and more evident as the days went by and found him still intact. Ukridge, when he called upon me to discuss the matter, was visibly perturbed. He sank into a chair beside the table at which I was beginning my modest morning meal, and, having drunk half my coffee, sighed deeply.

'Upon my Sam,' he moaned, 'it's a little disheartening. I strain my brain to think up schemes for getting us all a bit of money just at the moment when we are all needing it most, and when I hit on what is probably the simplest and yet ripest notion of our time, this blighter Weeks goes and lets me down by shirking his plain duty. It's just my luck that a fellow like that should have drawn the lot. And the worst of it is, laddie, that, now we've started with him, we've got to keep on. We can't possibly raise enough money to pay yearly subscriptions for anybody else. It's Weeks or nobody.'

'I suppose we must give him time.'

'That's what he says,' grunted Ukridge, morosely, helping himself to toast. 'He says he doesn't know how to start about it. To listen to him, you'd think that going and having a trifling accident was the sort of delicate and intricate job that required years of study and special preparation. Why, a child of six could do it on his head at five minutes' notice. The man's so infernally particular. You make helpful suggestions, and instead of accepting them in a broad, reasonable spirit of cooperation he comes back at you every time with some frivolous objection. He's so dashed fastidious. When we were out last night, we came on a couple of navvies scrapping. Good hefty fellows,

either of them capable of putting him in hospital for a month.
I told him to jump in and start separating them, and he said no;
it was a private dispute which was none of his business, and
he didn't feel justified in interfering. Finicky, I call it. I tell you,
laddie, this blighter is a broken reed. He has got cold feet. We
did wrong to let him into the drawing at all. We might have
known that a fellow like that would never give results. No
conscience. No sense of *esprit de corps*. No notion of putting
himself out to the most trifling extent for the benefit of the
community. Haven't you any more marmalade, laddie?'

'I have not.'

'Then I'll be going,' said Ukridge, moodily. 'I suppose,' he
added, pausing at the door, 'you couldn't lend me five bob?'

'How did you guess?'

'Then I'll tell you what,' said Ukridge, ever fair and reasonable; 'you can stand me dinner tonight.' He seemed cheered up
for the moment by this happy compromise, but gloom descended on him again. His face clouded. 'When I think,' he said, 'of all
the money that's locked up in that poor faint-hearted fish, just
waiting to be released, I could sob. Sob, laddie, like a little child.
I never liked that man – he has a bad eye and waves his hair.
Never trust a man who waves his hair, old horse.'

Ukridge's pessimism was not confined to himself. By the end
of a fortnight, nothing having happened to Teddy Weeks worse
than a slight cold which he shook off in a couple of days, the
general consensus of opinion among his apprehensive colleagues
in the Syndicate was that the situation had become desperate.
There were no signs whatever of any return on the vast capital
which we had laid out, and meanwhile meals had to be bought,
landladies paid, and a reasonable supply of tobacco acquired. It
was a melancholy task in these circumstances to read one's
paper of a morning.

All over the inhabited globe, so the well-informed sheet gave
one to understand, every kind of accident was happening every
day to practically everybody in existence except Teddy Weeks.
Farmers in Minnesota were getting mixed up with reaping-
machines, peasants in India were being bisected by crocodiles;
iron girders from skyscrapers were falling hourly on the heads

of citizens in every town from Philadelphia to San Francisco; and the only people who were not down with ptomaine poisoning were those who had walked over cliffs, driven motors into walls, tripped over manholes, or assumed on too slight evidence that the gun was not loaded. In a crippled world, it seemed, Teddy Weeks walked alone, whole and glowing with health. It was one of those grim, ironical, hopeless, grey, despairful situations which the Russian novelists love to write about, and I could not find it in me to blame Ukridge for taking direct action in this crisis. My only regret was that bad luck caused so excellent a plan to miscarry.

My first intimation that he had been trying to hurry matters on came when he and I were walking along the King's Road one evening, and he drew me into Markham Square, a dismal backwater where he had once had rooms.

'What's the idea?' I asked, for I disliked the place.

'Teddy Weeks lives here,' said Ukridge. 'In my old rooms.' I could not see that this lent any fascination to the place. Every day and in every way I was feeling sorrier and sorrier that I had been foolish enough to put money which I could ill spare into a venture which had all the earmarks of a wash-out, and my sentiments towards Teddy Weeks were cold and hostile.

'I want to inquire after him.'

'Inquire after him? Why?'

'Well, the fact is, laddie, I have an idea that he has been bitten by a dog.'

'What makes you think that?'

'Oh, I don't know,' said Ukridge, dreamily. 'I've just got the idea. You know how one gets ideas.'

The mere contemplation of this beautiful event was so inspiring that for awhile it held me silent. In each of the ten journals in which we had invested dog-bites were specifically recommended as things which every subscriber ought to have. They came about half-way up the list of lucrative accidents, inferior to a broken rib or a fractured fibula, but better value than an ingrowing toe-nail. I was gloating happily over the picture conjured up by Ukridge's words when an exclamation brought me back with a start to the realities of life. A revolting sight met my

eyes. Down the street came ambling the familiar figure of
Teddy Weeks, and one glance at his elegant person was enough
to tell us that our hopes had been built on sand. Not even a toy
Pomeranian had chewed this man.

'Hallo, you fellows!' said Teddy Weeks.

'Hallo!' we responded, dully.

'Can't stop,' said Teddy Weeks. 'I've got to fetch a doctor.'

'A doctor?'

'Yes. Poor Victor Beamish. He's been bitten by a dog.'

Ukridge and I exchanged weary glances. It seemed as if Fate
was going out of its way to have sport with us. What was the
good of a dog biting Victor Beamish? What was the good of a
hundred dogs biting Victor Beamish? A dog-bitten Victor Beamish had no market value whatever.

'You know that fierce brute that belongs to my landlady,'
said Teddy Weeks. 'The one that always dashes out into the
area and barks at people who come to the front door.' I remembered. A large mongrel with wild eyes and flashing fangs, badly
in need of a haircut. I had encountered it once in the street,
when visiting Ukridge, and only the presence of the latter, who
knew it well and to whom all dogs were as brothers, had saved
me from the doom of Victor Beamish. 'Somehow or other he
got into my bedroom this evening. He was waiting there
when I came home. I had brought Beamish back with me,
and the animal pinned him by the leg the moment I opened the
door.'

'Why didn't he pin you?' asked Ukridge, aggrieved.

'What I can't make out,' said Teddy Weeks, 'is how on earth
the brute came to be in my room. Somebody must have put him
there. The whole thing is very mysterious.'

'Why didn't he pin you?' demanded Ukridge again.

'Oh, I managed to climb on to the top of the wardrobe while
he was biting Beamish,' said Teddy Weeks. 'And then the
landlady came and took him away. But I can't stop here talking.
I must go and get that doctor.'

We gazed after him in silence as he tripped down the street.
We noted the careful manner in which he paused at the corner
to eye the traffic before crossing the road, the wary way in
which he drew back to allow a truck to rattle past.

'You heard that?' said Ukridge, tensely. 'He climbed on to the top of the wardrobe!'

'Yes.'

'And you saw the way he dodged that excellent truck?'

'Yes.'

'Something's got to be done,' said Ukridge, firmly. 'The man has got to be awakened to a sense of his responsibilities.'

Next day a deputation waited on Teddy Weeks.

Ukridge was our spokesman, and he came to the point with admirable directness.

'How about it?' asked Ukridge.

'How about what?' replied Teddy Weeks, nervously, avoiding his accusing eye.

'When do we get action?'

'Oh, you mean that accident business?'

'Yes.'

'I've been thinking about that,' said Teddy Weeks.

Ukridge drew the mackintosh which he wore indoors and out of doors and in all weathers more closely around him. There was in the action something suggestive of a member of the Roman Senate about to denounce an enemy of the State. In just such a manner must Cicero have swished his toga as he took a deep breath preparatory to assailing Clodius. He toyed for a moment with the ginger-beer wire which held his pince-nez in place, and endeavoured without success to button his collar at the back. In moments of emotion Ukridge's collar always took on a sort of temperamental jumpiness which no stud could restrain.

'And about time you *were* thinking about it,' he boomed, sternly.

We shifted appreciatively in our seats, all except Victor Beamish, who had declined a chair and was standing by the mantelpiece. 'Upon my Sam, it's about time you were thinking about it. Do you realize that we've invested an enormous sum of money in you on the distinct understanding that we could rely on you to do your duty and get immediate results? Are we to be forced to the conclusion that you are so yellow and few in the pod as to want to evade your honourable obligations? We thought better of you, Weeks. Upon my Sam, we thought better of you. We took you for a two-fisted, enterprising, big-souled, one hundred-per-cent he-man who would stand by his friends to the finish.'

'Yes, but –'

'Any bloke with a sense of loyalty and an appreciation of what it meant to the rest of us would have rushed out and found some means of fulfilling his duty long ago. You don't even grasp at the opportunities that come your way. Only yesterday I saw you draw back when a single step into the road would have had a truck bumping into you.'

'Well, it's not so easy to let a truck bump into you.'

'Nonsense. It only requires a little ordinary resolution. Use your imagination, man. Try to think that a child has fallen down in the street – a little golden-haired child,' said Ukridge, deeply affected. 'And a dashed great cab or something comes rolling up. The kid's mother is standing on the pavement, help-less, her hands clasped in agony. "Dammit," she cries, "will no one save my darling?" "Yes, by George," you shout, "*I* will." And out you jump and the thing's over in half a second. I don't know what you're making such a fuss about.'

'Yes, but –' said Teddy Weeks.

'I'm told, what's more, it isn't a bit painful. A sort of dull shock, that's all.'

'Who told you that?'

'I forget. Someone.'

'Well, you can tell him from me that he's an ass,' said Teddy Weeks, with asperity.

'All right. If you object to being run over by a truck there are lots of other ways. But, upon my Sam, it's pretty hopeless sug-gesting them. You seem to have no enterprise at all. Yesterday, after I went to all the trouble to put a dog in your room, a dog which would have done all the work for you – all you had to do was stand still and let him use his own judgement – what happened? You climbed on to –'

Victor Beamish interrupted, speaking in a voice husky with emotion.

'Was it you who put that damned dog in the room?'

'Eh?' said Ukridge. 'Why, yes. But we can have a good talk about all that later on,' he proceeded, hastily. 'The point at the

38

moment is how the dickens we're going to persuade this poor worm to collect our insurance money for us. Why, damme, I should have thought you would have –'

'All I can say –' began Victor Beamish, heatedly.

'Yes, yes,' said Ukridge; 'some other time. Must stick to business now, laddie. I was saying,' he resumed, 'that I should have thought you would have been as keen as mustard to put the job through for your own sake. You're always beefing that you haven't any clothes to impress managers with. Think of all you can buy with your share of the swag once you have summoned up a little ordinary determination and seen the thing through. Think of the suits, the boots, the hats, the spats. You're always talking about your dashed career, and how all you need to land you in a West-end production is good clothes. Well, here's your chance to get them.'

His eloquence was not wasted. A wistful look came into Teddy Weeks's eye, such a look as must have come into the eye of Moses on the summit of Pisgah. He breathed heavily! You could see that the man was mentally walking along Cork Street, weighing the merits of one famous tailor against another.

'I'll tell you what I'll do,' he said, suddenly. 'It's no use asking me to put this thing through in cold blood. I simply can't do it. I haven't the nerve. But if you fellows will give me a dinner tonight with lots of champagne I think it will key me up to it.'

A heavy silence fell upon the room. Champagne! The word was like a knell.

'How on earth are we going to afford champagne?' said Victor Beamish.

'Well, there it is,' said Teddy Weeks. 'Take it or leave it.'

'Gentlemen,' said Ukridge, 'it would seem that the company requires more capital. How about it, old horses? Let's get together in a frank, business-like cards-on-the-table spirit, and see what can be done. I can raise ten bob.'

'What!' cried the entire assembled company, amazed. 'How?'

'I'll pawn a banjo.'

'You haven't got a banjo.'

'No, but George Tupper has, and I know where he keeps it.'

Started in this spirited way, the subscriptions came pouring in. I contributed a cigarette-case, Betram Fox thought his landlady would let him owe for another week, Robert Dunhill had an uncle in Kensington who, he fancied, if tactfully approached, would be good for a quid, and Victor Beamish said that if the advertisement-manager of the O-So-Eesi Piano-Player was churlish enough to refuse an advance of five shillings against future work he misjudged him sadly. Within a few minutes, in short, the Lightning Drive had produced the impressive total of two pounds six shillings, and we asked Teddy Weeks if he thought that he could get adequately keyed up within the limits of that sum.

'I'll try,' said Teddy Weeks.

So, not unmindful of the fact that that excellent hostelry supplied champagne at eight shillings the quart bottle, we fixed the meeting for seven o'clock at Barolini's.

Considered as a social affair, Teddy Weeks's keying-up dinner was not a success. Almost from the start I think we all found it trying. It was not so much the fact that he was drinking deeply of Barolini's eight shilling champagne while we, from lack of funds, were compelled to confine ourselves to meaner beverages; what really marred the pleasantness of the function was the extraordinary effect the stuff had on Teddy. What was actually in the champagne supplied to Barolini and purveyed by him to the public, such as were reckless enough to drink it, at eight shillings the bottle remains a secret between its maker and his Maker; but three glasses of it were enough to convert Teddy Weeks from a mild and rather oily young man into a truculent swashbuckler.

He quarrelled with us all. With the soup he was tilting at Victor Beamish's theories of Art; the fish found him ridiculing Bertram Fox's views on the future of the motion-picture; and by the time the leg of chicken with dandelion salad arrived – or, as some held, string salad – opinions varied on this point – the hell-brew had so wrought on him that he had begun to lecture Ukridge on his mis-spent life and was urging him in accents audible across the street to go out and get a job and thus acquire sufficient self-respect to enable him to look himself in the face in a mirror without wincing. Not, added Teddy Weeks with what we all thought, uncalled-for offensiveness, that any amount of self-respect was likely to do that. Having said which, he called imperiously for another eight bobs'-worth.

We gazed at one another wanly. However excellent the end towards which all this was tending, there was no denying that it was hard to bear. But policy kept us silent. We recognized that this was Teddy Weeks's evening and that he must be humoured. Victor Beamish said meekly that Teddy had cleared up a lot of points which had been troubling him for a long time. Bertram Fox agreed that there was much in what Teddy had said about the future of the close-up. And even Ukridge, though his haughty soul was seared to its foundations by the latter's personal remarks, promised to take his homily to heart and act upon it at the earliest possible moment.

'You'd better!' said Teddy Weeks, belligerently, biting off the end of one of Barolini's best cigars. 'And there's another thing — don't let me hear of your coming and sneaking people's socks again.'

'Very well, laddie,' said Ukridge, humbly.

'If there is one person in the world that I despise,' said Teddy, bending a red-eyed gaze on the offender, 'it's a snock-seeker — a seek-snocker — a — well, you know what I mean.'

We hastened to assure him that we knew what he meant and he relapsed into a lengthy stupor, from which he emerged three-quarters of an hour later to announce that he didn't know what we intended to do, but that he was going. We said that we were going too, and we paid the bill and did so.

Teddy Weeks's indignation on discovering us gathered about him upon the pavement outside the restaurant was intense, and he expressed it freely. Among other things, he said — which was not true — that he had a reputation to keep up in Soho.

'It's all right, Teddy, old horse,' said Ukridge, soothingly. 'We just thought you would like to have all your old pals round you when you did it.'

'Did it? Did what?'

'Why, had the accident.'

Teddy Weeks glared at him truculently. Then his mood seemed to change abruptly, and he burst into a loud and hearty laugh.

'Well, of all the silly ideas!' he cried, amusedly. 'I'm not going to have an accident. You don't suppose I ever seriously

intended to have an accident, do you? It was just my fun.'
Then, with another sudden change of mood, he seemed to become a victim to an acute unhappiness. He stroked Ukridge's
arm affectionately, and a tear rolled down his cheek. 'Just my
fun,' he repeated. 'You don't mind my fun, do you?' he asked,
pleadingly. 'You like my fun, don't you? All my fun. Never
meant to have an accident at all. Just wanted dinner.' The gay
humour of it all overcame his sorrow once more. 'Funniest
thing ever heard,' he said cordially. 'Didn't want accident,
wanted dinner. Dinner daxident, danner dixident,' he added,
driving home his point. 'Well, good night all,' he said, cheerily.
And, stepping off the kerb on to a banana-skin, was instantly
knocked ten feet by a passing lorry.

'Two ribs and an arm,' said the doctor five minutes later,
superintending the removal proceedings. 'Gently with that
stretcher.'

It was two weeks before we were informed by the authorities
of Charing Cross Hospital that the patient was in a condition to
receive visitors. A whip-round secured the price of a basket of
fruit, and Ukridge and I were deputed by the shareholders to
deliver it with their compliments and kind inquiries.

'Hallo!' we said in a hushed, bedside manner when finally
admitted to his presence.

'Sit down, gentlemen,' replied the invalid.

I must confess even in that first moment to having experienced a slight feeling of surprise. It was not like Teddy Weeks
to call us gentlemen. Ukridge, however, seemed to notice nothing amiss.

'Well, well, well,' he said, buoyantly. 'And how are you,
laddie? We've brought you a few fragments of fruit.'

'I am getting along capitally,' replied Teddy Weeks, still in
that odd precise way which had made his opening words strike
me as curious. 'And I should like to say that in my opinion
England has reason to be proud of the alertness and enterprise
of her great journals. The excellence of their reading-matter, the
ingenuity of their various competitions, and, above all, the
go-ahead spirit which has resulted in this accident insurance
scheme are beyond praise. Have you got that down?' he
inquired.

Ukridge and I looked at each other. We had been told that Teddy was practically normal again, but this sounded like delirium.

'Have we got that down, old horse?' asked Ukridge, gently.

Teddy Weeks seemed surprised.

'Aren't you reporters?'

'How do you mean, reporters?'

'I thought you had come from one of these weekly papers that have been paying me insurance money, to interview me,' said Teddy Weeks.

Ukridge and I exchanged another glance. An uneasy glance this time. I think that already a grim foreboding had begun to cast its shadow over us.

'Surely you remember me, Teddy, old horse?' said Ukridge, anxiously.

Teddy Weeks knit his brow, concentrating painfully.

'Why, of course,' he said at last. 'You're Ukridge, aren't you?'

'That's right. Ukridge.'

'Of course. Ukridge.'

'Yes. Ukridge. Funny your forgetting me!'

'Yes,' said Teddy Weeks. 'It's the effect of the shock I got when that thing bowled me over. I must have been struck on the head, I suppose. It has had the effect of rendering my memory rather uncertain. The doctors here are very interested. They say it is a most unusual case. I can remember some things perfectly, but in some ways my memory is a complete blank.'

'Oh, but I say, old horse,' quavered Ukridge. 'I suppose you haven't forgotten about that insurance, have you?'

'Oh, no, I remember that.'

Ukridge breathed a relieved sigh.

'I was a subscriber to a number of weekly papers,' went on Teddy Weeks. 'They are paying me insurance money now.'

'Yes, yes, old horse,' cried Ukridge. 'But what I mean is you remember the Syndicate, don't you?'

Teddy Weeks raised his eyebrows.

'Syndicate? What Syndicate?'

'Why, when we all got together and put up the money to pay for the subscriptions to these papers and drew lots, to choose which of us should go out and have an accident and collect the money. And you drew it, don't you remember?'

Utter astonishment, and a shocked astonishment at that, spread itself over Teddy Weeks's countenance. The man seemed outraged.

'I certainly remember nothing of the kind,' he said, severely. 'I cannot imagine myself for a moment consenting to become a party to what from your own account would appear to have been a criminal conspiracy to obtain money under false pretences from a number of weekly papers.'

'But, laddie –'

'However,' said Teddy Weeks, 'if there is any truth in this story, no doubt you have documentary evidence to support it.'

Ukridge looked at me. I looked at Ukridge. There was a long silence.

'Shift-ho, old horse?' said Ukridge, sadly. 'No use staying on here.'

'No,' I replied, with equal gloom. 'May as well go.'

'Glad to have seen you,' said Teddy Weeks, 'and thanks for the fruit.'

The next time I saw the man he was coming out of a manager's office in the Haymarket. He had on a new Homburg hat of a delicate pearl grey, spats to match, and a new blue flannel suit, beautifully cut, with an invisible red twill. He was looking jubilant, and, as I passed him, he drew from his pocket a gold cigarette-case.

It was shortly after that, if you remember, that he made a big hit as the juvenile lead in that piece at the Apollo and started on his sensational career as a *matinée* idol.

Inside the church the organ had swelled into the familiar music of the *Wedding March*. A verger came out and opened the doors. The five cooks ceased their reminiscences of other and smarter weddings at which they had participated. The camera-men unshipped their cameras. The costermonger moved his barrow of vegetables a pace forward. A dishevelled and unshaven man at my side uttered a disapproving growl.

'Idle rich!' said the dishevelled man.

Out of the church came a beauteous being, leading attached to his arm another being, somewhat less beauteous.

44

There was no denying the spectacular effect of Teddy Weeks. He was handsomer than ever. His sleek hair, gorgeously waved, shone in the sun, his eyes were large and bright; his lissom frame, garbed in faultless morning-coat and trousers, was that of an Apollo. But his bride gave the impression that Teddy had married money. They paused in the doorway, and the camera-men became active and fussy.

'Have you got a shilling, laddie?' said Ukridge in a low, level voice.

'Why do you want a shilling?'

'Old horse,' said Ukridge, tensely, 'it is of the utmost vital importance that I have a shilling here and now.'

I passed it over. Ukridge turned to the dishevelled man, and I perceived that he held in his hand a large rich tomato of juicy and over-ripe appearance.

'Would you like to earn a bob?' Ukridge said.

'Would I!' replied the dishevelled man.

Ukridge sank his voice to a hoarse whisper.

The camera-men had finished their preparations. Teddy Weeks, his head thrown back in that gallant way which has endeared him to so many female hearts, was exhibiting his celebrated teeth. The cooks, in undertones, were making adverse comments on the appearance of the bride.

'Now, please,' said one of the camera-men.

Over the heads of the crowd, well and truly aimed, whizzed a large juicy tomato. It burst like a shell full between Teddy Weeks's expressive eyes, obliterating them in scarlet ruin. It spattered Teddy Weeks's collar, it dripped on Teddy Weeks's morning-coat. And the dishevelled man turned abruptly and raced off down the street.

Ukridge grasped my arm. There was a look of deep content in his eyes.

'Shift-ho?' said Ukridge.

Arm-in-arm, we strolled off in the pleasant June sunshine.

Chapter 3

The Début of Battling Billson

It becomes increasingly difficult, I have found, as time goes by, to recall the exact circumstances in which one first became acquainted with this man or that; for as a general thing I lay no claim to the possession of one of those hair-trigger memories which come from subscribing to the correspondence courses advertised in the magazines. And yet I can state without doubt or hesitation that the individual afterwards known as Battling Billson entered my life at half-past four on the afternoon of Saturday, September the tenth, two days after my twenty-seventh birthday. For there was that about my first sight of him which has caused the events to remain photographically lined on the tablets of my mind when a yesterday has faded from its page. Not only was our meeting dramatic and even startling, but it had in it something of the quality of the last straw, the final sling or arrow of outrageous Fortune. It seemed to put the lid on the sadness of life.

Everything had been going steadily wrong with me for more than a week. I had been away, paying a duty visit to uncongenial relatives in the country, and it had rained and rained and rained. There had been family prayers before breakfast and bezique after dinner. On the journey back to London my carriage had been full of babies, the train had stopped everywhere, and I had had nothing to eat but a bag of buns. And when finally I let myself into my lodgings in Ebury Street and sought the soothing haven of my sitting-room, the first thing I saw on opening the door was this enormous red-headed man lying on the sofa.

He made no move as I came in, for he was asleep; and I can best convey the instantaneous impression I got of his formidable physique by saying that I had no desire to wake him. The sofa was a small one, and he overflowed it in every direction. He had a broken nose, and his jaw was the jaw of a Wild West motion-picture star registering Determination. One hand was under his head; the other, hanging down to the floor, looked like a strayed ham congealed into stone. What he was doing in my sitting-room I did not know; but, passionately as I wished to know, I preferred not to seek first-hand information. There was something about him that seemed to suggest that he might be one of those men who are rather cross when they first wake up. I crept out and stole softly downstairs to make inquiries of Bowles, my landlord.

'Sir?' said Bowles, in his fruity ex-butler way, popping up from the depths accompanied by a rich smell of finnan haddie.

'There's someone in my room,' I whispered.

'That would be Mr Ukridge, sir.'

'It wouldn't be anything of the kind,' I replied, with asperity. I seldom had the courage to contradict Bowles, but this statement was so wildly inaccurate that I could not let it pass. 'It's a huge red-headed man.'

'Mr Ukridge's friend, sir. He joined Mr Ukridge here yesterday.'

'How do you mean, joined Mr Ukridge here yesterday?'

'Mr Ukridge came to occupy your rooms in your absence, sir, on the night after your departure. I assumed that he had your approval. He said, if I remember correctly, that "it would be all right."'

For some reason or other which I had never been able to explain, Bowles's attitude towards Ukridge from their first meeting had been that of an indulgent father towards a favourite son. He gave the impression now of congratulating me on having such a friend to rally round and sneak into my rooms when I went away.

'Would there be anything further, sir?' inquired Bowles, with a wistful half-glance over his shoulder. He seemed reluctant to tear himself away for long from the finnan haddie.

'No,' I said. 'Er – no. When do you expect Mr Ukridge back?'

'Mr Ukridge informed me that he would return for dinner, sir. Unless he has altered his plans, he is now at a *matinée* performance at the Gaiety Theatre.'

The audience was just beginning to leave when I reached the Gaiety. I waited in the Strand, and presently was rewarded by the sight of a yellow mackintosh working its way through the crowd.

'Hallo, laddie!' said Stanley Featherstonehaugh Ukridge, genially. 'When did you get back? I say, I want you to remember this tune, so that you can remind me of it tomorrow, when I'll be sure to have forgotten it. This is how it goes.' He poised himself flat-footedly in the surging tide of pedestrians and, shutting his eyes and raising his chin, began to yodel in a loud and dismal tenor. 'Tumty-tumty-tumty-tum, tum tum tum,' he concluded. 'And now, old horse, you may lead me across the street to the Coal Hole for a short snifter. What sort of a time have you had?'

'Never mind what sort of a time I've had. Who's the fellow you've dumped down in my rooms?'

'Red-haired man?'

'Good Lord! Surely even you wouldn't inflict more than one on me?'

Ukridge looked at me a little pained.

'I don't like this tone,' he said, leading me down the steps of the Coal Hole. 'Upon my Sam, your manner wounds me, old horse. I little thought that you would object to your best friend laying his head on your pillow.'

'I don't mind your head. At least I do, but I suppose I've got to put up with it. But when it comes to your taking in lodgers –'

'Order two tawny ports, laddie,' said Ukridge, 'and I'll explain all about that. I had an idea all along that you would want to know. It's like this,' he proceeded, when the tawny ports had arrived. 'That bloke's going to make my everlasting fortune.'

'Well, can't he do it somewhere else except in my sitting-room?'

'You know me, old horse,' said Ukridge, sipping luxuriously. 'Keen, alert, far-sighted. Brain never still. Always getting ideas – *bing* – like a flash. The other day I was in a pub down Chelsea way having a bit of bread and cheese, and a fellow came in smothered with jewels. Smothered, I give you my word. Rings on his fingers and a tie-pin you could have lit your cigar at. I made inquiries and found that he was Tod Bingham's manager.'

'Who's Tod Bingham?'

'My dear old son, you must have heard of Tod Bingham. The new middle-weight champion. Beat Alf Palmer for the belt a couple of weeks ago. And this bloke, as opulent-looking a bloke as ever I saw, was his manager. I suppose he gets about fifty per cent of everything Tod makes, and you know the sort of purses they give for big fights nowadays. And then there's music-hall tours and the movies and all that. Well, I see no reason why, putting the thing at the lowest figures, I shouldn't scoop in thousands. I got the idea two seconds after they told me who this fellow was. And what made the thing seem almost as if it was meant to be was the coincidence that I should have heard only that morning that the *Hyacinth* was in.'

The man seemed to me to be rambling. In my reduced and afflicted state his cryptic method of narrative irritated me.

'I don't know what you're talking about,' I said. 'What's the *Hyacinth*? In where?'

'Pull yourself together, old horse,' said Ukridge, with the air of one endeavouring to be patient with a half-witted child. 'You remember the *Hyacinth*, the tramp steamer I took that trip on a couple of years ago. Many's the time I've told you all about the *Hyacinth*. She docked in the Port of London the night before I met this opulent bloke, and I had been meaning to go down next day and have a chat with the lads. The fellow you found in your rooms is one of the trimmers. As decent a bird as ever you met. Not much conversation, but a heart of gold. And it came across me like a thunderbolt the moment they told me who the jewelled cove was that, if I could only induce this man Billson to take up scrapping seriously, with me as his manager, my fortune was made. Billson is the man who invented fighting.'

'He looks it.'

'Splendid chap – you'll like him.'

'I bet I shall. I made up my mind to like him the moment I saw him.'

'Never picks a quarrel, you understand – in fact, used to need the deuce of a lot of provocation before he would give of his best; but once he started – golly! I've seen that man clean out a bar at Marseilles in a way that fascinated you. A bar filled to overflowing with A.B.'s and firemen, mind you, and all capable of felling oxen with a blow. Six of them there were, and they kept swatting Billson with all the vim and heartiness at their disposal, but he just let them bounce off, and went on with the business in hand. The man's a champion, laddie, nothing less. You couldn't hurt him with a hatchet, and every time he hits anyone all the undertakers in the place jump up and make bids for the body. And the amazing bit of luck is that he was looking for a job ashore. It appears he's fallen in love with one of the barmaids at the Crown in Kennington. Not,' said Ukridge, so that all misapprehension should be avoided, 'the one with the squint. The other one. Flossie. The girl with yellow hair.'

'I don't know the barmaids at the Crown in Kennington,' I said.

'Nice girls,' said Ukridge, paternally. 'So it was all right, you see. Our interests were identical. Good old Billson isn't what you'd call a very intelligent chap, but I managed to make him understand after an hour or so, and we drew up the contract. I'm to get fifty per cent, of everything in consideration of managing him, fixing up fights, and looking after him generally.'

'And looking after him includes tucking him up on my sofa and singing him to sleep?'

Again that pained look came into Ukridge's face. He gazed at me as if I had disappointed him.

'You keep harping on that, laddie, and it isn't the right spirit. Anyone would think that we had polluted your damned room.'

'Well, you must admit that having this coming champion of yours in the home is going to make things a bit crowded.'

'Don't worry about that, my dear old man,' said Ukridge, reassuringly. 'We move to the White Hart at Barnes tomorrow, to start training. I've got Billson an engagement in one of the preliminaries down at Wonderland two weeks from tonight.'

'No; really?' I said, impressed by this enterprise. 'How did you manage it?'

'I just took him along and showed him to the management. They jumped at him. You see, the old boy's appearance rather speaks for itself. Thank goodness, all this happened just when I had a few quid tucked away. By the greatest good luck I ran into George Tupper at the very moment when he had had word

that they were going to make him an under-secretary or something – I can't remember the details, but it's something they give
these Foreign Office blokes when they show a bit of class – and
Tuppy parted with a tenner without a murmur. Seemed sort of
dazed. I believe now I could have had twenty if I'd had the
presence of mind to ask for it. Still,' said Ukridge, with a manly
resignation which did him credit, 'it can't be helped now, and
ten will see me through. The only thing that's worrying me at
the moment is what to call Billson.'

'Yes, I should be careful what I called a man like that.'

'I mean, what name is he to fight under?'

'Why not his own?'

'His parents, confound them,' said Ukridge, moodily, 'christ-
ened him Wilberforce. I ask you, can you see the crowd at
Wonderland having Wilberforce Billson introduced to them?'

'Willie Billson,' I suggested. 'Rather snappy.'

Ukridge considered the proposal seriously, with knit brows,
as becomes a manager.

'Too frivolous,' he decided at length. 'Might be all right for a
bantam, but – no, I don't like it. I was thinking of something
like Hurricane Hicks or Rock-Crusher Riggs.'

'Don't do it,' I urged, 'or you'll kill his career right from the
start. You never find a real champion with one of these fancy
names. Bob Fitzsimmons, Jack Johnson, James J. Corbett, James
J. Jeffries –'

'James J. Billson?'

'Rotten.'

'You don't think,' said Ukridge, almost with timidity, 'that
Wildcat Wix might do?'

'No fighter with an adjective in front of his name ever boxed
in anything except a three-round preliminary.'

'How about Battling Billson?'

I patted him on the shoulder.

'Go no farther,' I said. 'The thing is settled. Battling Billson
is the name.'

'Laddie,' said Ukridge in a hushed voice, reaching across
the table and grasping my hand, 'this is genius. Sheer genius.
Order another couple of tawny ports, old man.'

I did so, and we drank deep to the Battler's success.

My formal introduction to my godchild took place on our return to Ebury Street, and – great as had been my respect for the man before – it left me with a heightened appreciation of the potentialities for triumph awaiting him in his selected profession. He was awake by this time and moving ponderously about the sitting-room, and he looked even more impressive standing than he had appeared when lying down. At our first meeting, moreover, his eyes had been closed in sleep; they were now open, green in colour, and of a peculiarly metallic glint which caused them, as we shook hands, to seem to be exploring my person for good spots to hit. What was probably intended to be the smile that wins appeared to me a grim and sardonic twist of the lip. Take him for all in all, I had never met a man so calculated to convert the most truculent swashbuckler to pacifism at a glance; and when I recalled Ukridge's story of the little unpleasantness at Marseilles and realized that a mere handful of half a dozen able-bodied seamen had had the temerity to engage this fellow in personal conflict, it gave me a thrill of patriotic pride. There must be good stuff in the British Merchant Marine, I felt. Hearts of oak.

Dinner, which followed the introduction, revealed the Battler rather as a capable trencherman than as a sparkling conversationalist. His long reach enabled him to grab salt, potatoes, pepper, and other necessaries without the necessity of asking for them; and on other topics he seemed to possess no views which he deemed worthy of exploitation. A strong, silent man.

That there was a softer side to his character was, however, made clear to me when, after smoking one of my cigars and talking for awhile of this and that, Ukridge went out on one of those mysterious errands of his which were always summoning him at all hours and left my guest and myself alone together. After a bare half-hour's silence, broken only by the soothing gurgle of his pipe, the coming champion cocked an intimidating eye at me and spoke.

'You ever been in love, mister?'

I was thrilled and flattered. Something in my appearance, I told myself, some nebulous something that showed me a man of sentiment and sympathy, had appealed to this man, and he was about to pour out his heart in intimate confession. I said yes, I had been in love many times. I went on to speak of love as a noble emotion of which no man need be ashamed. I spoke at length and with fervour.

' 'R!' said Battling Billson.

Then, as if aware that he had been chattering in an undignified manner to a comparative stranger, he withdrew into the silence again and did not emerge till it was time to go to bed, when he said 'Good night, mister,' and disappeared. It was disappointing. Significant, perhaps, the conversation had been, but I had been rather hoping for something which could have been built up into a human document, entitled 'The Soul of the Abysmal Brute', and sold to some editor for that real money which was always so badly needed in the home.

Ukridge and his *protégé* left next morning for Barnes, and, as that riverside resort was somewhat off my beat, I saw no more of the Battler until the fateful night at Wonderland. From time to time Ukridge would drop in at my rooms to purloin cigars and socks, and on these occasions he always spoke with the greatest confidence of his man's prospects. At first, it seemed, there had been a little difficulty owing to the other's rooted idea that plug tobacco was an indispensable adjunct to training : but towards the end of the first week the arguments of wisdom had prevailed and he had consented to abandon smoking until after his début. By this concession the issue seemed to Ukridge to have been sealed as a certainty, and he was in sunny mood as he borrowed the money from me to pay our fares to the Underground station at which the pilgrim alights who wishes to visit that Mecca of East-end boxing, Wonderland.

The Battler had preceded us, and when we arrived was in the dressing-room, stripped to a breath-taking semi-nudity. I had not supposed that it was possible for a man to be larger than was Mr Billson when arrayed for the street, but in trunks and boxing shoes he looked like his big brother. Muscles resembling the hawsers of an Atlantic liner coiled down his arms and rippled along his massive shoulders. He seemed to dwarf altogether the by no means flimsy athlete who passed out of the room as we came in.

'That's the bloke,' announced Mr Billson, jerking his red head after this person.

We understood him to imply that the other was his opponent, and the spirit of confidence which had animated us waxed considerably. Where six of the pick of the Merchant Marine had failed, this stripling could scarcely hope to succeed.

'I been talkin' to 'im,' said Battling Billson.

I took this unwonted garrulity to be due to a slight nervousness natural at such a moment.

' 'E's 'ad a lot of trouble, that bloke,' said the Battler.

The obvious reply was that he was now going to have a lot more, but before either of us could make it a hoarse voice announced that Squiffy and the Toff had completed their three-round bout and that the stage now waited for our nominee. We hurried to our seats. The necessity of taking a look at our man in his dressing-room had deprived us of the pleasure of witnessing the passage of arms between Squiffy and the Toff, but I gathered that it must have been lively and full of entertainment, for the audience seemed in excellent humour. All those who were not too busy eating jellied eels were babbling happily or whistling between their fingers to friends in distant parts of the hall. As Mr Billson climbed into the ring in all the glory of his red hair and jumping muscles, the babble rose to a roar. It was plain that Wonderland had stamped our Battler with its approval on sight.

The audiences which support Wonderland are not disdainful of science. Neat footwork wins their commendation, and a skilful ducking of the head is greeted with knowing applause. But what they esteem most highly is the punch. And one sight of Battling Billson seemed to tell them that here was the Punch personified. They sent the fighters off to a howl of ecstasy, and settled back in their seats to enjoy the pure pleasure of seeing two of their fellow-men hitting each other very hard and often.

The howl died away.

I looked at Ukridge with concern. Was this the hero of Marseilles, the man who cleaned out bar-rooms and on whom undertakers fawned? Diffident was the only word to describe our Battler's behaviour in that opening round. He pawed lightly at his antagonist. He embraced him like a brother. He shuffled about the ring, innocuous.

'What's the matter with him?' I asked.

'He always starts slow,' said Ukridge, but his concern was manifest. He fumbled nervously at the buttons of his mackintosh. The referee was warning Battling Billson. He was speaking to him like a disappointed father. In the cheaper and baser parts of the house enraged citizens were whistling 'Comrades'. Everywhere a chill had fallen on the house. That first fine fresh enthusiasm had died away, and the sounding of the gong for the end of the round was greeted with censorious cat-calls. As Mr Billson lurched back to his corner, frank unfriendliness was displayed on all sides.

With the opening of the second round considerably more spirit was introduced into the affair. The same strange torpidity still held our Battler in its grip, but his opponent was another man. During round one he had seemed a little nervous and apprehensive. He had behaved as if he considered it prudent not to stir Mr Billson. But now this distaste for direct action had left him. There was jauntiness in his demeanour as he moved to the centre of the ring; and, having reached it, he uncoiled a long left and smote Mr Billson forcefully on the nose. Twice he smote him, and twice Mr Billson blinked like one who has had bad news from home. The man who had had a lot of trouble leaned sideways and brought his right fist squarely against the Battler's ear.

All was forgotten and forgiven. A moment before the audience had been solidly anti-Billson. Now they were as unanimously pro. For these blows, while they appeared to have affected him not at all physically, seemed to have awakened Mr Billson's better feelings as if somebody had turned on a tap. They had aroused in Mr Billson's soul that zest for combat which had been so sadly to seek in round one. For an instant after the receipt of that buffet on the ear the Battler stood motionless on his flat feet, apparently in deep thought. Then, with the air of one who has suddenly remembered an important appointment, he plunged forward. Like an animated windmill he cast himself upon the bloke of troubles. He knocked him here, he bounced him there. He committed mayhem upon his person. He did everything to him that a man can do who is hampered with boxing-gloves, until presently the troubled one was leaning heavily against the ropes, his head hanging dazedly, his whole attitude that of a man who would just as soon let the matter drop. It only remained for the Battler to drive home the final punch, and a hundred enthusiasts, rising to their feet, were pointing out to him desirable locations for it.

But once more that strange diffidence had descended upon our representative. While every other man in the building seemed to know the correct procedure and was sketching it out in nervous English, Mr Billson appeared the victim of doubt. He looked uncertainly at his opponent and inquiringly at the referee.

The referee, obviously a man of blunted sensibilities, was unresponsive. Do It Now was plainly his slogan. He was a business man, and he wanted his patrons to get good value for their money. He was urging Mr Billson to make a thorough job of it. And finally Mr Billson approached his man and drew back his right arm. Having done this, he looked over his shoulder once more at the referee.

It was a fatal blunder. The man who had had a lot of trouble may have been in poor shape, but, like most of his profession, he retained, despite his recent misadventures, a reserve store of energy. Even as Mr Billson turned his head, he reached down to the floor with his gloved right hand, then, with a final effort, brought it up in a majestic sweep against the angle of the other's jaw. And then, as the fickle audience, with swift change of sympathy, cheered him on, he buried his left in Mr Billson's stomach on the exact spot where the well-dressed man wears the third button of his waistcoat.

Of all human experiences this of being smitten in this precise locality is the least agreeable. Battling Billson drooped like a stricken flower, settled slowly down, and spread himself out. He lay peacefully on his back with outstretched arms like a man floating in smooth water. His day's work was done.

A wailing cry rose above the din of excited patrons of sport endeavouring to explain to their neighbours how it had all happened. It was the voice of Ukridge mourning over his dead.

At half-past eleven that night, as I was preparing for bed, a drooping figure entered my room. I mixed a silent, sympathetic Scotch and soda, and for awhile no word was spoken.

'How is the poor fellow?' I asked at length.

'He's all right,' said Ukridge, listlessly. 'I left him eating fish and chips at a coffee-stall.'

'Bad luck his getting pipped on the post like that.'

'Bad luck!' boomed Ukridge, throwing off his lethargy with a vigour that spoke of mental anguish. 'What do you mean, bad luck? It was just dam' bone-headedness. Upon my Sam, it's a little hard. I invest vast sums in this man, I support him in luxury for two weeks, asking nothing of him in return except to sail in and knock somebody's head off, which he could have done in two minutes if he had liked, and he lets me down purely and simply because the other fellow told him that he had been up all night looking after his wife who had burned her hand at the jam factory. Infernal sentimentalism!'

'Does him credit,' I argued.

'Bah!'

'Kind hearts,' I urged, 'are more than coronets.'

'Who the devil wants a pugilist to have a kind heart? What's the use of this man Billson being able to knock out an elephant if he's afflicted with this damned maudlin mushiness? Who ever heard of a mushy pugilist? It's the wrong spirit. It doesn't make for success.'

'It's a handicap, of course,' I admitted.

'What guarantee have I,' demanded Ukridge, 'that if I go to enormous trouble and expense getting him another match, he won't turn aside and brush away a silent tear in the first round because he's heard that the blighter's wife has got an ingrowing toenail?'

'You could match him only against bachelors.'

'Yes, and the first bachelor he met would draw him into a corner and tell him his aunt was down with whooping-cough, and the chump would heave a sigh and stick his chin out to be walloped. A fellow's got no business to have red hair if he isn't going to live up to it. And yet,' said Ukridge, wistfully, 'I've seen that man – it was in a dance-hall at Naples – I've seen him take on at least eleven Italians simultaneously. But then, one of them stuck a knife about three inches into his leg. He seems to need something like that to give him ambition.'

'I don't see how you are going to arrange to have him knifed just before each fight.'

'No,' said Ukridge, mournfully.

'What are you going to do about his future? Have you any plans?'

'Nothing definite. My aunt was looking for a companion to attend to her correspondence and take care of the canary last time I saw her. I might try to get the job for him.'

And with a horrid, mirthless laugh Stanley Featherstonehaugh Ukridge borrowed five shillings and passed out into the night.

I did not see Ukridge for the next few days, but I had news of him from our mutual friend George Tupper, whom I met prancing in uplifted mood down Whitehall.

'I say,' said George Tupper without preamble, and with a sort of dazed fervour, 'they've given me an under-secretaryship.'

I pressed his hand. I would have slapped him on the back, but one does not slap the backs of eminent Foreign Office officials in Whitehall in broad daylight, even if one has been at school with them.

'Congratulations,' I said. 'There is no one whom I would more gladly see under-secretarying. I heard rumours of this from Ukridge.'

'Oh, yes, I remember I told him it might be coming off. Good old Ukridge! I met him just now and told him the news, and he was delighted.'

'How much did he touch you for?'

'Eh? Oh, only five pounds. Till Saturday. He expects to have a lot of money by then.'

'Did you ever know the time when Ukridge didn't expect to have a lot of money?'

'I want you and Ukridge to come and have a bit of dinner with me to celebrate. How would Wednesday suit you?'

'Splendidly.'

'Seven-thirty at the Regent Grill, then. Will you tell Ukridge?'

'I don't know where he's got to. I haven't seen him for nearly a week. Did he tell you where he was?'

'Out at some place at Barnes. What was the name of it?'

'The White Hart?'

'That's it.'

'Tell me,' I said, 'how did he seem? Cheerful?'

'Very. Why?'

'The last time I saw him he was thinking of giving up the struggle. He had had reverses.'

I proceeded to the White Hart immediately after lunch. The fact that Ukridge was still at that hostelry and had regained his usual sunny outlook on life seemed to point to the fact that the clouds enveloping the future of Mr Billson had cleared away, and that the latter's hat was still in the ring. That this was so was made clear to me directly I arrived. Inquiring for my old friend, I was directed to an upper room, from which, as I approached, there came a peculiar thudding noise. It was caused, as I perceived on opening the door, by Mr Billson. Clad in flannel trousers and a sweater, he was earnestly pounding a large leather object suspended from a wooden platform. His manager, seated on a soap-box in a corner, regarded him the while with affectionate proprietorship.

'Hallo, old horse!' said Ukridge, rising as I entered. 'Glad to see you.'

The din of Mr Billson's bag-punching, from which my arrival had not caused him to desist, was such as to render conversation difficult. We moved to the quieter retreat of the bar downstairs, where I informed Ukridge of the under secretary's invitation.

'I'll be there,' said Ukridge. 'There's one thing about good old Billson, you can trust him not to break training if you take your eye off him. And, of course, he realizes that this is a big thing. It'll be the making of him.'

'Your aunt is considering engaging him, then?'

'My aunt? What on earth are you talking about? Collect yourself, laddie.'

'When you left me you were going to try to get him the job of looking after your aunt's canary.'

'Oh, I was feeling rather sore then. That's all over. I had an earnest talk with the poor zimp, and he means business from now on. And so he ought to, dash it, with a magnificent opportunity like this.'

'Like what?'

'We're on to a big thing now, laddie, the dickens of a big thing.'

'I hope you've made sure the other man's a bachelor. Who is he?'

'Tod Bingham.'

'Tod Bingham?' I groped in my memory. 'You don't mean the middle-weight champion?'

'That's the fellow.'

'You don't expect me to believe that you've got a match on with a champion already?'

'It isn't exactly a match. It's like this. Tod Bingham is going round the East-end halls offering two hundred quid to anyone who'll stay four rounds with him. Advertisement stuff. Good old Billson is going to unleash himself at the Shoreditch Empire next Saturday.'

'Do you think he'll be able to stay four rounds?'

'Stay four rounds!' cried Ukridge. 'Why, he could stay four rounds with a fellow armed with a Gatling-gun and a couple of pickaxes. That money's as good as in our pockets, laddie. And once we're through with this job, there isn't a boxing-place in England that won't jump at us. I don't mind telling you in confidence, old horse, that in a year from now I expect to be pulling in hundreds a week. Clean up a bit here first, you know, and then pop over to America and make an enormous fortune. Damme. I shan't know how to spend the money!'

'Why not buy some socks? I'm running a bit short of them.'

'Now, laddie, laddie,' said Ukridge, reprovingly, 'need we strike a jarring note? Is this the moment to fling your beastly socks in an old friend's face? A broader-minded spirit is what I would like to see.'

I was ten minutes late in arriving at the Regent Grill on the Wednesday of George Tupper's invitation, and the spectacle of George in person standing bare-headed at the Piccadilly entrance filled me with guilty remorse. George was the best fellow in the world, but the atmosphere of the Foreign Office had increased the tendency he had always had from boyhood to a sort of precise fussiness, and it upset him if his affairs did not run exactly on schedule. The thought that my unpunctuality should have marred this great evening sent me hurrying towards him full of apologies.

'Oh, there you are,' said George Tupper. 'I say, it's too bad –'

'I'm awfully sorry. My watch –'

'Ukridge!' cried George Tupper, and I perceived that it was not I who had caused his concern.

'Isn't he coming?' I asked, amazed. The idea of Ukridge evading a free meal was one of those that seem to make the solid foundations of the world rock.

'He's come. And he's brought a girl with him!'

'A *girl*!'

'In pink, with yellow hair,' wailed George Tupper. 'What am I to do?'

I pondered the point.

'It's a weird thing for even Ukridge to have done,' I said, 'but I suppose you'll have to give her dinner.'

'But the place is full of people I know, and this girl's so – so spectacular.'

I felt for him deeply, but I could see no way out of it.

'You don't think I could say I had been taken ill?'

'It would hurt Ukridge's feelings.'

'I should enjoy hurting Ukridge's feelings, curse him!' said George Tupper, fervently.

'And it would be an awful slam for the girl, whoever she is.'

George Tupper sighed. His was a chivalrous nature. He drew himself up as if bracing himself for a dreadful ordeal.

'Oh, well, I suppose there's nothing to do,' he said. 'Come along. I left them drinking cocktails in the lounge.'

George had not erred in describing Ukridge's addition to the festivities as spectacular. Flamboyant would have been a suitable word. As she preceded us down the long dining-room, her arm linked in George Tupper's – she seemed to have taken a liking to George – I had ample opportunity for studying her, from her patent-leather shoes to the mass of golden hair beneath her picture-hat. She had a loud, clear voice, and she was telling George Tupper the rather intimate details of an internal complaint which had recently troubled an aunt of hers. If George had been the family physician, she could not have been franker; and I could see a dull glow spreading over his shapely ears.

Perhaps Ukridge saw it, too, for he seemed to experience a slight twinge of conscience.

'I have an idea, laddie,' he whispered, 'that old Tuppy is a trifle peeved at my bringing Flossie along. If you get a chance, you might murmur to him that it was military necessity.'

'Who is she?' I asked.

'I told you about her. Flossie, the barmaid at the Crown in Kennington. Billson's *fiancée*.'

I looked at him in amazement.

'Do you mean to tell me that you're courting death by flirting with Battling Billson's girl?'

'My dear old man, nothing like that,' said Ukridge, shocked. 'The whole thing is, I've got a particular favour to ask of her – rather a rummy request – and it was no good springing it on her in cold blood. There had to be a certain amount of champagne in advance, and my funds won't run to champagne. I'm taking her on to the Alhambra after dinner. I'll look you up tonight and tell you all about it.'

We then proceeded to dine. It was not one of the pleasantest meals of my experience. The future Mrs Billson prattled agreeably throughout, and Ukridge assisted her in keeping the conversation alive; but the shattered demeanour of George Tupper would have taken the sparkle out of any banquet. From time to time he pulled himself together and endeavoured to play the host, but for the most part he maintained a pale and brooding silence; and it was a relief when Ukridge and his companion rose to leave.

'Well! –' began George Tupper in a strangled voice, as they moved away down the aisle.

I lit a cigar and sat back dutifully to listen.

Ukridge arrived in my rooms at midnight, his eyes gleaming through their pince-nez with a strange light. His manner was exuberant.

'It's all right,' he said.

'I'm glad you think so.'

'Did you explain to Tuppy?'

'I didn't get a chance. He was talking too hard.'

'About me?'

'Yes. He said everything I've always felt about you, only far, far better than I could ever have put it.'

Ukridge's face clouded for a moment, but cheerfulness returned.

'Oh, well, it can't be helped. He'll simmer down in a day or two. It had to be done, laddie. Life and death matter. And it's all right. Read this.'

I took the letter he handed me. It was written in a scrawly hand.

'What's this?'

'Read it, laddie. I think it will meet the case.'

I read.

' "Wilberforce." '

'Who on earth's Wilberforce?'

'I told you that was Billson's name.'

'Oh, yes.'

I returned to the letter.

WILBERFORCE,

I take my pen in hand to tell you that I can never be yours. You will no doubt be surprised to hear that I love another and a better man, so that it can never be. He loves me, and he is a better man than you.

Hoping this finds you in the pink as it leaves me at present.

Yours faithfully,
FLORENCE BURNS.

'I told her to keep it snappy,' said Ukridge.

'Well, she's certainly done it,' I replied, handing back the letter. 'I'm sorry. From the little I saw of her, I thought her a nice girl – for Billson. Do you happen to know the other man's address? Because it would be a kindly act to send him a post card advising him to leave England for a year or two.'

'The Shoreditch Empire will find him this week.'

'What!'

'The other man is Tod Bingham.'

'Tod Bingham!' The drama of the situation moved me. 'Do you mean to say that Tod Bingham is in love with Battling Billson's girl?'

'No. He's never seen her!'

'What do you mean?'

Ukridge sat down creakingly on the sofa. He slapped my knee with sudden and uncomfortable violence.

'Laddie,' said Ukridge, 'I will tell you all. Yesterday afternoon I found old Billson reading a copy of the *Daily Sportsman*. He isn't much of a reader as a rule, so I was rather interested to know what had gripped him. And do you know what it was, old horse?'

'I do not.'

'It was an article about Tod Bingham. One of those damned sentimental blurbs they print about pugilists nowadays, saying what a good chap he was in private life and how he always sent a telegram to his old mother after each fight and gave her half the purse. Damme, there ought to be a censorship of the Press. These blighters don't mind *what* they print. I don't suppose Tod Bingham has *got* an old mother, and if he has I'll bet he doesn't give her a bob. There were tears in that chump Billson's eyes as he showed me the article. Salt tears, laddie! "Must be a nice feller!" he said. Well, I ask you! I mean to say, it's a bit thick when the man you've been pouring out money for and watching over like a baby sister starts getting sorry for a champion three days before he's due to fight him. A champion, mark you! It was bad enough his getting mushy about that fellow at Wonderland, but when it came to being soft-hearted over Tod Bingham something had to be done. Well, you know me. Brain like a buzz-saw. I saw the only way of counteracting this pernicious stuff was to get him so mad with Tod Bingham that he would forget all about his old mother, so I suddenly thought: Why not get Flossie to pretend that Bingham had cut him out with her? Well, it's not the sort of thing you can ask a girl to do without preparing the ground a bit, so I brought her along to Tuppy's dinner. It was a master-stroke, laddie. There's nothing softens the delicately-nurtured like a good dinner, and there's no denying that old Tuppy did us well. She agreed the moment I put the thing to her, and sat down and wrote that letter without a blink. I think she thinks it's all a jolly practical joke. She's a light-hearted girl.'

'Must be.'

'It'll give poor old Billson a bit of a jar for the time being, I suppose, but it'll make him spread himself on Saturday night, and he'll be perfectly happy on Sunday morning when she tells him she didn't mean it and he realizes that he's got a hundred quid of Tod Bingham's in his trousers pocket.'

'I thought you said it was two hundred quid that Bingham was offering.'

'I get a hundred,' said Ukridge, dreamily.

'The only flaw is, the letter doesn't give the other man's name. How is Billson to know it's Tod Bingham?'

'Why, damme, laddie, do use your intelligence. Billson isn't going to sit down and yawn when he gets that letter. He'll buzz straight down to Kennington and ask Flossie.'

'And then she'll give the whole thing away.'

'No, she won't. I slipped her a couple of quid to promise she wouldn't. And that reminds me, old man, it has left me a bit short, so if you could possibly manage –'

'Good night,' I said.

'But, laddie –'

'And God bless you,' I added, firmly.

The Shoreditch Empire is a roomy house, but it was crowded to the doors when I reached it on the Saturday night. In normal circumstances I suppose there would always have been a large audience on a Saturday, and this evening the lure of Tod Bingham's personal appearance had drawn more than capacity. In return for my shilling I was accorded the privilege of standing against the wall at the back, a position from which I could not see a great deal of the performance.

From the occasional flashes which I got of the stage between the heads of my neighbours, however, and from the generally restless and impatient attitude of the audience I gathered that I was not missing much. The programme of the Shoreditch Empire that week was essentially a one-man affair. The patrons had the air of suffering the preliminary acts as unavoidable obstacles that stand between them and the head-liner. It was Tod Bingham whom they had come to see, and they were not cordial to the unfortunate serio-comics, tramp cyclists, jugglers, acrobats, and ballad singers who intruded themselves during the earlier part of the evening. The cheer that arose as the curtain fell on a dramatic sketch came from the heart, for the next number on the programme was that of the star.

A stout man in evening dress with a red handkerchief worn ambassadorially athwart his shirt-front stepped out from the wings.

'Ladies and gentlemen!'

' 'Ush!' cried the audience,

'Ladies and gentlemen!'

A Voice: 'Good ole Tod!' ('Cheese it!')

'Ladies and gentlemen,' said the ambassador for the third time. He scanned the house apprehensively. 'Deeply regret have unfortunate disappointment to announce. Tod Bingham unfortunately unable to appear before you tonight.'

A howl like the howl of wolves balked of their prey or of an amphitheatre full of Roman citizens on receipt of the news that the supply of lions had run out greeted these words. We stared at each other with a wild surmise. Could this thing be, or was it not too thick for human belief?

'Wot's the matter with 'im?' demanded the gallery, hoarsely.

'Yus, wot's the matter with 'im?' echoed we of the better element on the lower floor.

The ambassador sidled uneasily towards the prompt entrance. He seemed aware that he was not a popular favourite.

' 'E 'as 'ad an unfortunate accident,' he declared, nervousness beginning to sweep away his aitches wholesale. 'On 'is way 'ere to this 'all 'e was unfortunately run into by a truck, sustaining bruises and contusions which render 'im unfortunately unable to appear before you tonight. I beg to announce that 'is place will be taken by Professor Devine, who will render 'is marvellous imitations of various birds and familiar animals. Ladies and gentlemen,' concluded the ambassador, stepping nimbly off the stage, 'I thank you one and all.'

The curtain rose and a dapper individual with a waxed moustache skipped on.

'Ladies and gentlemen, my first imitation will be of that well-known songster, the common thrush – better known to some of you per'aps as the throstle. And in connexion with my performance I wish to state that I 'ave nothing whatsoever in my mouth. The effects which I produce –'

I withdrew, and two-thirds of the audience started to do the same. From behind us, dying away as the doors closed, came the plaintive note of the common thrush feebly competing with that other and sterner bird which haunts those places of entertainment where audiences are critical and swift to take offence.

Out in the street, a knot of Shoreditch's younger set were hanging on the lips of an excited orator in a battered hat and trousers which had been made for a larger man. Some stirring tale which he was telling held them spell-bound. Words came raggedly through the noise of the traffic.

'– like this. Then 'e 'its 'im another like that. Then they start – on the side of the jor –'

'Pass along, there,' interrupted an official voice. 'Come on, there, pass along.'

The crowd thinned and resolved itself into its elements. I found myself moving down the street in company with the wearer of the battered hat. Though we had not been formally introduced, he seemed to consider me a suitable recipient for his tale. He enrolled me at once as a nucleus for a fresh audience.

' 'E comes up, this bloke does, just as Tod is goin' in at the stage-door –'

'Tod?' I queried.

'Tod Bingham. 'E comes up just as 'e's goin' in at the stage-door, and 'e says " ' Ere!" and Tod says "Yus?" and this bloke 'e says "Put 'em up!" and Tod says "Put wot up?" and this bloke says "Yer 'ands," and Tod says "Wot, me?" – sort of surprised. An' the next minute they're fightin' all over the shop.'

'But surely Tod Bingham was run over by a truck?'

The man in the battered hat surveyed me with the mingled scorn and resentment which the devout bestow on those of heretical views.

'Truck! 'E wasn't run over by no truck. Wot mikes yer fink 'e was run over by a truck? Wot 'ud 'e be doin' bein' run over by a truck? 'E 'ad it put across 'im by this red-'eaded bloke, same as I'm tellin' yer.'

A great light shone upon me.

'Red-headed?' I cried.

'Yus.'

'A big man?'

'Yus.'

'And he put it across Tod Bingham?'

'Put it across 'im proper. 'Ad to go 'ome in a keb, Tod did. Funny a bloke that could fight like that bloke could fight 'adn't the sense to go and do it on the stige and get some money for it. That's wot I think.'

Across the street an arc-lamp shed its cold rays. And into its glare there strode a man draped in a yellow mackintosh. The light gleamed on his pince-nez and lent a gruesome pallor to his set face. It was Ukridge retreating from Moscow.

'Others,' I said, 'are thinking the same.'

And I hurried across the road to administer what feeble consolation I might. There are moments when a fellow needs a friend.

Chapter 4

First Aid for Dora

Never in the course of a long and intimate acquaintance having been shown any evidence to the contrary, I had always looked on Stanley Featherstonehaugh Ukridge, my boyhood chum, as a man ruggedly indifferent to the appeal of the opposite sex. I had assumed that, like so many financial giants, he had no time for dalliance with women – other and deeper matters, I supposed, keeping that great brain permanently occupied. It was a surprise, therefore, when, passing down Shaftesbury Avenue one Wednesday afternoon in June at the hour when *matinée* audiences were leaving the theatres, I came upon him assisting a girl in a white dress to mount an omnibus.

As far as this simple ceremony could be rendered impressive, Ukridge made it so. His manner was a blend of courtliness and devotion; and if his mackintosh had been a shade less yellow and his hat a trifle less disreputable, he would have looked just like Sir Walter Raleigh.

The bus moved on, Ukridge waved, and I proceeded to make inquiries. I felt that I was an interested party. There had been a distinctly 'object-matrimony' look about the back of his neck, it seemed to me; and the prospect of having to support a Mrs Ukridge and keep a flock of little Ukridges in socks and shirts perturbed me.

'Who was that?' I asked.

'Oh, hallo, laddie!' said Ukridge, turning. 'Where did you spring from? If you had come a moment earlier, I'd have introduced you to Dora.' The bus was lumbering out of sight into Piccadilly Circus, and the white figure on top turned and gave a final wave. 'That was Dora Mason,' said Ukridge, having flapped a large hand in reply. 'She's my aunt's secretary-companion. I used to see a bit of her from time to time when I was

69

living at Wimbledon. Old Tuppy gave me a couple of seats for that show at the Apollo, so I thought it would be a kindly act to ask her along. I'm sorry for that girl. Sorry for her, old horse.'

'What's the matter with her?'

'Hers is a grey life. She has few pleasures. It's an act of charity to give her a little treat now and then. Think of it! Nothing to do all day but brush the Pekingese and type out my aunt's rotten novels.'

'Does your aunt write novels?'

'The world's worst, laddie, the world's worst. She's been steeped to the gills in literature ever since I can remember. They've just made her president of the Pen and Ink Club. As a matter of fact, it was her novels that did me in when I lived with her. She used to send me to bed with the beastly things and ask me questions about them at breakfast. Absolutely without exaggeration, laddie, at breakfast. It was a dog's life, and I'm glad it's over. Flesh and blood couldn't stand the strain. Well, knowing my aunt, I don't mind telling you that my heart bleeds for poor little Dora. I know what a foul time she has, and I feel a better, finer man for having given her this passing gleam of sunshine. I wish I could have done more for her.'

'Well, you might have stood her tea after the theatre.'

'Not within the sphere of practical politics, laddie. Unless you can sneak out without paying, which is dashed difficult to do with these cashiers watching the door like weasels, tea even at an ABC shop punches the pocket-book pretty hard, and at the moment I'm down to the scrapings. But I'll tell you what, I don't mind joining you in a cup, if you were thinking of it.'

'I wasn't.'

'Come, come! A little more of the good old spirit of hospitality, old horse.'

'Why do you wear that beastly mackintosh in mid-summer?'

'Don't evade the point, laddie. I can see at a glance that you need tea. You're looking pale and fagged.'

'Doctors say that tea is bad for the nerves.'

'Yes, possibly there's something in that. Then I'll tell you what,' said Ukridge, never too proud to yield a point, 'we'll make it a whisky-and-soda instead. Come along over to the Criterion.'

It was a few days after this that the Derby was run, and a horse of the name of Gunga Din finished third. This did not interest the great bulk of the intelligentsia to any marked extent, the animal having started at a hundred to three, but it meant much to me, for I had drawn his name in the sweepstake at my club. After a monotonous series of blanks stretching back to the first year of my membership, this seemed to me the outstanding event of the century, and I celebrated my triumph by an informal dinner to a few friends. It was some small consolation to me later to remember that I had wanted to include Ukridge in the party, but failed to get hold of him. Dark hours were to follow, but at least Ukridge did not go through them bursting with my meat.

There is no form of spiritual exaltation so poignant as that which comes from winning even a third prize in a sweepstake. So tremendous was the moral uplift that, when eleven o'clock arrived, it seemed silly to sit talking in a club and still sillier to go to bed. I suggested spaciously that we should all go off and dress and resume the revels at my expense half an hour later at Mario's, where, it being an extension night, there would be music and dancing till three. We scattered in cabs to our various homes.

How seldom in this life do we receive any premonition of impending disaster. I hummed a gay air as I entered the house in Ebury Street where I lodged, and not even the usually quelling sight of Bowles, my landlord, in the hall as I came in could quench my bonhomie. Generally a meeting with Bowles had the effect on me which the interior of a cathedral has on the devout, but tonight I was superior to this weakness.

'Ah, Bowles,' I cried, chummily, only just stopping myself from adding 'Honest fellow!' 'Hallo, Bowles! I say, Bowles, I drew Gunga Din in the club sweep.'

'Indeed, sir?'

'Yes. He came in third, you know.'

'So I see by the evening paper, sir. I congratulate you.'

'Thank you, Bowles, thank you.'

'Mr Ukridge called earlier in the evening, sir,' said Bowles.

'Did he? Sorry I was out. I was trying to get hold of him. Did he want anything in particular?'

'Your dress-clothes, sir.'

'My dress-clothes, eh?' I laughed genially. 'Extraordinary fellow! You never know –' A ghastly thought smote me like a blow. A cold wind seemed to blow through the hall. 'He didn't *get* them, did he?' I quavered.

'Why, yes, sir.'

'Got my dress-clothes?' I muttered thickly, clutching for support at the hat-stand.

'He said it would be all right, sir,' said Bowles, with that sickening tolerance which he always exhibited for all that Ukridge said or did. One of the leading mysteries of my life was my landlord's amazing attitude towards this hell-hound. He fawned on the man. A splendid fellow like myself had to go about in a state of hushed reverence towards Bowles, while a human blot like Ukridge could bellow at him over the banisters without the slightest rebuke. It was one of those things which make one laugh cynically when people talk about the equality of man.

'He got my dress-clothes?' I mumbled.

'Mr Ukridge said that he knew you would be glad to let him have them, as you would not be requiring them tonight.'

'But I do require them, damn it!' I shouted, lost to all proper feeling. Never before had I let fall an oath in Bowles's presence. 'I'm giving half a dozen men supper at Mario's in a quarter of an hour.'

Bowles clicked his tongue sympathetically.

'What am I going to do?'

'Perhaps if you would allow me to lend you mine, sir?'

'Yours?'

'I have a very nice suit. It was given to me by his lordship the late Earl of Oxted, in whose employment I was for many years. I fancy it would do very well on you, sir. His lordship was about your height, though perhaps a little slenderer. Shall I fetch it, sir? I have it in a trunk downstairs.'

The obligations of hospitality are sacred. In fifteen minutes' time six jovial men would be assembling at Mario's, and what would they do, lacking a host? I nodded feebly.

'It's very kind of you,' I managed to say.

'Not at all, sir. It is a pleasure.'

If he was speaking the truth, I was glad of it. It is nice to think that the affair brought pleasure to someone.

That the late Earl of Oxted had indeed been a somewhat slenderer man than myself became manifest to me from the first pulling on of the trousers. Hitherto I had always admired the slim, small-boned type of aristocrat, but it was not long before I was wishing that Bowles had been in the employment of someone who had gone in a little more heartily for starchy foods. And I regretted, moreover, that the fashion of wearing a velvet collar on an evening coat, if it had to come in at all, had not lasted a few years longer. Dim as the light in my bedroom was, it was strong enough to make me wince as I looked in the mirror.

And I was aware of a curious odour.

'Isn't this room a trifle stuffy, Bowles?'

'No, sir. I think not.'

'Don't you notice an odd smell?'

'No, sir. But I have a somewhat heavy cold. If you are ready, sir, I will call a cab.'

Moth balls! That was the scent I had detected. It swept upon me like a wave in the cab. It accompanied me like a fog all the way to Mario's, and burst out in its full fragrance when I entered the place and removed my overcoat. The cloak-room waiter sniffed in startled way as he gave me my check, one or two people standing near hastened to remove themselves from my immediate neighbourhood, and my friends, when I joined them, expressed themselves with friend-like candour. With a solid unanimity they told me frankly that it was only the fact that I was paying for the supper that enabled them to tolerate my presence.

The leper-like feeling induced by this uncharitable attitude caused me after the conclusion of the meal to withdraw to the balcony to smoke in solitude. My guests were dancing merrily, but such pleasures were not for me. Besides, my velvet collar had already excited ribald comment, and I am a sensitive man. Crouched in a lonely corner of the balcony, surrounded by the outcasts who were not allowed on the lower floor because they were not dressed, I chewed a cigar and watched the revels with a jaundiced eye. The space reserved for dancing was crowded and couples either revolved warily or ruthlessly bumped a passage for themselves, using their partners as battering-rams. Prominent among the ruthless bumpers was a big man who was giving a realistic imitation of a steam-plough. He danced strongly and energetically, and when he struck the line, something had to give.

From the very first something about this man had seemed familiar; but owing to his peculiar crouching manner of dancing, which he seemed to have modelled on the ring-style of Mr James J. Jeffries, it was not immediately that I was able to see his face. But presently, as the music stopped and he straightened himself to clap his hands for an encore, his foul features were revealed to me.

It was Ukridge. Ukridge, confound him, with my dress-clothes fitting him so perfectly and with such unwrinkled smoothness that he might have stepped straight out of one of Ouida's novels. Until that moment I had never fully realized the meaning of the expression 'faultless evening dress'. With a passionate cry I leaped from my seat, and, accompanied by a rich smell of camphor, bounded for the stairs. Like Hamlet on a less impressive occasion, I wanted to slay this man when he was full of bread, with all his crimes, broad-blown, as flush as May, at drinking, swearing, or about some act that had no relish of salvation in it.

'But, laddie,' said Ukridge, backed into a corner of the lobby apart from the throng, 'be reasonable.'

I cleansed my bosom of a good deal of that perilous stuff that weighs upon the heart.

'How could I guess that you would want the things? Look at it from my position, old horse. I knew you, laddie, a good true friend who would be delighted to lend a pal his dress-clothes any time when he didn't need them himself, and as you weren't there when I called, I couldn't ask you, so I naturally simply borrowed them. It was all just one of those little misunderstandings which can't be helped. And, as it luckily turns out, you had a spare suit, so everything was all right, after all.'

'You don't think this poisonous fancy dress is mine, do you?'

'Isn't it?' said Ukridge, astonished.

'It belongs to Bowles. He lent it to me.'

'And most extraordinarily well you look in it, laddie,' said Ukridge. 'Upon my Sam, you look like a duke or something.'

'And smell like a second-hand clothes-store.'

'Nonsense, my dear old son, nonsense. A mere faint suggestion of some rather pleasant antiseptic. Nothing more. I like it. It's invigorating. Honestly, old man. it's really remarkable what an air that suit gives you. Distinguished. That's the word I was searching for. You look distinguished. All the girls are saying so. When you came in just now to speak to me, I heard one of them whisper "Who is it?" That shows you.'

'More likely "What is it?"'

'Ha, ha!' bellowed Ukridge, seeking to cajole me with sycophantic mirth. 'Dashed good! Deuced good! Not "Who is it?" but "What is it?" It beats me how you think of these things. Golly, if I had a brain like yours – But now, old son, if you don't mind, I really must be getting back to poor little Dora. She'll be wondering what has become of me.'

The significance of these words had the effect of making me forget my just wrath for a moment.

'Are you here with that girl you took to the theatre the other afternoon?'

'Yes. I happened to win a trifle on the Derby, so I thought it would be the decent thing to ask her out for an evening's pleasure. Hers is a grey life.'

'It must be, seeing you so much.'

'A little personal, old horse,' said Ukridge reprovingly. 'A trifle bitter. But I know you don't mean it. Yours is a heart of gold really. If I've said that once, I've said it a hundred times. Always saying it. Rugged exterior but heart of gold. My very words. Well, good-bye for the present, laddie. I'll look in to-morrow and return these things. I'm sorry there was any misunderstanding about them, but it makes up for everything, doesn't it, to feel that you've helped brighten life for a poor little downtrodden thing who has few pleasures.'

'Just one last word,' I said. 'One final remark.'

'Yes?'

'I'm sitting in that corner of the balcony over there,' I said. 'I mention the fact so that you can look out for yourself. If you come dancing underneath there, I shall drop a plate on you.

75

And if it kills you, so much the better. I'm a poor down-trodden little thing, and I have few pleasures.'

Owing to a mawkish respect for the conventions, for which I reproach myself, I did not actually perform this service to humanity. With the exception of throwing a roll at him – which missed him but most fortunately hit the member of my supper-party who had sniffed with the most noticeable offensiveness at my camphorated costume – I took no punitive measures against Ukridge that night. But his demeanour, when he called at my rooms next day, could not have been more crushed if I had dropped a pound of lead on him. He strode into my sitting-room with the sombre tread of the man who in a conflict with Fate has received the loser's end. I had been passing in my mind a number of good snappy things to say to him, but his appear-ance touched me to such an extent that I held them in. To abuse this man would have been like dancing on a tomb.

'For Heaven's sake what's the matter?' I asked. 'You look like a toad under the harrow.'

He sat down creakingly, and lit one of my cigars.

'Poor little Dora!'

'What about her?'

'She's got the push!'

'The push? From your aunt's, do you mean?'

'Yes.'

'What for?'

Ukridge sighed heavily.

'Most unfortunate business, old horse, and largely my fault. I thought the whole thing was perfectly safe. You see, my aunt goes to bed at half-past ten every night, so it seemed to me that if Dora slipped out at eleven and left a window open behind her she could sneak back all right when we got home from Mario's. But what happened? Some dashed officious ass,' said Ukridge, with honest wrath, 'went and locked the damned window. I don't know who it was. I suspect the butler. He has a nasty habit of going round the place late at night and shutting things. Upon my Sam, it's a little hard! If only people would leave things alone and not go snooping about –'

'What happened?'

'Why, it was the scullery window which we'd left open, and

when we got back at four o'clock this morning the infernal thing was shut as tight as an egg. Things looked pretty rocky, but Dora remembered that her bedroom window was always open, so we bucked up again for a bit. Her room's on the second floor, but I knew where there was a ladder, so I went and got it, and she was just hopping up as merry as dammit when somebody flashed a great beastly lantern on us, and there was a policeman, wanting to know what the game was. The whole trouble with the police force of London, laddie, the thing that makes them a hissing and a byword, is that they're snoopers to a man. Zeal, I suppose they call it. Why they can't attend to their own affairs is more than I can understand. Dozens of murders going on all the time, probably, all over Wimbledon, and all this bloke would do was stand and wiggle his infernal lantern and ask what the game was. Wouldn't be satisfied with a plain statement that it was all right. Insisted on rousing the house to have us identified.'

Ukridge paused, a reminiscent look of pain on his expressive face.

'And then?' I said.

'We were,' said Ukridge, briefly.

'What?'

'Identified. By my aunt. In a dressing-gown and a revolver. And the long and the short of it is, old man, that poor little Dora has got the sack.'

I could not find it in my heart to blame his aunt for what he evidently considered a high-handed and tyrannical outrage. If I were a maiden lady of regular views, I should relieve myself of the services of any secretary-companion who returned to roost only a few short hours in advance of the milk. But, as Ukridge plainly desired sympathy rather than an austere pronouncement on the relations of employer and employed, I threw him a couple of tuts, which seemed to soothe him a little. He turned to the practical side of the matter.

'What's to be done?'

'I don't see what you can do.'

'But I must do something. I've lost the poor little thing her job, and I must try to get it back. It's a rotten sort of job, but it's her bread and butter. Do you think George Tupper would biff round and have a chat with my aunt, if I asked him?'

'I suppose he would. He's the best-hearted man in the world. But I doubt if he'll be able to do much.'

'Nonsense, laddie,' said Ukridge, his unconquerable optimism rising bravely from the depths. 'I have the utmost confidence in old Tuppy. A man in a million. And he's such a dashed respectable sort of bloke that he might have her jumping through hoops and shamming dead before she knew what was happening to her. You never know. Yes, I'll try old Tuppy. I'll go and see him now.'

'I should.'

'Just lend me a trifle for a cab, old son, and I shall be able to get to the Foreign Office before one o'clock. I mean to say, even if nothing comes of it, I shall be able to get a lunch out of him. And I need refreshment, laddie, need it sorely. The whole business has shaken me very much.'

It was three days after this that, stirred by a pleasant scent of bacon and coffee, I hurried my dressing and, proceeding to my sitting-room, found that Ukridge had dropped in to take breakfast with me, as was often his companionable practice. He seemed thoroughly cheerful again, and was plying knife and fork briskly like the good trencherman he was.

'Morning, old horse,' he said agreeably.

'Good morning.'

'Devilish good bacon, this. As good as I've ever bitten. Bowles is cooking you some more.'

'That's nice. I'll have a cup of coffee, if you don't mind me making myself at home while I'm waiting.' I started to open the letters by my plate, and became aware that my guest was eyeing me with a stare of intense penetration through his pince-nez, which were all crooked as usual. 'What's the matter?'

'Matter?'

'Why,' I said, 'are you looking at me like a fish with lung-trouble?'

'Was I?' He took a sip of coffee with an overdone carelessness. 'Matter of fact, old son, I was rather interested. I see you've had a letter from my aunt.'

'What?'

I had picked up the last envelope. It was addressed in a

78

strong female hand, strange to me. I now tore it open. It was even as Ukridge had said. Dated the previous day and headed 'Heath House, Wimbledon Common', the letter ran as follows:

DEAR SIR, – I shall be happy to see you if you will call at this address the day after tomorrow (Friday) at four-thirty. – Yours faithfully, JULIA UKRIDGE.

I could make nothing of this. My morning mail, whether pleasant or the reverse, whether bringing a bill from a tradesman or a cheque from an editor, had had till now the uniform quality of being plain, straightforward, and easy to understand; but this communication baffled me. How Ukridge's aunt had become aware of my existence, and why a call from me should ameliorate her lot, were problems beyond my unravelling, and I brooded over it as an Egyptologist might over some newly-discovered hieroglyphic.

'What does she say?' inquired Ukridge.

'She wants me to call at half-past four tomorrow afternoon.'

'Splendid!' cried Ukridge. 'I knew she would bite.'

'What on earth are you talking about?'

Ukridge reached across the table and patted me affectionately on the shoulder. The movement involved the upsetting of a full cup of coffee, but I suppose he meant well. He sank back again in his chair and adjusted his pince-nez in order to get a better view of me. I seemed to fill him with honest joy, and he suddenly burst into a spirited eulogy, rather like some minstrel of old delivering an *ex-tempore* boost of his chieftain and employer.

'Laddie,' said Ukridge, 'if there's one thing about you that I've always admired it's your readiness to help a pal. One of the most admirable qualities a bloke can possess, and nobody has it to a greater extent than you. You're practically unique in that way. I've had men come up to me and ask me about you. "What sort of a chap is he?" they say. "One of the very best," I reply. "A fellow you can rely on. A man who would die rather than let you down. A bloke who would go through fire and water to do a pal a good turn. A bird with a heart of gold and a nature as true as steel." '

'Yes, I'm a splendid fellow,' I agreed, slightly perplexed by this panegyric. 'Get on.'

'I am getting on, old horse,' said Ukridge with faint reproach. 'What I'm trying to say is that I knew you would be delighted to tackle this little job for me. It wasn't necessary to ask you. I *knew*.'

A grim foreboding of an awful doom crept over me, as it had done so often before in my association with Ukridge.

'Will you kindly tell me what damned thing you've let me in for now?'

Ukridge deprecated my warmth with a wave of his fork. He spoke soothingly and with a winning persuasiveness. He practically cooed.

'It's nothing, laddie. Practically nothing. Just a simple little act of kindness which you will thank me for putting in your way. It's like this. As I ought to have foreseen from the first, that ass Tuppy proved a broken reed. In that matter of Dora, you know. Got no result whatever. He went to see my aunt the day before yesterday, and asked her to take Dora on again, and she gave him the miss-in-balk. I'm not surprised. I never had any confidence in Tuppy. It was a mistake ever sending him. It's no good trying frontal attack in a delicate business like this. What you need is strategy. You want to think what is the enemy's weak side and then attack from that angle. Now, what is my aunt's weak side, laddie? Her weak side, what is it? Now think. Reflect, old horse.'

'From the sound of her voice, the only time I ever got near her, I should say she hadn't one.'

'That's where you make your error, old son. Butter her up about her beastly novels, and a child could eat out of her hand. When Tuppy let me down I just lit a pipe and had a good think. And then suddenly I got it. I went to a pal of mine, a thorough sportsman – you don't know him. I must introduce you some day – and he wrote my aunt a letter from you, asking if you could come and interview her for *Woman's Sphere*. It's a weekly paper, which I happen to know she takes in regularly. Now, listen, laddie. Don't interrupt for a moment. I want you to get the devilish shrewdness of this. You go and interview her, and she's all over you. Tickled to death. Of course, you'll have to do a good deal of Young Disciple stuff, but you won't mind that. After you've soft-soaped her till she's purring like a dynamo, you get up to go. "Well," you say, "this has been the proudest occasion of my life, meeting one whose work I have so long admired." And she says, "The pleasure is mine, old horse." And you slop over each other a bit more. Then you say sort of casually, as if it had just occurred to you, "Oh, by the way, I believe my cousin – or sister – No, better make it cousin – I believe my cousin, Miss Dora Mason is your secretary, isn't she?" "She isn't any such dam' thing," replies my aunt. "I sacked her three days ago." That's your cue, laddie. Your face falls, you register concern, you're frightfully cut up. You start in to ask her to let Dora come back. And you're such pals by this time that she can refuse you nothing. And there you are! My dear old son, you can take it from me that if you only keep your head and do the Young Disciple stuff properly the thing can't fail. It's an iron-clad scheme. There isn't a flaw in it.'

'There is one.'

'I think you're wrong. I've gone over the thing very carefully. What is it?'

'The flaw is that I'm not going anywhere near your infernal aunt. So you can trot back to your forger chum and tell him he's wasted a good sheet of letter-paper.'

A pair of pince-nez tinkled into a plate. Two pained eyes blinked at me across the table. Stanley Featherstonehaugh Ukridge was wounded to the quick.

'You don't mean to say you're backing out?' he said, in a low, quivering voice.

'I never was in.'

'Laddie,' said Ukridge, weightily, resting an elbow on his last slice of bacon, 'I want to ask you one question. Just one simple question. Have you ever let me down? Has there been one occasion in our long friendship when I have relied upon you and been deceived? Not one!'

'Everything's got to have a beginning. I'm starting now.'

'But think of her. Dora! Poor little Dora. Think of poor little Dora.'

'If this business teaches her to keep away from you, it will be a blessing in the end.'

'But, laddie –'

I suppose there is some fatal weakness in my character, or

else the brand of bacon which Bowles cooked possessed a peculiarly mellowing quality. All I know is that, after being adamant for a good ten minutes, I finished breakfast committed to a task from which my soul revolted. After all, as Ukridge said, it was rough on the girl. Chivalry is chivalry. We must strive to lend a helping hand as we go through this world of ours, and all that sort of thing. Four o'clock on the following afternoon found me entering a cab and giving the driver the address of Heath House, Wimbledon Common.

My emotions on entering Heath House were such as I would have felt had I been keeping a tryst with a dentist who by some strange freak happened also to be a duke. From the moment when a butler of super-Bowles dignity opened the door and, after regarding me with ill-concealed dislike, started to conduct me down a long hall, I was in the grip of both fear and humility. Heath House is one of the stately homes of Wimbledon ; how beautiful they stand, as the poet says : and after the humble drabness of Ebury Street it frankly overawed me. Its keynote was an extreme neatness which seemed to sneer at my squashy collar and reproach my baggy trouser-leg. The farther I penetrated over the polished floor, the more vividly was it brought home to me that I was one of the submerged tenth and could have done with a hair-cut. I had not been aware when I left home that my hair was unusually long, but now I seemed to be festooned by a matted and offensive growth. A patch on my left shoe which had had a rather comfortable look in Ebury Street stood out like a blot on the landscape. No, I was not at my ease ; and when I reflected that in a few moments I was to meet Ukridge's aunt, that legendary figure, face to face, a sort of wistful admiration filled me for the beauty of the nature of one who would go through all this to help a girl he had never even met. There was no doubt about it – the facts spoke for themselves – I was one of the finest fellows I had ever known. Nevertheless, there was no getting away from it, my trousers did bag at the knee.

'Mr Corcoran,' announced the butler, opening the drawing-room door. He spoke with just that intonation of voice that seemed to disclaim all responsibility. If I had an appointment, he intimated, it was his duty, however repulsive, to show me in; but, that done, he dissociated himself entirely from the whole affair.

There were two women and six Pekingese dogs in the room. The Pekes I had met before, during their brief undergraduate days at Ukridge's dog college, but they did not appear to recognize me. The occasion when they had lunched at my expense seemed to have passed from their minds. One by one they came up, sniffed, and then moved away as if my bouquet had disappointed them. They gave the impression that they saw eye to eye with the butler in his estimate of the young visitor. I was left to face the two women.

Of these – reading from right to left – one was a tall, angular, hawk-faced female with a stony eye. The other, to whom I gave but a passing glance at the moment, was small, and so it seemed to me, pleasant-looking. She had bright hair faintly powdered with grey, and mild eyes of a china blue. She reminded me of the better class of cat. I took her to be some casual caller who had looked in for a cup of tea. It was the hawk on whom I riveted my attention. She was looking at me with a piercing and unpleasant stare, and I thought how exactly she resembled the picture I had formed of her in my mind from Ukridge's conversation.

'Miss Ukridge?' I said, sliding on a rug towards her and feeling like some novice whose manager, against his personal wishes, has fixed up with a match with the heavyweight champion.

'I am Miss Ukridge,' said the other woman. 'Miss Watterson, Mr Corcoran.'

It was a shock, but, the moment of surprise over, I began to feel something approaching mental comfort for the first time since I had entered this house of slippery rugs and supercilious butlers. Somehow I had got the impression from Ukridge that his aunt was a sort of stage aunt, all stiff satin and raised eyebrows. This half-portion with the mild blue eyes I felt I could tackle. It passed my comprehension why Ukridge should ever have found her intimidating.

'I hope you will not mind if we have our little talk before Miss Watterson,' she said with a charming smile. 'She has come to arrange the details of the Pen and Ink Club dance which we are giving shortly. She will keep quite quiet and not interrupt. You don't mind?'

'Not at all, not at all,' I said in my attractive way. It is not exaggerating to say that at this moment I felt debonair. 'Not at all, not at all. Oh, not at all.'

'Won't you sit down?'

'Thank you, thank you.'

The hawk moved over to the window, leaving us to ourselves.

'Now we are quite cosy,' said Ukridge's aunt.

'Yes, yes,' I agreed. Dash it, I liked this woman.

'Tell me, Mr Corcoran,' said Ukridge's aunt, 'are you on the staff of *Woman's Sphere*? It is one of my favourite papers. I read it every week.'

'The outside staff.'

'What do you mean by the outside staff?'

'Well, I don't actually work in the office, but the editor gives me occasional jobs.'

'I see. Who is the editor now?'

I began to feel slightly less debonair. She was just making conversation, of course, to put me at my ease, but I wished she would stop asking me these questions. I searched desperately in my mind for a name – any name – but as usual on these occasions every name in the English language had passed from me.

'Of course. I remember now,' said Ukridge's aunt, to my profound relief. 'It's Mr Jevons, isn't it? I met him one night at dinner.'

'Jevons,' I burbled. 'That's right. Jevons.'

'A tall man with a light moustache.'

'Well, fairly tall,' I said, judicially.

'And he sent you here to interview me?'

'Yes.'

'Well, which of my novels do you wish me to talk about?'

I relaxed with a delightful sense of relief. I felt on solid ground at last. And then it suddenly came to me that Ukridge in his woollen-headed way had omitted to mention the name of a single one of this woman's books.

'Er – oh, all of them,' I said hurriedly.

'I see. My general literary work.'

'Exactly,' I said. My feeling towards her now was one of positive affection.

She leaned back in her chair with her finger-tips together, a pretty look of meditation on her face.

'Do you think it would interest the readers of *Woman's Sphere* to know which novel of mine is my own favourite?'

'I am sure it would.'

'Of course,' said Ukridge's aunt, 'it is not easy for an author to answer a question like that. You see, one has moods in which first one book and then another appeals to one.'

'Quite,' I replied. 'Quite.'

'Which of my books do *you* like best, Mr Corcoran?'

There swept over me the trapped feeling one gets in nightmares. From six baskets the six Pekingese stared at me unwinkingly.

'Er – oh, all of them,' I heard a croaking voice reply. My voice, presumably, though I did not recognize it.

'How delightful!' said Ukridge's aunt. 'Now, I really do call that delightful. One or two of the critics have said that my work was uneven. It is so nice to meet someone who doesn't agree with them. Personally, I think my favourite is *The Heart of Adelaide*.'

I nodded my approval of this sound choice. The muscles which had humped themselves stiffly on my back began to crawl back into place again. I found it possible to breathe.

'Yes,' I said, frowning thoughtfully, 'I suppose *The Heart of Adelaide* is the best thing you have written. It has such human appeal,' I added, playing it safe.

'Have you read it, Mr Corcoran?'

'Oh, yes.'

'And you really enjoyed it?'

'Tremendously.'

'You don't think it is a fair criticism to say that it is a little broad in parts?'

'Most unfair.' I began to see my way. I do not know why, but I had been assuming that her novels must be the sort you find in seaside libraries. Evidently they belonged to the other class of female novels, the sort which libraries ban. 'Of course,'

I said, 'it is written honestly, fearlessly, and shows life as it is. But broad? No, no!'

'That scene in the conservatory?'

'Best thing in the book,' I said stoutly.

A pleased smile played about her mouth. Ukridge had been right. Praise her work, and a child could eat out of her hand. I found myself wishing that I had really read the thing, so that I could have gone into more detail and made her still happier.

'I'm so glad you like it,' she said. 'Really, it is most encouraging.'

'Oh, no,' I murmured modestly.

'Oh, but it is. Because I have only just started to write it, you see. I finished chapter one this morning.'

She was still smiling so engagingly that for a moment the full horror of these words did not penetrate my consciousness.

'*The Heart of Adelaide* is my next novel. The scene in the conservatory, which you like so much, comes towards the middle of it. I was not expecting to reach it till about the end of next month. How odd that you should know all about it!'

I had got it now all right, and it was like sitting down on the empty space where there should have been a chair. Somehow the fact that she was so pleasant about it all served to deepen my discomfiture. In the course of an active life I have frequently felt a fool, but never such a fool as I felt then. The fearful woman had been playing with me, leading me on, watching me entangle myself like a fly on fly-paper. And suddenly I perceived that I had erred in thinking of her eyes as mild. A hard gleam had come into them. They were like a couple of blue gimlets. She looked like a cat that had caught a mouse, and it was revealed to me in one sickening age-long instant why Ukridge went in fear of her. There was that about her which would have intimidated the Sheik.

'It seems so odd, too,' she tinkled on, 'that you should have come to interview me for *Woman's Sphere*. Because they published an interview with me only the week before last. I thought it so strange that I rang up my friend Miss Watterson, who is the editress, and asked her if there had not been some mistake. And she said she had never heard of you. *Have* you ever heard of Mr Corcoran, Muriel?'

'Never,' said the hawk, fixing me with a revolted eye.

'How strange!' said Ukridge's aunt. 'But then the whole thing is so strange. Oh, must you go, Mr Corcoran?'

My mind was in a slightly chaotic condition, but on that one point it was crystal-clear. Yes, I must go. Through the door if I could find it – failing that, through the window. And anybody who tried to stop me would do well to have a care.

'You will remember me to Mr Jevons when you see him, won't you?' said Ukridge's aunt.

I was fumbling at the handle.

'And, Mr Corcoran.' She was still smiling amiably, but there had come into her voice a note like that which it had had on a certain memorable occasion when summoning Ukridge to his doom from the unseen interior of his Sheep's Cray Cottage. 'Will you please tell my nephew Stanley that I should be glad if he would send no more of his friends to see me. Good afternoon.'

I suppose that at some point in the proceedings my hostess must have rung a bell, for out in the passage I found my old chum, the butler. With the uncanny telepathy of his species he appeared aware that I was leaving under what might be called a cloud, for his manner had taken on a warder-like grimness. His hand looked as if it was itching to grasp me by the shoulder, and when we reached the front door he eyed the pavement wistfully, as if thinking what a splendid spot it would be for me to hit with a thud.

'Nice day,' I said, with the feverish instinct to babble which comes to strong men in their agony.

He scorned to reply, and as I tottered down the sunlit street I was conscious of his gaze following me.

'A very vicious specimen,' I could fancy him saying. 'And mainly due to my prudence and foresight that he hasn't got away with the spoons.'

It was a warm afternoon, but to such an extent had the recent happenings churned up my emotions that I walked the whole way back to Ebury Street with a rapidity which caused more languid pedestrians to regard me with a pitying contempt. Reaching my sitting-room in an advanced state of solubility and fatigue, I found Ukridge stretched upon the sofa.

'Hallo, laddie!' said Ukridge, reaching out a hand for the cooling drink that lay on the floor beside him. 'I was wondering when you would show up. I wanted to tell you that it won't be necessary for you to go and see my aunt after all. It appears that Dora has a hundred quid tucked away in a bank, and she's been offered a partnership by a woman she knows who runs one of these typewriting places. I advised her to close with it. So she's all right.'

He quaffed deeply of the bowl and breathed a contented sigh. There was a silence.

'When did you hear of this?' I asked at length.

'Yesterday afternoon,' said Ukridge. 'I meant to pop round and tell you, but somehow it slipped my mind.'

Chapter 5

The Return of Battling Billson

It was a most embarrassing moment, one of those moments which plant lines on the face and turn the hair a distinguished grey at the temples. I looked at the barman. The barman looked at me. The assembled company looked at us both impartially.

'Ho!' said the barman.

I am very quick. I could see at once that he was not in sympathy with me. He was a large, profuse man, and his eye as it met mine conveyed the impression that he regarded me as a bad dream come true. His mobile lips curved slightly, showing a gold tooth; and the muscles of his brawny arms, which were strong as iron bands, twitched a little.

'Ho!' he said.

The circumstances which had brought me into my present painful position were as follows. In writing those stories for the popular magazines which at that time were causing so many editors so much regret, I was accustomed, like one of my brother-authors, to take mankind for my province. Thus, one day I would be dealing with dukes in their castles, the next I would turn right round and start tackling the submerged tenth in their slums. Versatile. At the moment I happened to be engaged upon a rather poignant little thing about a girl called Liz, who worked in a fried-fish shop in the Ratcliff Highway, and I had accordingly gone down there to collect local colour. For whatever Posterity may say of James Corcoran, it can never say that he shrank from inconvenience where his Art was concerned.

The Ratcliff Highway is an interesting thoroughfare, but on a warm day it breeds thirst. After wandering about for an hour or so, therefore, I entered the Prince of Wales public-house, called for a pint of beer, drained it at a draught, reached in my pocket for coin, and found emptiness. I was in a position to add to my notes on the East End of London one to the effect that pocket-pickery flourishes there as a fine art.

'I'm awfully sorry,' I said, smiling an apologetic smile and endeavouring to put a debonair winsomeness into my voice. 'I find I've got no money.'

It was at this point that the barman said 'Ho!' and moved out into the open through a trick door in the counter.

'I think my pocket must have been picked,' I said.

'Oh, do you?' said the barman.

He gave me the idea of being rather a soured man. Years of association with unscrupulous citizens who tried to get drinks for nothing had robbed him of that fine fresh young enthusiasm with which he had started out on his career of barmanship.

'I had better leave my name and address,' I suggested.

'Who,' inquired the barman, coldly, 'wants your blinking name and address?'

These practical men go straight to the heart of a thing. He had put his finger on the very hub of the matter. Who did want my blinking name and address? No one.

'I will send –' I was proceeding, when things began to happen suddenly. An obviously expert hand gripped me by the back of the neck, another closed upon the seat of my trousers, there was a rush of air, and I was rolling across the pavement in the direction of a wet and unsavoury gutter. The barman, gigantic against the dirty white front of the public-house, surveyed me grimly.

I think that, if he had confined himself to mere looks – however offensive – I would have gone no farther into the matter. After all, the man had right on his side. How could he be expected to see into my soul and note its snowy purity? But, as I picked myself up, he could not resist the temptation to improve the occasion.

'That's what comes of tryin' to snitch drinks,' he said, with what seemed to me insufferable priggishness.

Those harsh words stung me to the quick. I burned with generous wrath. I flung myself on that barman. The futility of attacking such a Colossus never occurred to me. I forgot entirely that he could put me out of action with one hand.

A moment later, however, he had reminded me of this fact. Even as I made onslaught an enormous fist came from nowhere and crashed into the side of my head. I sat down again.

''Ullo!'

I was aware, dimly, that someone was speaking to me, someone who was not the barman. That athlete had already dismissed me as a spent force and returned to his professional duties. I looked up and got a sort of general impression of bigness and blue serge, and then I was lifted lightly to my feet.

My head had begun to clear now, and I was able to look more steadily at my sympathizer. And, as I looked, the feeling came to me that I had seen him before somewhere. That red hair, those glinting eyes, that impressive bulk – it was my old friend Wilberforce Billson and no other – Battling Billson, the coming champion, whom I had last seen fighting at Wonderland under the personal management of Stanley Featherstonehaugh Ukridge.

'Did 'e 'it yer?' inquired Mr Billson.

There was only one answer to this. Disordered though my faculties were, I was clear upon this point. I said 'Yes, he did hit me.'

''R!' said Mr Billson, and immediately passed into the hostelry.

It was not at once that I understood the significance of this move. The interpretation I placed upon his abrupt departure was that, having wearied of my society, he had decided to go and have some refreshment. Only when the sound of raised voices from within came pouring through the door did I begin to suspect that in attributing to it such callousness I might have wronged that golden nature. With the sudden reappearance of the barman – who shot out as if impelled by some imperious force and did a sort of backwards fox-trot across the pavement – suspicion became certainty.

The barman, as becomes a man plying his trade in the Ratcliff Highway, was made of stern stuff. He was no poltroon. As soon as he managed to stop himself from pirouetting, he dabbed at his right cheek-bone in a delicate manner, soliloquized for a moment, and then dashed back into the bar. And it was after the door had swung to again behind him that the proceedings may have been said formally to have begun.

What precisely was going on inside that bar I was still too enfeebled to go and see. It sounded like an earthquake, and no meagre earthquake at that. All the glassware in the world seemed to be smashing simultaneously, the populations of several cities were shouting in unison, and I could almost fancy that I saw the walls of the building shake and heave. And then somebody blew a police-whistle.

There is a magic about the sound of a police-whistle. It acts like oil on the most troubled waters. This one brought about an instant lull in the tumult. Glasses ceased to break, voices were hushed, and a moment later out came Mr Billson, standing not upon the order of his going. His nose was bleeding a little and there was the scenario of a black eye forming on his face, but otherwise there seemed nothing much the matter with him. He cast a wary look up and down the street and sprinted for the nearest corner. And I, shaking off the dreamy after-effects of my encounter with the barman, sprinted in his wake. I was glowing with gratitude and admiration. I wanted to catch this man up and thank him formally. I wanted to assure him of my undying esteem. Moreover, I wanted to borrow sixpence from him. The realization that he was the only man in the whole wide East End of London who was likely to lend me the money to save me having to walk back to Ebury Street gave me a rare burst of speed.

It was not easy to overtake him, for the sound of my pursuing feet evidently suggested to Mr Billson that the hunt was up, and he made good going. Eventually, however, when in addition to running I began to emit a plaintive 'Mr Billson! I say, Mr Billson!' at every second stride, he seemed to gather that he was among friends.

'Oh, it's you, is it?' he said, halting.

He was plainly relieved. He produced a murky pipe and lit it. I delivered my speech of thanks. Having heard me out, he removed his pipe and put into a few short words the moral of the whole affair.

'Nobody don't dot no pals of mine not when I'm around,' said Mr Billson.

'It was awfully good of you to trouble,' I said with feeling.

'No trouble,' said Mr Billson.

'You must have hit that barman pretty hard. He came out at forty miles an hour.'

'I dotted him,' agreed Mr Billson.

'I'm afraid he has hurt your eye,' I said, sympathetically.

'Him!' said Mr Billson, expectorating with scorn. 'That wasn't him. That was his pals. Six or seven of 'em there was.'

'And did you dot them too?' I cried, amazed at the prowess of this wonder-man.

''R!' said Mr Billson. He smoked awhile. 'But I dotted 'im most,' he proceeded. He looked at me with honest warmth, his chivalrous heart plainly stirred to its depths. 'The idea,' he said, disgustedly, 'of a — — — 'is size' – he defined the barman crisply and, as far as I could judge after so brief an acquaintanceship, accurately – 'goin' and dottin' a little — like you!'

The sentiment was so admirable that I could not take exception to its phraseology. Nor did I rebel at being called 'little'. To a man of Mr Billson's mould I supposed most people looked little.

'Well, I'm very much obliged,' I said.

Mr Billson smoked in silence.

'Have you been back long?' I asked, for something to say. Outstanding as were his other merits, he was not good at keeping a conversation alive.

'Back?' said Mr Billson.

'Back in London. Ukridge told me that you had gone to sea again.'

'Say, mister,' exclaimed Mr Billson, for the first time seeming to show real interest in my remarks, 'you seen 'im lately?'

'Ukridge? Oh, yes, I see him nearly every day.'

'I been tryin' to find 'im.'

'I can give you his address,' I said. And I wrote it down on the back of an envelope. Then, having shaken his hand, I thanked him once more for his courteous assistance and borrowed my fare back to Civilization on the Underground, and we parted with mutual expressions of good will.

The next step in the march of events was what I shall call the Episode of the Inexplicable Female. It occurred two days later. Returning shortly after lunch to my rooms in Ebury Street, I was met in the hall by Mrs Bowles, my landlord's wife.

I greeted her a trifle nervously, for, like her husband, she always exercised a rather oppressive effect on me. She lacked Bowles's ambassadorial dignity, but made up for it by a manner so peculiarly sepulchral that strong men quailed before her pale gaze. Scotch by birth, she had an eye that looked as if it was for ever searching for astral bodies wrapped in winding-sheets – this, I believe, being a favourite indoor sport among certain sets in North Britain.

'Sir,' said Mrs Bowles, 'there is a body in your sitting-room.'

'A body!' I am bound to say that this Phillips-Oppenheim-like opening to the conversation gave me something of a shock. Then I remembered her nationality. 'Oh, you mean a man?'

'A woman,' corrected Mrs Bowles. 'A body in a pink hat.'

I was conscious of a feeling of guilt. In this pure and modest house, female bodies in pink hats seemed to require explanation. I felt that the correct thing to do would have been to call upon Heaven to witness that this woman was nothing to me, nothing.

'I was to give you this letter, sir.'

I took it and opened the envelope with a sigh. I had recognized the handwriting of Ukridge, and for the hundredth time in our close acquaintance there smote me like a blow the sad suspicion that this man had once more gone and wished upon me some frightful thing.

MY DEAR OLD HORSE,

It's not often I ask you to do anything for me . . .

I laughed hollowly.

MY DEAR OLD HORSE,

It's not often I ask you to do anything for me, laddie, but I beg and implore you to rally round now and show yourself the true friend I know you are. The one thing I've always said about you, Corky my boy, is that you're a real pal who never lets a fellow down.

The bearer of this – a delightful woman, you'll like her – is Flossie's mother. She's up for the day by excursion from the North, and it is absolutely vital that she be lushed up and seen off at Euston at six-forty-five. I can't look after her myself, as unfortunately I'm laid up with a sprained ankle. Otherwise I wouldn't trouble you.

94

This is a life and death matter, old man, and I'm relying on you. I can't possibly tell you how important it is that this old bird should be suitably entertained. The gravest issues hang on it. So shove on your hat and go to it, laddie, and blessings will reward you. Tell you all the details when we meet.

Yours ever,
S. F. UKRIDGE.

P.S. – I will defray all expenses later.

Those last words did wring a faint, melancholy smile from me, but apart from them this hideous document seemed to me to be entirely free from comic relief. I looked at my watch and found that it was barely two-thirty. This female, therefore, was on my hands for a solid four hours and a quarter. I breathed maledictions – futile, of course, for it was a peculiar characteristic of the demon Ukridge on these occasions that, unless one were strong-minded enough to disregard his frenzied pleadings altogether (a thing which was nearly always beyond me), he gave one no chance of escape. He sprang his foul schemes on one at the very last moment, leaving no opportunity for a graceful refusal.

I proceeded slowly up the stairs to my sitting-room. It would have been a distinct advantage, I felt, if I had known who on earth this Flossie was of whom he wrote with such airy familiarity. The name, though Ukridge plainly expected it to touch a chord in me, left me entirely unresponsive. As far as I was aware, there was no Flossie of any description in my life. I thought back through the years. Long-forgotten Janes and Kates and Muriels and Elizabeths rose from the murky depths of my memory as I stirred it, but no Flossie. It occurred to me as I opened the door that, if Ukridge was expecting pleasant reminiscences of Flossie to form a tender bond between me and her mother, he was building on sandy soil.

The first impression I got on entering the room was that Mrs Bowles possessed the true reporter's gift for picking out the detail that really mattered. One could have said many things about Flossie's mother, as, for instance, that she was stout, cheerful, and far more tightly laced than a doctor would have considered judicious; but what stood out above all the others was the fact that she was wearing a pink hat. It was the largest, gayest, most exuberantly ornate specimen of head-wear that I had ever seen, and the prospect of spending four hours and a quarter in its society added the last touch to my already poignant gloom. The only gleam of sunshine that lightened my darkness was the reflection that, if we went to a picture-palace, she would have to remove it.

'Er – how do you do?' I said, pausing in the doorway.

' 'Ow do you do?' said a voice from under the hat. 'Say " 'Ow-do-you-do?" to the gentleman, Cecil.'

I perceived a small, shiny boy by the window. Ukridge, realizing with the true artist's instinct that the secret of all successful prose is the knowledge of what to omit, had not mentioned him in his letter; and, as he turned reluctantly to go through the necessary civilities, it seemed to me that the burden was more than I could bear. He was a rat-faced, sinister-looking boy, and he gazed at me with a frigid distaste which reminded me of the barman at the Prince of Wales public-house in Ratcliff Highway.

'I brought Cecil along,' said Flossie's (and presumably Cecil's) mother, after the stripling, having growled a cautious greeting, obviously with the mental reservation that it committed him to nothing, had returned to the window, 'because I thought it would be nice for 'im to say he had seen London.'

'Quite, quite,' I replied, while Cecil, at the window, gazed darkly out at London as if he did not think much of it.

'Mr Ukridge said you would trot us round.'

'Delighted, delighted,' I quavered, looking at the hat and looking swiftly away again. 'I think we had better go to a picture-palace, don't you?'

'Naw!' said Cecil. And there was that in his manner which suggested that when he said 'Naw!' it was final.

'Cecil wants to see the sights,' explained his mother. 'We can see all the pictures back at home. 'E's been lookin' forward to seein' the sights of London. It'll be an education for 'im, like, to see all the sights.'

'Westminster Abbey?' I suggested. After all, what could be better for the lad's growing mind than to inspect the memorials of the great past and, if disposed, pick out a suitable site for his own burial at some later date? Also, I had a fleeting notion, which a moment's reflection exploded before it could bring me much comfort, that women removed their hats in Westminster Abbey.

'Naw!' said Cecil.

''E wants to see the murders,' explained Flossie's mother.

She spoke as if it were the most reasonable of boyish desires, but it sounded to me impracticable. Homicides do not publish formal programmes of their intended activities. I had no notion what murders were scheduled for today.

''E always reads up all the murders in the Sunday paper,' went on the parent, throwing light on the matter.

'Oh, I understand,' I said. 'Then Madame Tussaud's is the spot he wants. They've got all the murderers.'

'Naw!' said Cecil.

'It's the places 'e wants to see,' said Flossie's mother, amiably tolerant of my density. 'The places where all them murders was committed. 'E's clipped out the addresses and 'e wants to be able to tell 'is friends when he gets back that 'e's seen 'em.'

A profound relief surged over me.

'Why, we can do the whole thing in a cab,' I cried. 'We can stay in a cab from start to finish. No need to leave the cab at all.'

'Or a bus?'

'Not a bus,' I said firmly. I was quite decided on a cab – one with blinds that would pull down, if possible.

''Ave it your own way,' said Flossie's mother agreeably. 'Speaking as far as I'm personally concerned, I'm shaw there's nothing I would rather prefer than a nice ride in a keb. Jear what the gentleman says, Cecil? You're goin' to ride in a keb.'

'Urgh!' said Cecil, as if he would believe it when he saw it. A sceptical boy.

It was not an afternoon to which I look back as among the happiest I have spent. For one thing, the expedition far exceeded my hasty estimates in the matter of expense. Why it should be so I cannot say, but all the best murders appear to take place in remote spots like Stepney and Canning Town, and cab-fares to these places run into money. Then, again, Cecil's was not one of those personalities which become more attractive with familiarity. I should say at a venture that those who liked him best were those who saw the least of him. And, finally, there was a monotony about the entire proceedings which soon began to afflict my nerves. The cab would draw up outside some mouldering house in some desolate street miles from civilization, Cecil would thrust his unpleasant head out of the window and drink the place in for a few moments of silent ecstasy, and then he would deliver his lecture. He had evidently read well and thoughtfully. He had all the information.

'The Canning Town 'Orror,' he would announce.

'Yes, dearie?' His mother cast a fond glance at him and a proud one at me. 'In this very 'ouse, was it?'

'In this very 'ouse,' said Cecil, with the gloomy importance of a confirmed bore about to hold forth on his favourite subject. 'Jimes Potter 'is nime was. 'E was found at seven in the morning underneaf the kitchen sink wiv 'is froat cut from ear to ear. It was the landlady's brother done it. They 'anged 'im at Pentonville.'

Some more data from the child's inexhaustible store, and then on to the next historic site.

'The Bing Street 'Orror!'

'In this very 'ouse, dearie?'

'In this very 'ouse. Body was found in the cellar in an advanced stige of dee-cawm-po-sition wiv its 'ead bashed in, pre-zoomably by some blunt instrument.'

At six-forty-six, ignoring the pink hat which protruded from the window of a third-class compartment and the stout hand that waved a rollicking farewell, I turned from the train with a pale, set face, and, passing down the platform of Euston Station, told a cabman to take me with all speed to Ukridge's lodgings in Arundel Street, Leicester Square. There had never, so far as I knew, been a murder in Arundel Street, but I was strongly of opinion that that time was ripe. Cecil's society and conversation had done much to neutralize the effects of a gentle upbringing and I toyed almost luxuriously with the thought of supplying him with an Arundel Street Horror for his next visit to the Metropolis.

'Aha, laddie,' said Ukridge, as I entered. 'Come in, old horse. Glad to see you. Been wondering when you would turn up.'

He was in bed, but that did not remove the suspicion which

had been growing in me all the afternoon that he was a low malingerer. I refused to believe for a moment in that sprained ankle of his. My view was that he had had the advantage of a first look at Flossie's mother and her engaging child and had shrewdly passed them on to me.

'I've been reading your book, old man,' said Ukridge, breaking a pregnant silence with an overdone carelessness. He brandished winningly the only novel I had ever written, and I can offer no better proof of the black hostility of my soul than the statement that even this did not soften me. 'It's immense, laddie. No other word for it. Immense. Damme, I've been crying like a child.'

'It is supposed to be a humorous novel,' I pointed out, coldly.

'Crying with laughter,' explained Ukridge, hurriedly.

I eyed him with loathing.

'Where do you keep your blunt instruments?' I asked.

'My what?'

'Your blunt instrument. I want a blunt instrument. Give me a blunt instrument. My God! Don't tell me you have no blunt instrument.'

'Only a safety razor.'

I sat down wearily on the bed.

'Hi! Mind my ankle!'

'Your ankle!' I laughed a hideous laugh, the sort of laugh the landlady's brother might have emitted before beginning operations on James Potter. 'A lot there is the matter with your ankle.'

'Sprained it yesterday, old man. Nothing serious,' said Ukridge, reassuringly. 'Just enough to lay me up for a couple of days.'

'Yes, till that ghastly female and her blighted boy had got well away.'

Pained astonishment was written all over Ukridge's face.

'You don't mean to say you didn't like her? Why, I thought you two would be all over each other.'

'And I suppose you thought that Cecil and I would be twin souls?'

'Cecil?' said Ukridge, doubtfully. 'Well, to tell you the truth, old man, I'm not saying that Cecil doesn't take a bit of knowing. He's the sort of boy you have to be patient with and bring out, if you understand what I mean. I think he grows on you.'

'If he ever tries to grow on me, I'll have him amputated.'

'Well, putting all that on one side,' said Ukridge, 'how did things go off?'

I described the afternoon's activities in a few tense words.

'Well, I'm sorry, old horse,' said Ukridge, when I had finished. 'Can't say more than that, can I? I'm sorry. I give you my solemn word I didn't know what I was letting you in for. But it was a life and death matter. There was no other way out. Flossie insisted on it. Wouldn't budge an inch.'

In my anguish I had forgotten all about the impenetrable mystery of Flossie.

'Who the devil is Flossie?' I asked.

'What! Flossie? You don't know who Flossie is? My dear old man, collect yourself. You must remember Flossie. The barmaid at the Crown in Kennington. The girl Battling Billson is engaged to. Surely you haven't forgotten Flossie? Why, she was saying only yesterday that you had nice eyes.'

Memory awoke. I felt ashamed that I could ever have forgotten a girl so bounding and spectacular.

'Of course! The blister you brought with you that night George Tupper gave us dinner at the Regent Grill. By the way, has George ever forgiven you for that?'

'There is still a little coldness,' admitted Ukridge, ruefully. 'I'm bound to say old Tuppy seems to be letting the thing rankle a bit. The fact of the matter is, old horse, Tuppy has his limitations. He isn't a real friend like you. Delightful fellow, but lacks vision. Can't understand that there are certain occasions when it is simply imperative that man's pals rally round him. Now you –'

'Well, I'll tell you one thing. I am hoping that what I went through this afternoon really was for some good cause. I should be sorry, now that I am in a cooler frame of mind, to have to strangle you where you lie. Would you mind telling me exactly what was the idea behind all this?'

'It's like this, laddie. Good old Billson blew in to see me the other day.'

'I met him down in the East End and he asked for your address.'

'Yes, he told me.'

'What's going on? Are you still managing him?'

'Yes. That's what he wanted to see me about. Apparently the contract has another year to run and he can't fix up anything without my O.K. And he's just had an offer to fight a bloke called Alf Todd at the Universal.'

'That's a step up from Wonderland,' I said, for I had a solid respect for this Mecca of the boxing world. 'How much is he getting this time?'

'Two hundred quid.'

'Two hundred quid! But that's a lot for practically an unknown man.'

'Unknown man?' said Ukridge, hurt. 'What do you mean, unknown man? If you ask my opinion, I should say the whole pugilistic world is seething with excitement about old Billson. Literally seething. Didn't he slosh the middleweight champion?'

'Yes, in a rough-and-tumble in a back alley. And nobody saw him do it.'

'Well, these things get about.'

'But two hundred pounds!'

'A fleabite, laddie, a fleabite. You can take it from me that we shall be asking a lot more than a measly couple of hundred for our services pretty soon. Thousands, thousands! Still, I'm not saying it won't be something to be going on with. Well, as I say, old Billson came to me and said he had had this offer, and how about it? And when I realized that I was in halves, I jolly soon gave him my blessing and told him to go as far as he liked. So you can imagine how I felt when Flossie put her foot down like this.'

'Like what? About ten minutes ago when you started talking, you seemed to be on the point of explaining about Flossie. How does she come to be mixed up with the thing? What did she do?'

'Only wanted to stop the whole business, laddie, that was all. Just put the kibosh on the entire works. Said he mustn't fight!'

'Mustn't fight?'

'That was what she said. Just in that airy, careless way, as if the most stupendous issues didn't hang on his fighting as he had never fought before. Said – if you'll believe me, laddie; I shan't blame you if you don't – that she didn't want his looks spoiled.' Ukridge gazed at me with lifted eyebrows while he let this evidence of feminine perverseness sink in. 'His looks, old man! You got the word correctly? His looks! She didn't want his looks spoiled. Why, damme, he hasn't got any looks. There isn't any possible manner in which you could treat that man's face without improving it. I argued with her by the hour, but no, she couldn't see it. Avoid women, laddie, they have no intelligence.'

'Well, I'll promise to avoid Flossie's mother, if that'll satisfy you. How does she come into the thing?'

'Now, there's a woman in a million, my boy. She saved the situation. She came along at the eleventh hour and snatched your old friend out of the soup. It seems she has a habit of popping up to London at intervals, and Flossie, while she loves and respects her, finds that from ten minutes to a quarter of an hour of the old dear gives her the pip to such an extent that she's a nervous wreck for days.'

I felt my heart warm to the future Mrs Billson. Despite Ukridge's slurs, a girl, it seemed to me, of the soundest intelligence.

'So when Flossie told me – with tears in her eyes, poor girl – that mother was due today, I had the inspiration of a lifetime. Said I would take her off her hands from start to finish if she would agree to let Billson fight at the Universal. Well, it shows you what family affection is, laddie; she jumped at it. I don't mind telling you she broke down completely and kissed me on both cheeks. The rest, old horse, you know.'

'Yes. The rest I do know.'

'Never,' said Ukridge, solemnly, 'never, old son, till the sands of the desert grow cold, shall I forget how you have stood by me this day!'

'Oh, all right. I expect in about a week from now you will be landing me with something equally foul.'

'Now, laddie –'

'When does this fight come off?'

'A week from tonight. I'm relying on you to be at my side.

Tense nervous strain, old man; shall want a pal to see me through.'

'I wouldn't miss it for worlds. I'll give you dinner before we go there, shall I?'

'Spoken like a true friend,' said Ukridge, warmly. 'And on the following night I will stand you the banquet of your life. A banquet which will ring down the ages. For, mark you, laddie, I shall be in funds. In funds, my boy.'

'Yes, if Billson wins. What does he get if he loses?'

'Loses? He won't lose. How the deuce can he lose? I'm surprised at you talking in that silly way when you've seen him only a few days ago. Didn't he strike you as being pretty fit when you saw him?'

'Yes, by Jove, he certainly did.'

'Well, then! Why, it looks to me as if the sea air had made him tougher than ever. I've only just got my fingers straightened out after shaking hands with him. He could win the heavy-weight championship of the world tomorrow without taking his pipe out of his mouth. Alf Todd,' said Ukridge, soaring to an impressive burst of imagery, 'has about as much chance as a one-armed blind man in a dark room trying to shove a pound of melted butter into a wild-cat's left ear with a red-hot needle.'

Although I knew several of the members, for one reason or another I had never been inside the Universal Sporting Club, and the atmosphere of the place when we arrived on the night of the fight impressed me a good deal. It was vastly different from Wonderland, the East End home of pugilism where I had witnessed the Battler make his début. There, a certain laxness in the matter of costume had been the prevailing note; here, white shirt-fronts gleamed on every side. Wonderland, more-over, had been noisy. Patrons of sport had so far forgotten them-selves as to whistle through their fingers and shout badinage at distant friends. At the Universal one might have been in church. In fact, the longer I sat, the more ecclesiastical did the atmos-phere seem to become. When we arrived, two acolytes in the bantam class were going devoutly through the ritual under the eye of the presiding minister, while a large congregation looked on in hushed silence. As we took our seats, this portion of the service came to an end and the priest announced that Nippy

Coggs was the winner. A reverent murmur arose for an instant from the worshippers, Nippy Coggs disappeared into the vestry, and after a pause of a few minutes I perceived the familiar form of Battling Billson coming up the aisle.

There was no doubt about it, the Battler did look good. His muscles seemed more cable-like than ever, and a recent hair-cut had given a knobby, bristly appearance to his head which put him even more definitely than before in the class of those with whom the sensible man would not lightly quarrel. Mr Todd, his antagonist, who followed him a moment later, was no beauty – the almost complete absence of any division between his front hair and his eyebrows would alone have prevented him being that – but he lacked a certain *je-ne-sais-quoi* which the Battler pre-eminently possessed. From the first instant of his appearance in the public eye our man was a warm favourite. There was a pleased flutter in the pews as he took his seat, and I could hear whispered voices offering substantial bets on him.

'Six-round bout,' announced the *padre*. 'Battling Billson (Bermondsey) versus Alf Todd (Marylebone). Gentlemen will kindly stop smoking.'

The congregation relit their cigars and the fight began.

Bearing in mind how vitally Ukridge's fortunes were bound up in his protégé's success tonight, I was relieved to observe that Mr Todd opened the proceedings in a manner that seemed to offer little scope for any display of Battling Billson's fatal kind-heartedness. I had not forgotten how at Wonderland our Battler, with the fight in hand, had allowed victory to be snatched from him purely through a sentimental distaste for being rough with his adversary, a man who had had a lot of trouble and had touched Mr Billson's heart thereby. Such a disaster was unlikely to occur tonight. It was difficult to see how anyone in the same ring with him could possibly be sorry for Alf Todd. A tender pity was the last thing his behaviour was calculated to rouse in the bosom of an opponent. Directly the gong sounded, he tucked away what little forehead Nature had given him beneath his fringe, breathed loudly through his nose, and galloped into the fray. He seemed to hold no bigoted views as to which hand it was best to employ as a medium of attack.

Right or left, it was all one to Alf. And if he could not hit Mr Billson with his hands, he was perfectly willing, so long as the eye of authority was not too keenly vigilant, to butt him with his head. Broad-minded – that was Alf Todd.

Wilberforce Billson, veteran of a hundred fights on a hundred water-fronts, was not backward in joining the revels. In him Mr Todd found a worthy and a willing playmate. As Ukridge informed me in a hoarse whisper while the vicar was reproaching Alf for placing an elbow where no elbow should have been, this sort of thing was as meat and drink to Wilberforce. It was just the kind of warfare he had been used to all his life, and precisely the sort most calculated to make him give of his best – a dictum which was strikingly endorsed a moment later, when, after some heated exchanges in which, generous donor though he was, he had received more than he had bestowed, Mr Todd was compelled to slither back and do a bit of fancy side-stepping. The round came to an end with the Battler distinctly leading on points, and so spirited had it been that applause broke out in various parts of the edifice.

The second round followed the same general lines as the first. The fact that up to now he had been foiled in his attempts to resolve Battling Billson into his component parts had had no damping effect on Alf Todd's ardour. He was still the same active, energetic soul, never sparing himself in his efforts to make the party go. There was a whole-hearted abandon in his rushes which reminded one of a short-tempered gorilla trying to get at its keeper. Occasionally some extra warmth on the part of his antagonist would compel him to retire momentarily into a clinch, but he always came out of it as ready as ever to resume the argument. Nevertheless, at the end of round two he was still a shade behind. Round three added further points to the Battler's score, and at the end of round four Alf Todd had lost so much ground that the most liberal odds were required to induce speculators to venture their cash on his chances.

And then the fifth round began, and those who a minute before had taken odds of three to one on the Battler and openly proclaimed the money as good as in their pockets, stiffened in their seats or bent forward with pale and anxious faces. A few brief moments back it had seemed to them incredible that this sure thing could come unstitched. There was only this round and the next to go – a mere six minutes of conflict; and Mr Billson was so far ahead on points that nothing but the accident of his being knocked out could lose him the decision. And you had only to look at Wilberforce Billson to realize the absurdity of his being knocked out. Even I, who had seen him go through the process at Wonderland, refused to consider the possibility. If ever there was a man in the pink, it was Wilberforce Billson.

But in boxing there is always the thousandth chance. As he came out of his corner for round five, it suddenly became plain that things were not well with our man. Some chance blow in that last mêlée of round four must have found a vital spot, for he was obviously in bad shape. Incredible as it seemed, Battling Billson was groggy. He shuffled rather than stepped; he blinked in a manner damping to his supporters; he was clearly finding increasing difficulty in foiling the boisterous attentions of Mr Todd. Sibilant whispers arose; Ukridge clutched my arm in an agonized grip; voices were offering to bet on Alf; and in the Battler's corner, their heads peering through the ropes, those members of the minor clergy who had been told off to second our man were wan with apprehension.

Mr Todd, for his part, was a new man. He had retired to his corner at the end of the preceding round with the moody step of one who sees failure looming ahead. 'I'm always chasing rainbows,' Mr Todd's eye had seemed to say as it rested gloomily on the resined floor. 'Another dream shattered!' And he had come out for round five with the sullen weariness of the man who has been helping to amuse the kiddies at a children's party and has had enough of it. Ordinary politeness rendered it necessary for him to see this uncongenial business through to the end, but his heart was no longer in it.

And then, instead of the steel and india-rubber warrior who had smitten him so sorely at their last meeting, he found this sagging wreck. For an instant sheer surprise seemed to shackle Mr Todd's limbs, then he adjusted himself to the new conditions. It was as if somebody had grafted monkey-glands on to Alfred Todd. He leaped at Battling Billson, and Ukridge's grip on my arm became more painful than ever.

A sudden silence fell upon the house. It was a tense, expectant silence, for affairs had reached a crisis. Against the ropes near his corner the Battler was leaning, heedless of the well-meant counsel of his seconds, and Alf Todd, with his fringe now almost obscuring his eyes, was feinting for an opening. There is a tide in the affairs of men which, taken at the flood, leads on to fortune; and Alf Todd plainly realized this. He fiddled for an instant with his hands, as if he were trying to mesmerize Mr Billson, then plunged forward.

A great shout went up. The congregation appeared to have lost all sense of what place this was that they were in. They were jumping up and down in their seats and bellowing deplorably. For the crisis had been averted. Somehow or other Wilberforce Billson had contrived to escape from that corner, and now he was out in the middle of the ring, respited.

And yet he did not seem pleased. His usually expressionless face was contorted with pain and displeasure. For the first time in the entire proceedings he appeared genuinely moved. Watching him closely, I could see his lips moving, perhaps in prayer. And as Mr Todd, bounding from the ropes, advanced upon him, he licked those lips. He licked them in a sinister meaning way, and his right hand dropped slowly down below his knee.

Alf Todd came on. He came jauntily and in the manner of one moving to a feast or festival. This was the end of a perfect day, and he knew it. He eyed Battling Billson as if the latter had been a pot of beer. But for the fact that he came of a restrained and unemotional race, he would doubtless have burst into song. He shot out his left and it landed on Mr Billson's nose. Nothing happened. He drew back his right and poised it almost lovingly for a moment. It was during this moment that Battling Billson came to life.

To Alf Todd it must have seemed like a resurrection. For the last two minutes he had been testing in every way known to science his theory that this man before him no longer possessed the shadow of a punch, and the theory had seemed proven up to the hilt. Yet here he was now behaving like an unleashed whirlwind. A disquieting experience. The ropes collided with the small of Alf Todd's back. Something else collided with his chin. He endeavoured to withdraw, but a pulpy glove took him on the odd fungoid growth which he was accustomed laughingly to call his ear. Another glove impinged upon his jaw. And there the matter ended for Alf Todd.

'Battling Billson is the winner,' intoned the vicar.

'Wow!' shouted the congregation.

'Whew!' breathed Ukridge in my ear.

It had been a near thing, but the old firm had pulled through at the finish.

Ukridge bounded off to the dressing-room to give his Battler a manager's blessing; and presently, the next fight proving something of an anti-climax after all the fevered stress of its predecessor, I left the building and went home. I was smoking a last pipe before going to bed when a violent ring at the front-door bell broke in on my meditations. It was followed by the voice of Ukridge in the hall.

I was a little surprised. I had not been expecting to see Ukridge again tonight. His intention when we parted at the Universal had been to reward Mr Billson with a bit of supper; and, as the Battler had a coy distaste for the taverns of the West End, this involved a journey to the far East, where in congenial surroundings the coming champion would drink a good deal of beer and eat more hard-boiled eggs than you would have believed possible. The fact that the host was now thundering up my stairs seemed to indicate that the feast had fallen through. And the fact that the feast had fallen through suggested that something had gone wrong.

'Give me a drink, old horse,' said Ukridge, bursting into the room.

'What on earth's the matter?'

'Nothing, old horse, nothing. I'm a ruined man, that's all.'

He leaped feverishly at the decanter and siphon which Bowles had placed upon the table. I watched him with concern. This could be no ordinary tragedy that had changed him thus from the ebullient creature of joy who had left me at the Universal. A thought flashed through my mind that Battling Billson must have been disqualified – to be rejected a moment later, when I remembered that fighters are not disqualified as an after-thought half an hour after the fight. But what else could have brought about this anguish? If ever there was an occasion for solemn rejoicing, now would have seemed to be the time.

'What's the matter?' I asked again.

'Matter? I'll tell you what's the matter,' moaned Ukridge. He splashed seltzer into his glass. He reminded me of King Lear. 'Do you know how much I get out of that fight tonight? Ten quid! Just ten rotten contemptible sovereigns! That's what's the matter.'

'I don't understand.'

'The purse was thirty pounds. Twenty for the winner. My share is ten. Ten, I'll trouble you! What in the name of everything infernal is the good of ten quid?'

'But you said Billson told you –'

'Yes, I know I did. Two hundred was what he told me he was to get. And the weak-minded, furtive, under-handed son of Belial didn't explain that he was to get it for losing!'

'Losing?'

'Yes. He was to get it for losing. Some fellows who wanted a chance to do some heavy betting persuaded him to sell the fight.'

'But he didn't sell the fight.'

'I know that, dammit. That's the whole trouble. And do you know why he didn't? I'll tell you. Just as he was all ready to let himself be knocked out in that fifth round, the other bloke happened to tread on his ingrowing toe-nail, and that made him so mad that he forgot about everything else and sailed in and hammered the stuffing out of him. I ask you, laddie! I appeal to you as a reasonable man. Have you ever in your life heard of such a footling, idiotic, woollen-headed proceeding? Throwing away a fortune, an absolute dashed fortune, purely to gratify a momentary whim! Hurling away wealth beyond the dreams of avarice simply because a bloke stamped on his ingrowing toe-nail. His ingrowing toe-nail!' Ukridge laughed raspingly. 'What right has a boxer to *have* an ingrowing toe-nail? And if he has an ingrowing toe-nail, surely – my gosh! – he can stand a little trifling discomfort for half a minute. The fact of the matter is, old horse, boxers aren't what they were. Degenerate, laddie, absolutely degenerate. No heart. No courage. No self-respect. No vision. The old bulldog breed has disappeared entirely.'

And with a moody nod Stanley Featherstonehaugh Ukridge passed out into the night.

Chapter 6

Ukridge Sees Her Through

The girl from the typewriting and stenographic bureau had a quiet but speaking eye. At first it had registered nothing but enthusiasm and the desire to please. But now, rising from that formidable notebook, it met mine with a look of exasperated bewilderment. There was an expression of strained sweetness on her face, as of a good woman unjustly put upon. I could read what was in her mind as clearly as if she had been impolite enough to shout it. She thought me a fool. And as this made the thing unanimous, for I had been feeling exactly the same myself for the last quarter of an hour, I decided that the painful exhibition must now terminate.

It was Ukridge who had let me in for the thing. He had fired my imagination with tales of authors who were able to turn out five thousand words a day by dictating their stuff to a stenographer instead of writing it; and though I felt at the time that he was merely trying to drum up trade for the typewriting bureau in which his young friend Dora Mason was now a partner, the lure of the idea had gripped me. Like all writers, I had a sturdy distaste for solid work, and this seemed to offer a pleasant way out, turning literary composition into a jolly *tête-à-tête* chat. It was only when those gleaming eyes looked eagerly into mine and that twitching pencil poised itself to record the lightest of my golden thoughts that I discovered what I was up against. For fifteen minutes I had been experiencing all the complex emotions of a nervous man who, suddenly called upon to make a public speech, realizes too late that his brain has been withdrawn and replaced by a cheap cauliflower substitute: and I was through.

'I'm sorry,' I said, 'but I'm afraid it's not much use going on. I don't seem able to manage it.'

Now that I had come frankly out into the open and admitted my idiocy, the girl's expression softened. She closed her note-book forgivingly.

'Lots of people can't,' she said. 'It's just a knack.'

'Everything seems to go out of my head.'

'I've often thought it must be very difficult to dictate.'

Two minds with but a single thought, in fact. Her sweet reasonableness, combined with the relief that the thing was over, induced in me a desire to babble. One has the same feeling when the dentist lets one out of his chair.

'You're from the Norfolk Street Agency, aren't you?' I said. A silly question, seeing that I had expressly rung them up on the telephone and asked them to send somebody round; but I was still feeling the effects of the ether.

'Yes.'

'That's in Norfolk Street, isn't it? I mean,' I went on hurriedly, 'I wonder if you know a Miss Mason there? Miss Dora Mason.'

She seemed surprised.

'My name is Dora Mason,' she said.

I was surprised, too. I had not supposed that partners in type-writing businesses stooped to going out on these errands. And I was conscious of a return of my former embarrassment, feeling – quite unreasonably, for I had only seen her once in my life, and then from a distance – that I ought to have remembered her. 'We were short-handed at the office,' she explained, 'so I came along. But how do you know my name?'

'I am a great friend of Ukridge's.'

'Why, of course! I was wondering why your name was so familiar. I've heard him talk so much about you.'

And after that we really did settle down to the cosy *tête-à-tête* of which I had had visions. She was a nice girl, the only noticeable flaw in her character being an absurd respect for Ukridge's intelligence and abilities. I, who had known that foe of the human race from boyhood up and was still writhing beneath the memory of the night when he had sneaked my dress clothes, could have corrected her estimate of him, but it seemed unkind to shatter her girlish dreams.

'He was wonderful about this type-writing business,' she said.

'It was such a splendid opportunity, and but for Mr Ukridge I should have had to let it slip. You see, they were asking two hundred pounds for the partnership, and I only had a hundred. And Mr Ukridge insisted on putting up the rest of the money. You see – I don't know if he told you – he insisted that he ought to do something because he says he lost me the position I had with his aunt. It wasn't his fault at all, really, but he kept saying that if I hadn't gone to that dance with him I shouldn't have got back late and been dismissed. So –'

She was a rapid talker, and it was only now that I was able to comment on the amazing statement which she had made in the opening portion of her speech. So stunning had been the effect of those few words on me that I had hardly heard her subsequent remarks.

'Did you say that Ukridge insisted on finding the rest?' I gasped.

'Yes. Wasn't it nice of him?'

'He gave you a hundred pounds? Ukridge!'

'Guaranteed it,' said Miss Mason. 'I arranged to pay a hundred pounds down and the rest in sixty days.'

'But suppose the rest is not paid in sixty days?'

'Well, then I'm afraid I should lose my hundred. But it will be, of course. Mr Ukridge told me to have no anxiety about that at all. Well, good-bye, Mr Corcoran. I must be going now. I'm sorry we didn't get better results with the dictating. I should think it must be very difficult to do till you get used to it.'

Her cheerful smile as she went out struck me as one of the most pathetic sights I had ever seen. Poor child, bustling off so brightly when her whole future rested on Ukridge's ability to raise a hundred pounds! I presumed that he was relying on one of those Utopian schemes of his which were to bring him in thousands – 'at a conservative estimate, laddie!' – and not for the first time in a friendship of years the reflection came to me that Ukridge ought to be in some sort of a home. A capital fellow in many respects, but not a man lightly to be allowed at large.

I was pursuing this train of thought when the banging of the front door, followed by a pounding of footsteps on the stairs and a confused noise without, announced his arrival.

'I say, laddie,' said Ukridge, entering the room, as was his habit, like a north-easterly gale, 'was that Dora Mason I saw going down the street? It looked like her back. Has she been here?'

'Yes. I asked her agency to send someone to take dictation, and she came.'

Ukridge reached out for the tobacco jar, filled his pipe, replenished his pouch, sank comfortably on to the sofa, adjusted the cushions, and bestowed an approving glance upon me.

'Corky, my boy,' said Ukridge, 'what I like about you and the reason why I always maintain that you will be a great man one of these days is that you have Vision. You have the big, broad, flexible outlook. You're not too proud to take advice. I say to you, "Dictate your stuff, it'll pay you," and, damme, you go straight off and do it. No arguing or shilly-shallying. You just go and do it. It's the spirit that wins to success. I like to see it. Dictating will add thousands a year to your income. I say it advisedly, laddie – thousands. And if you continue leading a steady and sober life and save your pennies, you'll be amazed at the way your capital will pile up. Money at five per cent compound interest doubles itself every fourteen years. By the time you're forty –'

It seemed churlish to strike a jarring note after all these compliments, but it had to be done.

'Never mind about what's going to happen to me when I'm forty,' I said. 'What I want to know is what is all this I hear about you guaranteeing Miss Mason a hundred quid?'

'Ah, she told you? Yes,' said Ukridge, airily, 'I guaranteed it. Matter of conscience, old son. Man of honour, no alternative. You see, there's no getting away from it, it was my fault that she got sacked by my aunt. Got to see her through, laddie, got to see her through.'

I goggled at the man.

'Look here,' I said, 'let's get this thing straight. A couple of days ago you touched me for five shillings and said it would save your life.'

'It did, old man, it did.'

'And now you're talking of scattering hundred quids about the place as if you were Rothschild. Do you smoke it or inject it with a hypodermic needle?'

There was pain in Ukridge's eyes as he sat up and gazed at me through the smoke.

'I don't like this tone, laddie,' he said, reproachfully. 'Upon my Sam, it wounds me. It sounds as if you had lost faith in me, in my vision.'

'Oh, I know you've got vision. And the big, broad, flexible outlook. Also snap, ginger, enterprise, and ears that stick out at right angles like the sails of a windmill. But that doesn't help me to understand where on earth you expect to get a hundred quid.'

Ukridge smiled tolerantly.

'You don't suppose I would have guaranteed the money for poor little Dora unless I knew where to lay my hands on it, do you? If you ask me, Have I got the stuff at this precise moment? I candidly reply, No, I haven't. But it's fluttering on the horizon, laddie, fluttering on the horizon. I can hear the beating of its wings.'

'Is Battling Billson going to fight someone and make your fortune again?'

Ukridge winced, and the look of pain flitted across his face once more.

'Don't mention that man's name to me, old horse,' he begged. 'Every time I think of him everything seems to go all black. No, the thing I have on hand now is a real solid business proposition. Gilt-edged, you might call it. I ran into a bloke the other day whom I used to know out in Canada.'

'I didn't know you had ever been in Canada,' I interrupted.

'Of course I've been in Canada. Go over there and ask the first fellow you meet if I was ever in Canada. Canada! I should say I had been in Canada. Why, when I left Canada, I was seen off on the steamer by a couple of policemen. Well, I ran into this bloke in Piccadilly. He was wandering up and down and looking rather lost. Couldn't make out what the deuce he was doing over here, because, when I knew him, he hadn't a cent. Well, it seems that he got fed up with Canada and went over to America to try and make his fortune. And, by Jove, he did, first crack out of the box. Bought a bit of land about the size of a pocket-handkerchief in Texas or Oklahoma or somewhere, and one morning, when he was hoeing the soil or planting turnips or something, out buzzed a whacking great oil-well. Apparently that sort of thing's happening every day out there. If I could get a bit of capital together, I'm dashed if I wouldn't go to Texas myself. Great open spaces where men are men, laddie – suit me down to the ground. Well, we got talking, and he said that he intended to settle in England. Came from London as a kid, but couldn't stick it at any price now because they had altered it so much. I told him the thing for him to do was to buy a house in the country with a decent bit of shooting, and he said, "Well, how do you buy a house in the country with a decent bit of shooting?" and I said, "Leave it entirely in my hands, old horse. I'll see you're treated right." So he told me to go ahead, and I went to Farmingdons, the house-agent blokes in Cavendish Square. Had a chat with the manager. Very decent old bird with moth-eaten whiskers. I said I'd got a millionaire looking for a house in the country. "Find him one, laddie," I said, "and we split the commish." He said "Right-o," and any day now I expect to hear that he's dug up something suitable. Well, you can see for yourself what that's going to mean. These house-agent fellows take it as a personal affront if a client gets away from them with anything except a collar-stud and the clothes he stands up in, and I'm in halves. Reason it out, my boy, reason it out.'

'You're sure this man really has money?'

'Crawling with it, laddie. Hasn't found out yet there's anything smaller than a five-pound note in circulation. He took me to lunch, and when he tipped the waiter the man burst into tears and kissed him on both cheeks.'

I am bound to admit that I felt easier in my mind, for it really did seem as though the fortunes of Miss Mason rested on firm ground. I had never supposed that Ukridge could be associated with so sound a scheme, and I said so. In fact, I rather overdid my approval, for it encouraged him to borrow another five shillings; and before he left we were in treaty over a further deal which was to entail my advancing him half a sovereign in one solid payment. Business breeds business.

For the next ten days I saw nothing of Ukridge. As he was in the habit of making these periodical disappearances, I did not worry unduly as to the whereabouts of my wandering boy, but

I was conscious from time to time of a mild wonder as to what had become of him. The mystery was solved one night when I was walking through Pall Mall on my way home after a late session with an actor acquaintance who was going into vaudeville, and to whom I hoped, – mistakenly, as it turned out – to sell a one-act play.

I say night, but it was nearly two in the morning. The streets were black and deserted, silence was everywhere, and all London slept except Ukridge and a friend of his whom I came upon standing outside Hardy's fishing tackle shop. That is to say, Ukridge was standing outside the shop. His friend was sitting on the pavement with his back against a lamp-post.

As far as I could see in the uncertain light, he was a man of middle age, rugged of aspect and grizzled about the temples. I was able to inspect his temples because – doubtless from the best motives – he was wearing his hat on his left foot. He was correctly clad in dress clothes, but his appearance was a little marred by a splash of mud across his shirt-front and the fact that at some point earlier in the evening he had either thrown away or been deprived of his tie. He gazed fixedly at the hat with a poached-egg-like stare. He was the only man I had ever seen who was smoking two cigars at the same time.

Ukridge greeted me with the warmth of a beleaguered garrison welcoming the relieving army.

'My dear old horse! Just the man I wanted!' he cried, as if he had picked me out of a number of competing applicants. 'You can give me a hand with Hank, laddie.'

'Is this Hank?' I inquired, glancing at the recumbent sportsman, who had now closed his eyes as if the spectacle of the hat had begun to pall.

'Yes. Hank Philbrick. This is the bloke I was telling you about, the fellow who wants the house.'

'He doesn't seem to want any house. He looks quite satisfied with the great open spaces.'

'Poor old Hank's a bit under the weather,' explained Ukridge, regarding his stricken friend with tolerant sympathy. 'It takes him this way. The fact is, old man, it's a mistake for these blokes to come into money. They overdo things. The only thing Hank ever got to drink for the first fifty years of his life was water, with buttermilk as a treat on his birthday, and he's trying to make up for lost time. He's only just discovered that there are such things as liqueurs in the world, and he's making them rather a hobby. Says they're such a pretty colour. It wouldn't be so bad if he stuck to one at a time, but he likes making experiments. Mixes them, laddie. Orders the whole lot and blends them in a tankard. Well, I mean to say,' said Ukridge reasonably, 'you can't take more than five or six tankards of mixed benedictine, chartreuse, kummel, crème de menthe, and old brandy without feeling the strain a bit. Especially if you stoke up on champagne and burgundy.'

A strong shudder ran through me at the thought. I gazed at the human cellar on the pavement with a feeling bordering on awe.

'Does he really?'

'Every night for the last two weeks. I've been with him most of the time. I'm the only pal he's got in London, and he likes to have me round.'

'What plans have you for his future? His immediate future, I mean. Do we remove him somewhere or is he going to spend the night out here under the quiet stars?'

'I thought, if you would lend a hand, old man, we could get him to the Carlton. He's staying there.'

'He won't be long, if he comes in in this state.'

'Bless you, my dear old man, they don't mind. He tipped the night-porter twenty quid yesterday and asked me if I thought it was enough. Lend a hand, laddie. Let's go.'

I lent a hand, and we went.

The effect which that nocturnal encounter had upon me was to cement the impression that in acting as agent for Mr Philbrick in the purchase of a house Ukridge was on to a good thing. What little I had seen of Hank had convinced me that he was not the man to be finicky about price. He would pay whatever they asked him without hesitation. Ukridge would undoubtedly make enough out of his share of the commission to pay off Dora Mason's hundred without feeling it. Indeed, for the first time in his life he would probably be in possession of that bit of capital of which he was accustomed to speak so wistfully. I ceased, therefore, to worry about Miss Mason's future and concentrated myself on my own troubles.

They would probably have seemed to anyone else minor troubles, but nevertheless they were big enough to depress me. Two days after my meeting with Ukridge and Mr Philbrick in Pall Mall I had received rather a disturbing letter.

There was a Society paper for which at that time I did occasional work and wished to do more; and the editor of this paper had sent me a ticket for the forthcoming dance of the Pen and Ink Club, with instructions to let him have a column and a half of bright descriptive matter. It was only after I had digested the pleasant reflection that here was a bit of badly needed cash dropping on me out of a clear sky that I realized why the words Pen and Ink Club seemed to have a familiar ring. It was the club of which Ukridge's aunt Julia was the popular and energetic president, and the thought of a second meeting with that uncomfortable woman filled me with a deep gloom. I had not forgotten – and probably would never forget – my encounter with her in her drawing-room at Wimbledon.

I was not in a financial position, however, to refuse editors their whims, so the thing had to be gone through; but the prospect damped me, and I was still brooding on it when a violent ring at the front-door bell broke in on my meditations. It was followed by the booming of Ukridge's voice inquiring if I were in. A moment later he had burst into the room. His eyes were wild, his pince-nez at an angle of forty-five, and his collar separated from its stud by a gap of several inches. His whole appearance clearly indicated some blow of fate, and I was not surprised when his first words revealed an aching heart.

'Hank Philbrick,' said Ukridge without preamble, ' is a son of Belial, a leper, and a worm.'

'What's happened now?'

'He's let me down, the weak-minded Tishbite! Doesn't want that house in the country after all. My gosh, if Hank Philbrick is the sort of man Canada is producing nowadays, Heaven help the British Empire.'

I shelved my petty troubles. They seemed insignificant beside this majestic tragedy.

'What made him change his mind?' I asked.

'The wobbling, vacillating hell-hound! I always had a feeling that there was something wrong with that man. He had a nasty, shifty eye. You'll bear me out, laddie, in that? Haven't I spoken to you a hundred times about his shifty eye?'

'Certainly. Why did he change his mind?'

'Didn't I always say he wasn't to be trusted?'

'Repeatedly. What made him change his mind?'

Ukridge laughed with a sharp bitterness that nearly cracked the window-pane. His collar leaped like a live thing. Ukridge's collar was always a sort of thermometer that registered the warmth of his feelings. Sometimes, when his temperature was normal, it would remain attached to its stud for minutes at a time; but the slightest touch of fever sent it jumping up, and the more he was moved the higher it jumped.

'When I knew Hank out in Canada,' he said, 'he had the constitution of an ox. Ostriches took his correspondence course in digestion. But directly he comes into a bit of money – Laddie,' said Ukridge earnestly, 'when I'm a rich man, I want you to stand at my elbow and watch me very carefully. The moment you see signs of degeneration speak a warning word. Don't let me coddle myself. Don't let me get fussy about my health. Where was I? Oh, yes. Directly this man comes into a bit of money he gets the idea that he's a sort of fragile, delicate flower.'

'I shouldn't have thought so from what you were telling me the other night.'

'What happened the other night was the cause of all the trouble. Naturally he woke up with a bit of a head.'

'I can quite believe it.'

'Yes, but my gosh, what's a head! In the old days he would have gone and worked it off by taking a dose of pain-killer and chopping down half a dozen trees. But now what happens? Having all this money, he wouldn't take a simple remedy like that. No, sir! He went to one of those Harley Street sharks who charge a couple of guineas for saying "Well, how are we this morning?" A fatal move, laddie. Naturally, the shark was all over him. Tapped him here and prodded him there, said he was run down, and finally told him he ought to spend six months

in a dry, sunny climate. Recommended Egypt. Egypt, I'll trouble
you, for a bloke who lived fifty years thinking that it was a
town in Illinois. Well, the long and the short of it is that he's
gone off for six months, doesn't want a place in England, and I
hope he gets bitten by a crocodile. And the lease all drawn out
and ready to sign. Upon my Sam, it's a little hard. Sometimes
I wonder whether it's worth while going on struggling.'

A sombre silence fell upon us. Ukridge, sunk in gloomy
reverie, fumbled absently at his collar stud. I smoked with a
heavy heart.

'What will your friend Dora do now?' I said at length.

'That's what's worrying me,' said Ukridge, lugubriously.
'I've been trying to think of some other way of raising that
hundred, but at the moment I don't mind confessing I am baffled. I can see no daylight.'

Nor could I. His chance of raising a hundred pounds by any
means short of breaking into the Mint seemed slight indeed.

'Odd the way things happen,' I said. I gave him the editor's
letter. 'Look at that.'

'What's this?'

'He's sending me to do an article on the Pen and Ink Club
dance. If only I had never been to see your aunt –'

'And made such a mess of it.'

'I didn't make a mess of it. It just happened that –'

'All right, laddie, all right,' said Ukridge, tonelessly. 'Don't
let's split straws. The fact remains, whether it's your fault or
not, the thing was a complete frost. What were you saying?'

'I was saying that, if only I had never been to your aunt, I
could have met her in a perfectly natural way at this dance.'

'Done Young Disciple stuff,' said Ukridge, seizing on the idea.
'Rubbed in the fact that you could do her a bit of good by
boosting her in the paper.'

'And asked her to re-engage Miss Mason as her secretary.'

Ukridge fiddled with the letter.

'You don't think even now –'

I was sorry for him and sorrier for Dora Mason, but on this
point I was firm.

'No, I don't.'

'But consider, laddie,' urged Ukridge. 'At this dance she may well be in malleable mood. The lights, the music, the laughter, the jollity.'

'No,' I said. 'It can't be done. I can't back out of going to the affair, because if I did I'd never get any more work to do for this paper. But I'll tell you one thing. I mean to keep quite clear of your aunt. That's final. I dream of her in the night sometimes and wake up screaming. And in any case it wouldn't be any use my tackling her. She wouldn't listen to me. It's too late. You weren't there that afternoon at Wimbledon, but you can take it from me that I'm not one of her circle of friends.'

'That's the way it always happens,' sighed Ukridge. 'Everything comes too late. Well, I'll be popping off. Lot of heavy thinking to do, laddie. Lot of heavy thinking.'

And he left without borrowing even a cigar, a sure sign that his resilient spirit was crushed beyond recuperation.

The dance of the Pen and Ink Club was held, like so many functions of its kind, at the Lotus Rooms, Knightsbridge, that barrack-like building which seems to exist only for these sad affairs. The Pen and Ink evidently went in for quality in its membership rather than quantity; and the band, when I arrived, was giving out the peculiarly tinny sound which bands always produce in very large rooms that are only one-sixth part full. The air was chilly and desolate and a general melancholy seemed to prevail. The few couples dancing on the broad acres of floor appeared sombre and introspective, as if they were meditating on the body upstairs and realizing that all flesh is as grass. Around the room on those gilt chairs which are only seen in subscription-dance halls weird beings were talking in undertones, probably about the trend of Scandinavian literature. In fact, the only bright spot on the whole gloomy business was that it occurred before the era of tortoiseshell-rimmed spectacles.

That curious grey hopelessness which always afflicts me when I am confronted with literary people in the bulk was not lightened by the reflection that at any moment I might encounter Miss Julia Ukridge. I moved warily about the room, keenly alert, like a cat that has wandered into a strange alley and sees in every shadow the potential hurler of a half-brick. I could envisage nothing but awkwardness and embarrassment springing from such a meeting. The lesson which I had drawn from my previous encounter with her was that happiness for me lay in keeping as far away from Miss Julia Ukridge as possible.

'Excuse me!'

My precautions had been in vain. She had sneaked up on me from behind.

'Good evening,' I said.

It is never any good rehearsing these scenes in advance. They always turn out so differently. I had been assuming, when I slunk into this hall, that if I met this woman I should feel the same shrinking sense of guilt and inferiority which had proved so disintegrating at Wimbledon. I had omitted to make allowances for the fact that that painful episode had taken place on her own ground, and that right from the start my conscience had been far from clear. Tonight the conditions were different.

'Are you a member of the Pen and Ink Club?' said Ukridge's aunt, frostily.

Her stony blue eyes were fixed on me with an expression that was not exactly loathing, but rather a cold and critical contempt. So might a fastidious cook look at a black-beetle in her kitchen.

'No,' I replied, 'I am not.'

I felt bold and hostile. This woman gave me a pain in the neck, and I endeavoured to express as much in the language of the eyes.

'Then will you please tell me what you are doing here? This is a private dance.'

One has one's moments. I felt much as I presume Battling Billson must have felt in his recent fight with Alf Todd, when he perceived his antagonist advancing upon him wide-open, inviting the knock-out punch.

'The editor of *Society* sent me a ticket. He wanted an article written about it.'

If I was feeling like Mr Billson, Ukridge's aunt must have felt very like Mr Todd. I could see that she was shaken. In a flash I had changed from a black-beetle to a god-like creature, able, if conciliated, to do a bit of that log-rolling which is so dear to the heart of the female novelist. And she had not conciliated me. Of all sad words of tongue or pen, the saddest are these: It might have been. It is too much to say that her jaw fell, but certainly the agony of this black moment caused her lips to part in a sort of twisted despair. But there was good stuff in this woman. She rallied gamely.

'A Press ticket,' she murmured.

'A Press ticket,' I echoed.

'May I see it?'

'Certainly.'

'Thank you.'

'Not at all.'

She passed on.

I resumed my inspection of the dancers with a lighter heart. In my present uplifted mood they did not appear so bad as they had a few minutes back. Some of them, quite a few of them, looked almost human. The floor was fuller now, and whether owing to my imagination or not, the atmosphere seemed to have taken on a certain cheeriness. The old suggestion of a funeral still lingered, but now it was possible to think of it as a less formal, rather jollier funeral. I began to be glad that I had come.

'Excuse me!'

I had thought that I was finished with this sort of thing for the evening, and I turned with a little impatience. It was a refined tenor voice that had addressed me, and it was a refined tenor-looking man whom I saw. He was young and fattish, with a Jovian coiffure and pince-nez attached to a black cord.

'Pardon me,' said this young man, 'but are you a member of the Pen and Ink Club?'

My momentary annoyance vanished, for it suddenly occurred to me that, looked at in the proper light, it was really extremely flattering, this staunch refusal on the part of these people to entertain the belief that I could be one of them. No doubt, I felt, they were taking up the position of the proprietor of a certain night-club, who, when sued for defamation of character by a young lady to whom he had refused admittance on the ground that she was not a fit person to associate with his members, explained to the court that he had meant it as a compliment.

'No, thank Heaven!' I replied.

'Then what –'

'Press ticket,' I explained.

'Press ticket? What paper?'

'*Society.*'

There was nothing of the Julia Ukridge spirit in this young man, no ingrained pride which kept him aloof and outwardly indifferent. He beamed like the rising sun. He grasped my arm and kneaded it. He gambolled about me like a young lamb in the springtime.

'My dear fellow!' he exclaimed, exuberantly, and clutched my arm more firmly, lest even now I might elude him. 'My dear fellow, I really must apologize. I would not have questioned you, but there are some persons present who were not invited. I met a man only a moment ago who said that he had bought a ticket. Some absurd mistake. There were no tickets for sale. I was about to question him further, but he disappeared into the crowd and I have not seen him since. This is a quite private dance, open only to members of the club. Come with me, my dear fellow, and I will give you a few particulars which you may find of use for your article.'

He led me resolutely into a small room off the floor, closed the door to prevent escape, and, on the principle on which you rub a cat's paws with butter to induce it to settle down in a new home, began to fuss about with whisky and cigarettes.

'Do, do sit down.'

I sat down.

'First, about this club. The Pen and Ink Club is the only really exclusive organization of its kind in London. We pride ourselves on the fact. We are to the literary world what Brooks's and the Carlton are to the social. Members are elected solely by invitation. Election, in short, you understand, is in the nature of an accolade. We have exactly one hundred members, and we include only those writers who in our opinion possess vision.'

'And the big, broad, flexible outlook?'

'I beg your pardon?'

'Nothing.'

'The names of most of those here tonight must be very familiar to you.'

'I know Miss Ukridge, the president,' I said.

A faint, almost imperceptible shadow passed over the stout young man's face. He removed his pince-nez and polished them with a touch of disfavour. There was a rather flat note in his voice.

'Ah, yes,' he said, 'Julia Ukridge. A dear soul, but between ourselves, strictly between ourselves, not a great deal of help in an executive capacity.'

'No!'

'No. In confidence, I do all the work. I am the club's secretary. My name, by the way, is Charlton Prout. You may know it?'

He eyed me wistfully, and I felt that something ought to be done about him. He was much too sleek, and he had no right to do his hair like that.

'Of course,' I said. 'I have read all your books.'

'Really?'

'*A Shriek in the Night. Who Killed Jasper Blossom?* – all of them.'

He stiffened austerely.

'You must be confusing me with some other – ah – writer,' he said. 'My work is on somewhat different lines. The reviewers usually describe the sort of thing I do as Pastels in Prose. My best-liked book, I believe, is *Grey Myrtles*. Dunstable's brought it out last year. It was exceedingly well received. And I do a good deal of critical work for the better class of review.' He paused. 'If you think it would interest your readers,' he said, with a deprecating wave of the hand, 'I will send you a photograph. Possibly your editor would like to use it.'

'I bet he would.'

'A photograph somehow seems to – as it were – set off an article of this kind.'

'That,' I replied, cordially, 'is what it doesn't do nothing else but.'

'And you won't forget *Grey Myrtles*. Well, if you have finished your cigarette, we might be returning to the ballroom. These people rather rely on me to keep things going, you know.'

A burst of music greeted us as he opened the door, and even

in that first moment I had an odd feeling that it sounded different. That tinny sound had gone from it. And as we debouched from behind a potted palm and came in sight of the floor, I realized why.

The floor was full. It was crammed, jammed, and overflowing. Where couples had moved as single spies, they were now in battalions. The place was alive with noise and laughter. These people might, as my companion had said, be relying on him to keep things going, but they seemed to have been getting along uncommonly well in his absence. I paused and surveyed the mob in astonishment. I could not make the man's figures balance.

'I thought you said the Pen and Ink Club had only a hundred members.'

The secretary was fumbling for his glasses. He had an almost Ukridge-like knack of dropping his pince-nez in moments of emotion.

'It – it has,' he stammered.

'Well, reading from left to right, I make it nearer seven hundred.'

'I cannot understand it.'

'Perhaps they have been having a new election and letting in some writers without vision,' I suggested.

I was aware of Miss Ukridge bearing down upon us, bristling.

'Mr Prout!'

The talented young author of *Grey Myrtles* leaped convulsively.

'Yes, Miss Ukridge?'

'Who are all these people?'

'I – I don't know,' said the talented young man.

'You don't know! It's your business to know. You are the secretary of the club. I suggest that you find out as quickly as possible who they are and what they imagine they are doing here.'

The goaded secretary had something of the air of a man leading a forlorn hope, and his ears had turned bright pink, but he went at it bravely. A serene-looking man with a light moustache and a made-up tie was passing, and he sprang upon him like a stoutish leopard.

'Excuse me, sir.'

'Eh?'

'Will you kindly – would you mind – pardon me if I ask –'

'What are you doing here?' demanded Miss Ukridge, curtly, cutting in on his flounderings with a masterful impatience. 'How do you come to be at this dance?'

The man seemed surprised.

'Who, me?' he said. 'I came with the rest of 'em.'

'What do you mean, the rest of them?'

'The members of the Warner's Stores Social and Outing Club.'

'But this is the dance of the Pen and Ink Club,' bleated Mr Prout.

'Some mistake,' said the other, confidently. 'It's a bloomer of some kind. Here,' he added, beckoning to a portly gentleman of middle age who was bustling by, 'you'd better have a talk with our hon. sec. He'll know. Mr Biggs, this gentleman seems to think there's been some mistake about this dance.'

Mr Biggs stopped, looked, and listened. Seen at close range, he had a forceful, determined air. I liked his looks.

'May I introduce Mr Charlton Prout?' I said. 'Author of *Grey Myrtles*. Mr Prout,' I went on, as this seemed to make little or no sensation, 'is the secretary of the Pen and Ink Club.'

'I'm the secretary of the Warner's Stores Social and Outing Club,' said Mr Biggs.

The two secretaries eyed each other warily, like two dogs.

'But what are you doing here?' moaned Mr Prout, in a voice like the wind in the tree-tops. 'This is a private dance.'

'Nothing of the kind,' said Mr Biggs, resolutely. 'I personally bought tickets for all my members.'

'But there were no tickets for sale. The dance was for the exclusive –'

'It's perfectly evident that you have come to the wrong hall or chosen the wrong evening,' snapped Miss Ukridge, abruptly superseding Mr Prout in the supreme command. I did not blame her for feeling a little impatient. The secretary was handling the campaign very feebly.

The man behind the Warner's Stores Social and Outing Club cocked a polite but belligerent eye at this new enemy. I liked his looks more than ever. This was a man who would fight it out on these lines if it took all the summer.

'I have not the honour of this lady's acquaintance,' he said, smoothly, but with a gradually reddening eye. The Biggses, that eye seemed to say, were loath to war upon women, but if the women asked for it they could be men of iron, ruthless. 'Might I ask who this lady is?'

'This is our president.'

'Happy to meet you, ma'am.'

'Miss Ukridge,' added Mr Prout, completing the introduction.

The name appeared to strike a chord in Mr Biggs. He bent forward and a gleam of triumph came into his eyes.

'Ukridge, did you say?'

'Miss Julia Ukridge.'

'Then it's all right,' said Mr Biggs, briskly. 'There's been no mistake. I bought our tickets from a gentleman named Ukridge. I got seven hundred at five bob apiece, reduction for taking a quantity and ten per cent discount for cash. If Mr Ukridge acted contrary to instructions, it's too late to remedy the matter now. You should have made it clear to him what you wanted him to do before he went and did it.'

And with this extremely sound sentiment the honorary secretary of the Warner's Stores Social and Outing Club turned on the heel of his shining dancing-pump and was gone. And I, too, sauntered away. There seemed nothing to keep me. As I went, I looked over my shoulder. The author of *Grey Myrtles* appeared to be entering upon the opening stages of what promised to be a painful *tête-à-tête*. My heart bled for him. If ever a man was blameless, Mr Prout was, but the president of the Pen and Ink Club was not the woman to allow a trifle like that to stand in her way.

'Oh, it just came to me, laddie,' said Stanley Featherstonehaugh Ukridge modestly, interviewed later by our representative. 'You know me. One moment mind a blank, then – *bing!* – some dashed colossal idea. It was your showing me that ticket for the dance that set me thinking. And I happened to meet a bloke in a pub who worked in Warner's Stores. Nice fellow, with a fair amount of pimples. Told me their Social and Outing

Club was working up for its semi-annual beano. One thing led to another, I got him to introduce me to the hon. sec., and we came to terms. I liked the man, laddie. Great treat to meet a bloke with a good, level business head. We settled the details in no time. Well, I don't mind telling you, Corky my boy, that at last for the first time in many years I begin to see my way clear. I've got a bit of capital now. After sending poor little Dora her hundred, I shall have at least fifty quid left over. Fifty quid! My dear old son, you may take it from me that there's no limit – absolutely no limit – to what I can accomplish with fifty o'goblins in my kick. From now on I see my way clear. My feet are on solid ground. The world, laddie, is my oyster. Nothing can stop me from making a colossal fortune. I'm not exaggerating, old horse – a colossal fortune. Why, by a year from now I calculate, at a conservative estimate –'

Our representative then withdrew.

Chapter 7

No Wedding Bells for Him

To Ukridge, as might be expected from one of his sunny optimism, the whole affair has long since come to present itself in the light of yet another proof of the way in which all things in this world of ours work together for good. In it, from start to finish, he sees the finger of Providence; and, when marshalling evidence to support his theory that a means of escape from the most formidable perils will always be vouchsafed to the righteous and deserving, this is the episode which he advances as Exhibit A.

The thing may be said to have had its beginning in the Haymarket one afternoon towards the middle of the summer. We had been lunching at my expense at the Pall Mall Restaurant, and as we came out a large and shiny car drew up beside the kerb, and the chauffeur, alighting, opened the bonnet and began to fiddle about in its interior with a pair of pliers. Had I been alone, a casual glance in passing would have contented me, but for Ukridge the spectacle of somebody else working always had an irresistible fascination, and, gripping my arm, he steered me up to assist him in giving the toiler moral support. About two minutes after he had started to breathe earnestly on the man's neck, the latter, seeming to become aware that what was tickling his back hair was not some wandering June zephyr, looked up with a certain petulance.

' 'Ere!' he said, protestingly. Then his annoyance gave place to something which – for a chauffeur – approached cordiality. ' 'Ullo!' he observed.

'Why, hallo, Frederick,' said Ukridge. 'Didn't recognize you. Is this the new car?'

'Ah,' nodded the chauffeur.

'Pal of mine,' explained Ukridge to me in a brief aside. 'Met him in a pub.' London was congested with pals whom Ukridge had met in pubs. 'What's the trouble?'

'Missing,' said Frederick the chauffeur. 'Soon 'ave her right.'

His confidence in his skill was not misplaced. After a short interval he straightened himself, closed the bonnet, and wiped his hands.

'Nice day,' he said.

'Terrific,' agreed Ukridge. 'Where are you off to?'

'Got to go to Addington. Pick up the guv'nor playin' golf there.' He seemed to hesitate for a moment, then the mellowing influence of the summer sunshine asserted itself. 'Like a ride as far as East Croydon? Get a train back from there.'

It was a handsome offer, and one which neither Ukridge nor myself disposed to decline. We climbed in, Frederick trod on the self-starter, and off we bowled, two gentlemen of fashion taking their afternoon airing. Speaking for myself, I felt tranquil and debonair, and I have no reason to suppose that Ukridge was otherwise. The deplorable incident which now occurred was thus rendered doubly distressing. We had stopped at the foot of the street to allow the north-bound traffic to pass, when our pleasant after-luncheon torpidity was shattered by a sudden and violent shout.

'Hi!'

That the shouter was addressing us there was no room for doubt. He was standing on the pavement not four feet away, glaring unmistakably into our costly tonneau – a stout, bearded man of middle age, unsuitably clad, considering the weather and the sartorial prejudices of Society, in a frock-coat and a bowler hat. 'Hi! You!' he bellowed, to the scandal of all good passers-by.

Frederick the chauffeur, after one swift glance of god-like disdain out of the corner of his left eye, had ceased to interest himself in this undignified exhibition on the part of one of the lower orders, but I was surprised to observe that Ukridge was betraying all the discomposure of some wild thing taken in a trap. His face had turned crimson and assumed a bulbous expression, and he was staring straight ahead of him with a piteous effort to ignore what manifestly would not be ignored.

'I'd like a word with you,' boomed the bearded one.

And then matters proceeded with a good deal of rapidity. The traffic had begun to move on now, and as we moved with it, travelling with increasing speed, the man appeared to realize that if 'twere done 'twere well 'twere done quickly. He executed a cumbersome leap and landed on our running-board; and Ukridge, coming suddenly to life, put out a large flat hand and pushed. The intruder dropped off, and the last I saw of him he was standing in the middle of the road, shaking his fist, in imminent danger of being run over by a number three omnibus.

'Gosh!' sighed Ukridge, with some feverishness.

'What was it all about?' I inquired.

'Bloke I owe a bit of money to,' explained Ukridge, tersely.

'Ah!' I said, feeling that all had been made clear. I had never before actually seen one of Ukridge's creditors in action, but he had frequently given me to understand that they lurked all over London like leopards in the jungle, waiting to spring on him. There were certain streets down which he would never walk for fear of what might befall.

'Been trailing me like a bloodhound for two years,' said Ukridge. 'Keeps bobbing up when I don't expect him and turning my hair white to the roots.'

I was willing to hear more, and even hinted as much, but he relapsed into a moody silence. We were moving at a brisk clip into Clapham Common when the second of the incidents occurred which were to make this drive linger in the memory. Just as we came in sight of the Common, a fool of a girl loomed up right before our front wheels. She had been crossing the road, and now, after the manner of her species, she lost her head. She was a large, silly-looking girl, and she darted to and fro like a lunatic hen; and as Ukridge and I rose simultaneously from our seats, clutching each other in agony, she tripped over her feet and fell. But Frederick, master of his craft, had the situation well in hand. He made an inspired swerve, and when we stopped a moment later, the girl was picking herself up, dusty, but still in one piece.

These happenings affect different men in different ways. In Frederick's cold grey eye as he looked over his shoulder and backed the car there was only the weary scorn of a superman for the never-ending follies of a woollen-headed proletariat. I, on the other hand, had reacted in a gust of nervous profanity. And Ukridge, I perceived as I grew calmer, the affair had touched on his chivalrous side. All the time we were backing he was mumbling to himself, and he was out of the car, bleating apologies, almost before we had stopped.

'Awfully sorry. Might have killed you. Can't forgive myself.'

The girl treated the affair in still another way. She giggled. And somehow that brainless laugh afflicted me more than anything that had gone before. It was not her fault, I suppose. This untimely mirth was merely due to disordered nerves. But I had taken a prejudice against her at first sight.

'I do hope,' babbled Ukridge, 'you aren't hurt? Do tell me you aren't hurt.'

The girl giggled again. And she was at least twelve pounds too heavy to be a giggler. I wanted to pass on and forget her.

'No, reely, thanks.'

'But shaken, what?'

'I did come down a fair old bang,' chuckled this repellent female.

'I thought so. I was afraid so. Shaken. Ganglions vibrating. You just let me drive you home.'

'Oh, it doesn't matter.'

'I insist. Positively I insist!'

' 'Ere!' said Frederick the chauffeur, in a low, compelling voice.

'Eh?'

'Got to get on to Addington.'

'Yes, yes, yes,' said Ukridge, with testy impatience, quite the seigneur resenting interference from an underling. 'But there's plenty of time to drive this lady home. Can't you see she's shaken? Where can I take you?'

'It's only just round the corner in the next street. Balbriggan the name of the house is.'

'Balbriggan, Frederick, in the next street,' said Ukridge, in a tone that brooked no argument.

I suppose the spectacle of the daughter of the house rolling up to the front door in a Daimler is unusual in Peabody Road, Clapham Common. At any rate, we had hardly drawn up when Balbriggan began to exude its occupants in platoons. Father, mother, three small sisters, and a brace of brothers were on the steps in the first ten seconds. They surged down the garden path in a solid mass.

Ukridge was at his most spacious. Quickly establishing himself on the footing of a friend of the family, he took charge of the whole affair. Introductions sped to and fro, and in a few moving words he explained the situation, while I remained mute and insignificant in my corner and Frederick the chauffeur stared at his oil-gauge with a fathomless eye.

'Couldn't have forgiven myself, Mr Price, if anything had happened to Miss Price. Fortunately my chauffeur is an excellent driver and swerved just in time. You showed great presence of mind, Frederick,' said Ukridge, handsomely, 'great presence of mind.'

Frederick continued to gaze aloofly at his oil-gauge.

'What a lovely car, Mr Ukridge!' said the mother of the family.

'Yes?' said Ukridge, airily. 'Yes, quite a good old machine.'

'Can you drive yourself?' asked the smaller of the two small brothers, reverently.

'Oh, yes. Yes. But I generally use Frederick for town work.'

'Would you and your friend care to come in for a cup of tea?' said Mrs Price.

I could see Ukridge hesitate. He had only recently finished an excellent lunch, but there was that about the offer of a free meal which never failed to touch a chord in him. At this point, however, Frederick spoke.

' 'Ere!' said Frederick.

'Eh?'

'Got to get on to Addington,' said Frederick, firmly.

Ukridge started as one waked from a dream. I really believe he had succeeded in persuading himself that the car belonged to him.

'Of course, yes. I was forgetting. I have to be at Addington almost immediately. Promised to pick up some golfing friends. Some other time, eh?'

'Any time you're in the neighbourhood, Mr Ukridge,' said Mr Price, beaming upon the popular pet.

'Thanks, thanks.'

'Tell me, Mr Ukridge,' said Mrs Price. 'I've been wondering ever since you told me your name. It's such an unusual one. Are you any relation to the Miss Ukridge who writes books?'

'My aunt,' beamed Ukridge.

'No, really? I do love her stories so. Tell me –'

Frederick, whom I could not sufficiently admire, here broke off what promised to be a lengthy literary discussion by treading on the self-starter, and we drove off in a flurry of good wishes and invitations. I rather fancy I heard Ukridge, as he leaned over the back of the car, promising to bring his aunt round to Sunday supper some time. He resumed his seat as we turned the corner and at once began to moralize.

'Always sow the good seed, laddie. Absolutely nothing to beat the good seed. Never lose the chance of establishing yourself. It is the secret of a successful life. Just a few genial words, you see, and here I am with a place I can always pop into for a bite when funds are low.'

I was shocked at his sordid outlook, and said so. He rebuked me out of his larger wisdom.

'It's all very well to take that attitude, Corky my boy, but do you realize that a family like that has cold beef, baked potatoes, pickles, salad, blanc-mange, and some sort of cheese every Sunday night after Divine service? There are moments in a man's life, laddie, when a spot of cold beef with blanc-mange to follow means more than words can tell.'

It was about a week later that I happened to go to the British Museum to gather material for one of those brightly informative articles of mine which appeared from time to time in the weekly papers. I was wandering through the place, accumulating data, when I came upon Ukridge with a small boy attached to each hand. He seemed a trifle weary, and he welcomed me with something of the gratification of the shipwrecked mariner who sights a sail.

'Run along and improve your bally minds, you kids,' he said to the children. 'You'll find me here when you've finished.'

'All right, Uncle Stanley,' chorused the children.

'Uncle Stanley?' I said, accusingly.

He winced a little. I had to give him credit for that.

'Those are the Price kids. From Clapham.'

'I remember them.'

'I'm taking them out for the day. Must repay hospitality, Corky my boy.'

'Then you have really been inflicting yourself on those unfortunate people?'

'I have looked in from time to time,' said Ukridge, with dignity.

'It's just over a week since you met them. How often have you looked in?'

'Couple of times, perhaps. Maybe three.'

'To meals?'

'There was a bit of browsing going on,' admitted Ukridge.

'And now you're Uncle Stanley!'

'Fine, warm-hearted people,' said Ukridge, and it seemed to me that he spoke with a touch of defiance. 'Made me one of the family right from the beginning. Of course, it cuts both ways. This afternoon, for instance, I got landed with those kids. But, all in all, taking the rough with the smooth, it has worked out distinctly on the right side of the ledger. I own I'm not over-keen on the hymns after Sunday supper, but the supper, laddie, is undeniable. As good a bit of cold beef,' said Ukridge, dreamily, 'as I ever chewed.'

'Greedy brute,' I said, censoriously.

'Must keep body and soul together, old man. Of course, there are one or two things about the business that are a bit embarrassing. For instance, somehow or other they seem to have got the idea that that car we turned up in that day belongs to me, and the kids are always pestering me to take them for a ride. Fortunately I've managed to square Frederick, and he thinks he can arrange for a spin or two during the next few days. And then Mrs Price keeps asking me to bring my aunt round for a cup of tea and a chat, and I haven't the heart to tell her that my aunt absolutely and finally disowned me the day after that business of the dance.'

'You didn't tell me that.'

'Didn't I? Oh, yes. I got a letter from her saying that as far as she was concerned I had ceased to exist. I thought it showed a nasty, narrow spirit, but I can't say I was altogether surprised. Still, it makes it awkward when Mrs Price wants to get matey with her. I've had to tell her that my aunt is a chronic invalid and never goes out, being practically bedridden. I find all this a bit wearing, laddie.'

'I suppose so.'

'You see,' said Ukridge, 'I dislike subterfuge.'

There seemed no possibility of his beating this, so I left the man and resumed my researches.

After this I was out of town for a few weeks, taking my annual vacation. When I got back to Ebury Street, Bowles, my landlord, after complimenting me in a stately way on my sunburned appearance, informed me that George Tupper had called several times while I was away.

'Appeared remarkably anxious to see you, sir.'

I was surprised at this. George Tupper was always glad – or seemed to be glad – to see an old school friend when I called upon him, but he rarely sought me out in my home.

'Did he say what he wanted?'

'No, sir. He left no message. He merely inquired as to the probable date of your return and expressed a desire that you would visit him as soon as convenient.'

'I'd better go and see him now.'

'It might be advisable, sir.'

I found George Tupper at the Foreign Office, surrounded by important-looking papers.

'Here you are at last!' cried George, resentfully, it seemed to me. 'I thought you were never coming back.'

'I had a splendid time, thanks very much for asking,' I replied. 'Got the roses back to my cheeks.'

George, who seemed far from his usual tranquil self, briefly cursed my cheeks and their roses.

'Look here,' he said, urgently, 'something's got to be done. Have you seen Ukridge yet?'

'Not yet. I thought I would look him up this evening.'

'You'd better. Do you know what has happened? That poor ass has gone and got himself engaged to be married to a girl at Clapham!'

'What?'

'Engaged! Girl at Clapham. Clapham Common,' added George Tupper, as if in his opinion that made the matter even worse.

'You're joking!'

'I'm not joking,' said George peevishly. 'Do I look as if I were joking? I met him in Battersea Park with her, and he introduced me. She reminded me,' said George Tupper, shivering slightly, for that fearful evening had seared his soul deeply, 'of that ghastly female in pink he brought with him the night I gave you two dinner at the Regent Grill – the one who talked at the top of her voice all the time about her aunt's stomach-trouble.'

Here I think he did Miss Price an injustice. She had struck me during our brief acquaintance as something of a blister, but I had never quite classed her with Battling Billson's Flossie.

'Well, what do you want me to do?' I asked, not, I think, unreasonably.

'You've got to think of some way of getting him out of it. I can't do anything. I'm busy all day.'

'So am I busy.'

'Busy my left foot!' said George Tupper, who in moments of strong emotion was apt to relapse into the phraseology of school days and express himself in a very un-Foreign Official manner. 'About once a week you work up energy enough to write a rotten article for some rag of a paper on "Should Curates Kiss?" or some silly subject, and the rest of the time you loaf about with Ukridge. It's obviously your job to disentangle the poor idiot.'

'But how do you know he wants to be disentangled? It seems to me you're jumping pretty readily to conclusions. It's all very well for you bloodless officials to sneer at the holy passion, but it's love, as I sometimes say, that makes the world go round. Ukridge probably feels that until now he never realized what true happiness could mean.'

'Does he?' snorted George Tupper. 'Well, he didn't look it when I met him. He looked like – well, do you remember when he went in for the heavyweights at school and that chap in Seymour's house hit him in the wind in the first round? That's how he looked when he was introducing the girl to me.'

I am bound to say the comparison impressed me. It is odd how these little incidents of one's boyhood linger in the memory. Across the years I could see Ukridge now, half doubled up,

one gloved hand caressing his diaphragm, a stunned and horri-
fied bewilderment in his eyes. If his bearing as an engaged man
had reminded George Tupper of that occasion, it certainly did
seem as if the time had come for his friends to rally round
him.

'You seem to have taken on the job of acting as a sort of
unofficial keeper to the man,' said George. 'You'll have to help
him now.'

'Well, I'll go and see him.'

'The whole thing is too absurd,' said George Tupper. 'How
can Ukridge get married to anyone! He hasn't a bob in the
world.'

'I'll point that out to him. He's probably overlooked it.'

It was my custom when I visited Ukridge at his lodgings to
stand underneath his window and bellow his name – upon
which, if at home and receiving, he would lean out and drop
me down his latchkey, thus avoiding troubling his landlady to
come up from the basement to open the door. A very judicious
proceeding, for his relations with that autocrat were usually in
a somewhat strained condition. I bellowed now, and his head
popped out.

'Hallo, laddie!'

It seemed to me, even at this long range, that there was something peculiar about his face, but it was not till I had climbed
the stairs to his room that I was able to be certain. I then perceived that he had somehow managed to acquire a black eye,
which, though past its first bloom, was still of an extraordinary
richness.

'Great Scott!' I cried, staring at this decoration. 'How and
when?'

Ukridge drew at his pipe moodily.

'It's a long story,' he said. 'Do you remember some people
named Price at Clapham –'

'You aren't going to tell me your *fiancée* has biffed you in the
eye already?'

'Have you heard?' said Ukridge, surprised. 'Who told you
I was engaged?'

'George Tupper. I've just been seeing him.'

'Oh, well, that saves a lot of explanation. Laddie,' said

Ukridge, solemnly, 'let this be a warning to you. Never –'

I wanted facts, not moralizings.

'How did you get the eye?' I interrupted.

Ukridge blew out a cloud of smoke and his other eye glowed sombrely.

'That was Ernie Finch,' he said, in a cold voice.

'Who is Ernie Finch? I've never heard of him.'

'He's a sort of friend of the family, and as far as I can make out was going rather strong as regards Mabel till I came along. When we got engaged he was away, and no one apparently thought it worth while to tell him about it, and he came along one night and found me kissing her good-bye in the front garden. Observe how these things work out, Corky. The sight of him coming along suddenly gave Mabel a start, and she screamed; the fact that she screamed gave this man Finch a totally wrong angle on the situation; and this caused him, blast him, to rush up, yank off my glasses with one hand, and hit me with the other right in the eye. And before I could get at him the family were roused by Mabel's screeches and came out and separated us and explained that I was engaged to Mabel. Of course, when he heard that, the man apologized. And I wish you could have seen the beastly smirk he gave when he was doing it. Then there was a bit of a row and old Price forbade him the house. A fat lot of good that was. I've had to stay indoors ever since waiting for the colour-scheme to dim a bit.'

'Of course,' I urged, 'one can't help being sorry for the chap in a way.'

'*I* can,' said Ukridge, emphatically. 'I've reached the conclusion that there is not room in this world for Ernie Finch and myself, and I'm living in the hope of meeting him one of these nights down in a dark alley.'

'You sneaked his girl,' I pointed out.

'I don't want his beastly girl,' said Ukridge, with ungallant heat.

'Then you really do want to get out of this thing?'

'Of course I want to get out of it.'

'But, if you feel like that, how on earth did you ever let it happen?'

'I simply couldn't tell you, old horse,' said Ukridge, frankly.

'It's all a horrid blur. The whole affair was the most ghastly shock to me. It came absolutely out of a blue sky. I had never so much as suspected the possibility of such a thing. All I know is that we found ourselves alone in the drawing-room after Sunday supper, and all of a sudden the room became full of Prices of every description babbling blessings. And there I was!'

'But you must have given them something to go on.'

'I was holding her hand. I admit that.'

'Ah!'

'Well, my gosh, I don't see why there should have been such a fuss about that. What does a bit of hand-holding amount to? The whole thing, Corky, my boy, boils down to the question, Is any man safe? It's got so nowadays,' said Ukridge with a strong sense of injury, 'that you've only to throw a girl a kindly word, and the next thing you know you're in the Lord Warden Hotel at Dover, picking the rice out of your hair.'

'Well, you must own that you were asking for it. You rolled up in a new Daimler and put on enough dog for half a dozen millionaires. And you took the family for rides, didn't you?'

'Perhaps a couple of times.'

'And talked about your aunt, I expect, and how rich she was?'

'I may have touched on my aunt occasionally.'

'Well, naturally these people thought you were sent from heaven. The wealthy son-in-law.' Ukridge projected himself from the depths sufficiently to muster up the beginnings of a faint smile of gratification at the description. Then his troubles swept him back again. 'All you've got to do, if you want to get out of it, is to confess to them that you haven't a bob.'

'But, laddie, that's the difficulty. It's a most unfortunate thing, but, as it happens, I am on the eve of making an immense fortune, and I'm afraid I hinted as much to them from time to time.'

'What do you mean?'

'Since I saw you last I've put all my money in a bookmaker's business.'

'How do you mean – all your money? Where did you get any money?'

'You haven't forgotten the fifty quid I made selling tickets for my aunt's dance? And then I collected a bit more here and there out of some judicious bets. So there it is. The firm is in a small way at present, but with the world full of mugs shoving and jostling one another to back losers, the thing is a potential gold-mine, and I'm a sleeping partner. It's no good my trying to make these people believe I'm hard up. They would simply laugh in my face and rush off and start breach-of-promise actions. Upon my Sam, it's a little hard! Just when I have my foot firmly planted on the ladder of success, this has to happen.' He brooded in silence for awhile. 'There's just one scheme that occurred to me,' he said at length. 'Would you have any objection to writing an anonymous letter?'

'What's the idea?'

'I was just thinking that, if you were to write them an anonymous letter, accusing me of all sorts of things – Might say I was married already.'

'Not a bit of good.'

'Perhaps you're right,' said Ukridge, gloomily, and after a few minutes more of thoughtful silence I left him. I was standing on the front steps when I heard him clattering down the stairs.

'Corky, old man!'

'Hallo?'

'I think I've got it,' said Ukridge, joining me on the steps. 'Came to me in a flash a second ago. How would it be if someone were to go down to Clapham and pretend to be a detective making inquiries about me? Dashed sinister and mysterious, you know. A good deal of meaning nods and shakes of the head. Give the impression that I was wanted for something or other. You get the idea? You would ask a lot of questions and take notes in a book –'

'How do you mean – *I* would?'

Ukridge looked at me in pained surprise.

'Surely, old horse, you wouldn't object to doing a trifling service like this for an old friend?'

'I would, strongly. And in any case, what would be the use of my going? They've seen me.'

'Yes, but they wouldn't recognize you. Yours,' said Ukridge, ingratiatingly, 'is an ordinary, meaningless sort of face. Or one of those theatrical costumier people would fit you out with a disguise –'

'No!' I said, firmly. 'I'm willing to do anything in reason to help you out of this mess, but I refuse to wear false whiskers for you or anyone.'

'All right then,' said Ukridge, despondently; 'in that case, there's nothing to be –'

At this moment he disappeared. It was so swiftly done that he seemed to have been snatched up to heaven. Only the searching odour of his powerful tobacco lingered to remind me that he had once been at my side, and only the slam of the front door told me where he had gone. I looked about, puzzled to account for this abrupt departure, and as I did so heard galloping footsteps and perceived a stout, bearded gentleman of middle age, clad in a frock-coat and a bowler hat. He was one of those men who, once seen, are not readily forgotten; and I recognized him at once. It was the creditor, the bloke Ukridge owed a bit of money to, the man who had tried to board our car in the Haymarket. Halting on the pavement below me, he removed the hat and dabbed at his forehead with a large coloured silk handkerchief.

'Was that Mr Smallweed you were talking to?' he demanded, gustily. He was obviously touched in the wind.

'No,' I replied, civilly. 'No. Not Mr Smallweed.'

'You're lying to me, young man!' cried the creditor, his voice rising in a too-familiar shout. And at the words, as if they had been some magic spell, the street seemed suddenly to wake from slumber. It seethed with human life. Maids popped out of windows, areas disgorged landladies, the very stones seemed to belch forth excited spectators. I found myself the centre of attraction – and, for some reason which was beyond me, cast for the *rôle* of the villain of the drama. What I had actually done to the poor old man, nobody appeared to know; but the school of thought which held that I had picked his pocket and brutally assaulted him had the largest number of adherents, and there was a good deal of informal talk of lynching me. Fortunately a young man in a blue flannel suit, who had been one of the earliest arrivals on the scene, constituted himself a peacemaker.

'Come along, o' man,' he said, soothingly, his arm weaving itself into that of the fermenting creditor. 'You don't want to make yourself conspicuous, do you?'

'In there!' roared the creditor, pointing at the door.

The crowd seemed to recognize that there had been an error in its diagnosis. The prevalent opinion now was that I had kidnapped the man's daughter and was holding her prisoner behind that sinister door. The movement in favour of lynching me became almost universal.

'Now, now!' said the young man, whom I was beginning to like more every minute.

'I'll kick the door in!'

'Now, now! You don't want to go doing anything silly or foolish,' pleaded the peacemaker. 'There'll be a policeman along before you know where you are, and you'll look foolish if he finds you kicking up a silly row.'

I must say that, if I had been in the bearded one's place and had had right so indisputably on my side, this argument would not have influenced me greatly, but I suppose respectable citizens with a reputation to lose have different views on the importance of colliding with the police, however right they may be. The creditor's violence began to ebb. He hesitated. He was plainly trying to approach the matter in the light of pure reason.

'You know where the fellow lives,' argued the young man. 'See what I mean? Meantersay, you can come and find him whenever you like.'

This, too, sounded thin to me. But it appeared to convince the injured man. He allowed himself to be led away, and presently, the star having left the stage, the drama ceased to attract. The audience melted away. Windows closed, areas emptied themselves, and presently the street was given over once more to the cat lunching in the gutter and the coster hymning his brussels sprouts.

A hoarse voice spoke through the letter-box.

'Has he gone, laddie?'

I put my mouth to the slit, and we talked together like Pyramus and Thisbe.

'Yes.'

'You're sure?'

'Certain.'

'He isn't lurking round the corner somewhere, waiting to pop out?'

'No. He's gone.'

The door opened and an embittered Ukridge emerged.

'It's a little hard!' he said, querulously. 'You would scarcely credit it, Corky, but all that fuss was about a measly one pound two and threepence for a rotten little clockwork man that broke the first time I wound it up. Absolutely the first time, old man! It's not as if it had been a tandem bicycle, an enlarging camera, a Kodak, and a magic lantern.'

I could not follow him.

'Why should a clockwork man be a tandem bicycle and the rest of it?'

'It's like this,' said Ukridge. 'There was a bicycle and photograph shop down near where I lived a couple of years ago, and I happened to see a tandem bicycle there which I rather liked the look of. So I ordered it provisionally from this cove. Absolutely provisionally, you understand. Also an enlarging camera, a Kodak, and a magic lantern. The goods were to be delivered when I had made up my mind about them. Well, after about a week the fellow asks if there are any further particulars I want to learn before definitely buying the muck. I say I am considering the matter, and in the meantime will he be good enough to let me have that little clockwork man in his window which walks when wound up?'

'Well?'

'Well, damme,' said Ukridge, aggrieved, 'it didn't walk. It broke the first time I tried to wind it. Then a few weeks went by and this bloke started to make himself dashed unpleasant. Wanted me to pay him money! I reasoned with the blighter. I said: "Now look here, my man, need we say any more about this? Really, I think you've come out of the thing extremely well. Which," I said, "would you rather be owed for? A clockwork man, or a tandem bicycle, an enlarging camera, a Kodak, and a magic lantern?" You'd think that would have been simple enough for the meanest intellect, but no, he continued to make a fuss, until finally I had to move out of the neighbourhood. Fortunately, I had given him a false name –'

'Why?'

'Just an ordinary business precaution,' explained Ukridge.

'I see.'

'I looked on the matter as closed. But ever since then he has been bounding out at me when I least expect him. Once, by gad, he nearly nailed me in the middle of the Strand, and I had to leg it like a hare up Burleigh Street and through Covent Garden. I'd have been collared to a certainty, only he tripped over a basket of potatoes. It's persecution, damme, that's what it is – persecution!'

'Why don't you pay the man?' I suggested.

'Corky, old horse,' said Ukridge, with evident disapproval of these reckless fiscal methods, 'talk sense. How can I pay the man? Apart from the fact that at this stage of my career it would be madness to start flinging money right and left, there's the principle of the thing!'

The immediate result of this disturbing episode was that Ukridge, packing his belongings in a small suit-case and reluctantly disgorging a week's rent in lieu of notice, softly and silently vanished away from his own lodgings and came to dwell in mine, to the acute gratification of Bowles, who greeted his arrival with a solemn joy and brooded over him at dinner the first night like a father over a long-lost son. I had often given him sanctuary before in his hour of need, and he settled down with the easy smoothness of an old campaigner. He was good enough to describe my little place as a home from home, and said that he had half a mind to stay on and end his declining years there.

I cannot say that this suggestion gave me the rapturous pleasure it seemed to give Bowles, who nearly dropped the potato dish in his emotion; but still I must say that on the whole the man was not an exacting guest. His practice of never rising before lunch-time ensured me those mornings of undisturbed solitude which are so necessary to the young writer if he is to give *Interesting Bits* of his best; and if I had work to do in the evenings he was always ready to toddle downstairs and smoke a pipe with Bowles, whom he seemed to find as congenial a companion as Bowles found him. His only defect, indeed, was the habit he had developed of looking in on me in my bedroom at all hours of the night to discuss some new scheme designed to relieve him of his honourable obligations to Miss Mabel Price, of Balbriggan, Peabody Road, Clapham Common. My outspoken remarks on this behaviour checked him for forty-eight hours, but at three o'clock on the Sunday morning that ended the first week of his visit light flashing out above my head told me that he was in again.

'I think, laddie,' I heard a satisfied voice remark, as a heavy weight descended on my toes, 'I think, laddie, that at last I have hit the bull's-eye and rung the bell. Hats off to Bowles, without whom I would never have got the idea. It was only when he told me the plot of that story he is reading that I began to see daylight. Listen, old man,' said Ukridge, settling himself more comfortably on my feet, 'and tell me if you don't think I am on to a good thing. About a couple of days before Lord Claude Tremaine was to marry Angela Bracebridge, the most beautiful girl in London –'

'What the devil are you talking about? And do you know what the time is?'

'Never mind the time, Corky, my boy. Tomorrow is the day of rest and you can sleep on till an advanced hour. I was telling you the plot of this Primrose Novelette thing that Bowles is reading.'

'You haven't woken me up at three in the morning to tell me the plot of a rotten novelette!'

'You haven't been listening, old man,' said Ukridge, with gentle reproach. 'I was saying that it was this plot that gave me my big idea. To cut it fairly short, as you seem in a strange mood, this Lord Claude bloke, having had a rummy pain in his left side, went to see a doctor a couple of days before the wedding, and the doc gave him the start of his young life by telling him that he had only six months to live. There's a lot more of it, of course, and in the end it turns out that the fool of a doctor was all wrong; but what I'm driving at is that this development absolutely put the bee on the wedding. Everybody sympathized with Claude and said it was out of the question that he could dream of getting married. So it suddenly occurred to me, laddie, that here was the scheme of a lifetime. I'm going to supper at Balbriggan tomorrow, and what I want you to do is simply to –'

'You can stop right there,' I said, with emotion. 'I know what you want me to do. You want me to come along with you, disguised in a top-hat and a stethoscope, and explain to these people that I am a Harley Street specialist, and have been sounding you and have discovered that you are in the last stages of heart-disease.'

'Nothing of the kind, old man, nothing of the kind. I wouldn't dream of asking you to do anything like that.'

'Yes, you would, if you had happened to think of it.'

'Well, as a matter of fact, since you mention it,' said Ukridge, thoughtfully, 'it wouldn't be a bad scheme. But if you don't feel like taking it on –'

'I don't.'

'Well, then, all I want you to do is to come to Balbriggan at about nine. Supper will be over by then. No sense,' said Ukridge, thoughtfully, 'in missing supper. Come to Balbriggan at about nine, ask for me, and tell me in front of the gang that my aunt is dangerously ill.'

'What's the sense in that?'

'You aren't showing that clear, keen intelligence of which I have often spoken so highly, Corky. Don't you see? The news is a terrible shock to me. It bowls me over. I clutch at my heart –'

'They'll see through it in a second.'

'I ask for water –'

'Ah, that's a convincing touch. That'll make them realize you aren't yourself.'

'And after a while we leave. In fact, we leave as quickly as we jolly well can. You see what happens? I have established the fact that my heart is weak, and in a few days I write and say I've been looked over and the wedding must unfortunately be off because –'

'Damned silly idea!'

'Corky my boy,' said Ukridge gravely, 'to a man as up against it as I am no idea is silly that looks as if it might work. Don't you think this will work?'

'Well, it might, of course,' I admitted.

'Then I shall have a dash at it. I can rely on you to do your part?'

'How am I supposed to know that your aunt is ill?'

'Perfectly simple. They 'phoned from her house, and you are the only person who knows where I'm spending the evening.'

'And will you swear that this is really all you want me to do?'

'Absolutely all.'

'No getting me there and letting me in for something foul?'

'My dear old man!'

'All right,' I said. 'I feel in my bones that something's going to go wrong, but I suppose I've got to do it.'

'Spoken like a true friend,' said Ukridge.

At nine o'clock on the following evening I stood on the steps of Balbriggan waiting for my ring at the bell to be answered. Cats prowled furtively in the purple dusk, and from behind a lighted window on the ground floor of the house came the tinkle of a piano and the sound of voices raised in one of the more mournful types of hymn. I recognized Ukridge's above the rest. He was expressing with a vigour which nearly cracked the glass a desire to be as a little child washed clean of sin, and it somehow seemed to deepen my already substantial gloom. Long experience of Ukridge's ingenious schemes had given me a fatalistic feeling with regard to them. With whatever fair prospects I started out to cooperate with him on these occasions, I almost invariably found myself entangled sooner or later in some nightmare imbroglio.

The door opened. A maid appeared.

'Is Mr Ukridge here?'

'Yes, sir.'

'Could I see him for a moment?'

I followed her into the drawing-room.

'Gentleman to see Mr Ukridge, please,' said the maid, and left me to do my stuff.

I was aware of a peculiar feeling. It was a sort of dry-mouthed panic, and I suddenly recognized it as the same helpless stage-fright which I had experienced years before on the occasion when, the old place presumably being short of talent,

I had been picked on to sing a solo at the annual concert at school. I gazed upon the roomful of Prices, and words failed me. Near the bookshelf against the wall was a stuffed seagull of blackguardly aspect, suspended with outstretched wings by a piece of string. It had a gaping gamboge beak and its eye was bright and sardonic. I found myself gazing at it in a hypnotized manner. It seemed to see through me at a glance.

It was Ukridge who came to the rescue. Incredibly at his ease in this frightful room, he advanced to welcome me, resplendent in a morning-coat, patent-leather shoes, and tie, all of which I recognized as my property. As always when he looted my wardrobe, he exuded wealth and respectability.

'Want to see me, laddie?'

His eye met mine meaningly, and I found speech. We had rehearsed this little scene with a good deal of care over the luncheon-table, and the dialogue began to come back to me. I was able to ignore the seagull and proceed.

'I'm afraid I have serious news, old man,' I said, in a hushed voice.

'Serious news?' said Ukridge, trying to turn pale.

'Serious news!'

I had warned him during rehearsals that this was going to sound uncommonly like a vaudeville cross-talk act of the Argumentative College Chums type, but he had ruled out the objection as far-fetched. Nevertheless, that is just what it did sound like, and I found myself blushing warmly.

'What is it?' demanded Ukridge, emotionally, clutching me by the arm in a grip like the bite of a horse.

'Ouch!' I cried. 'Your aunt!'

'My aunt?'

'They telephoned from the house just now,' I proceeded, warming to my work, 'to say that she had had a relapse. Her condition is very serious. They want you there at once. Even now it may be too late.'

'Water!' said Ukridge, staggering back and clawing at his waistcoat – or rather at my waistcoat, which I had foolishly omitted to lock up. 'Water!'

It was well done. Even I, much as I wished that he would

stop wrenching one of my best ties all out of shape, was obliged
to admit that. I suppose it was his lifelong training in staggering under the blows of Fate that made him so convincing. The
Price family seemed to be shaken to its foundations. There was
no water in the room, but a horde of juvenile Prices immediately rushed off in quest of some, and meanwhile the rest of
the family gathered about the stricken man, solicitous and sympathetic.

'My aunt! Ill!' moaned Ukridge.

'I shouldn't worry, o' man,' said a voice at the door.

So sneering and altogether unpleasant was this voice that for
a moment I almost thought that it must have been the seagull
that had spoken. Then, turning, I perceived a young man in a
blue flannel suit. A young man whom I had seen before. It was
the Peacemaker, the fellow who had soothed and led away the
infuriated bloke to whom Ukridge owed a bit of money.

'I shouldn't worry,' he said again, and looked malevolently
upon Ukridge. His advent caused a sensation. Mr Price, who
had been kneading Ukridge's shoulder with a strong man's silent
sympathy, towered as majestically as his five feet six would per-
mit him.

'Mr Finch,' he said, 'may I inquire what you are doing in my
house?'

'All right, all right –'

'I thought I told you –'

'All right, all right,' repeated Ernie Finch, who appeared to
be a young man of character. 'I've only come to expose an impostor.'

'Impostor!'

'Him!' said young Mr Finch, pointing a scornful finger at Ukridge.

I think Ukridge was about to speak, but he seemed to change
his mind. As for me, I had edged out of the centre of things,
and was looking on as inconspicuously as I could from behind a
red plush sofa. I wished to dissociate myself entirely from the
proceedings.

'Ernie Finch,' said Mrs Price, swelling, 'what do you mean?'

The young man seemed in no way discouraged by the general

atmosphere of hostility. He twirled his small moustache and smiled a frosty smile.

'I mean,' he said, feeling in his pocket and producing an envelope, 'that this fellow here hasn't got an aunt. Or, if he has, she isn't Miss Julia Ukridge, the well-known and wealthy novelist. I had my suspicions about this gentleman right from the first, I may as well tell you, and ever since he came to this house I've been going round making a few inquiries about him. The first thing I did was to write his aunt – the lady he says is his aunt – making out I wanted her nephew's address, me being an old school chum of his. Here's what she writes back – you can see it for yourselves if you want to: "Miss Ukridge acknowledges receipt of Mr Finch's letter, and in reply wishes to state that she has no nephew." No nephew! That's plain enough, isn't it?' He raised a hand to check comment. 'And here's another thing,' he proceeded. 'That motor-car he's been swanking about in. It doesn't belong to him at all. It belongs to a man named Fillimore. I noted the number and made investigations. This fellow's name isn't Ukridge at all. It's Smallweed. He's a penniless imposter who's been pulling all your legs from the moment he came into the house; and if you let Mabel marry him you'll be making the biggest bloomer of your lives!'

There was an awestruck silence. Price looked upon Price in dumb consternation.

'I don't believe you,' said the master of the house at length, but he spoke without conviction.

'Then, perhaps,' retorted Ernie Finch, 'you'll believe this gentleman. Come in, Mr Grindlay.'

Bearded, frock-coated, and sinister beyond words, the Creditor stalked into the room.

'You tell 'em,' said Ernie Finch.

The Creditor appeared more than willing. He fixed Ukridge with a glittering eye, and his bosom heaved with pent-up emotion.

'Sorry to intrude on a family on Sunday evening,' he said, 'but this young man told me I should find Mr Smallweed here, so I came along. I've been hunting for him high and low for two years and more about a matter of one pound two and threepence for goods supplied.'

'He owes you money?' faltered Mr Price.

'He bilked me,' said the Creditor, precisely.

'Is this true?' said Mr Price, turning to Ukridge.

Ukridge had risen and seemed to be wondering whether it was possible to sidle unobserved from the room. At this question he halted, and a weak smile played about his lips.

'Well –' said Ukridge.

The head of the family pursued his examination no further. His mind appeared to be made up. He had weighed the evidence and reached a decision. His eyes flashed. He raised a hand and pointed to the door.

'Leave my house!' he thundered.

'Right-o!' said Ukridge, mildly.

'And never enter it again!'

'Right-o!' said Ukridge.

Mr Price turned to his daughter.

'Mabel,' he said, 'this engagement of yours is broken. Broken, do you understand? I forbid you ever to see this scoundrel again. You hear me?'

'All right, pa,' said Miss Price, speaking for the first and last time. She seemed to be of a docile and equable disposition. I fancied I caught a not-displeased glance on its way to Ernie Finch.

'And now, sir,' cried Mr Price, 'go!'

'Right-o!' said Ukridge.

But here the Creditor struck a business note.

'And what,' he inquired, 'about my one pound two and three-pence?'

It seemed for a moment that matters were about to become difficult. But Ukridge, ever ready-witted, found the solution.

'Have you got one pound two and threepence on you, old man?' he said to me.

And with my usual bad luck I had.

We walked together down Peabody Road. Already Ukridge's momentary discomfiture had passed.

'It just shows, laddie,' he said, exuberantly, 'that one should never despair. However black the outlook, old horse, never, never despair. That scheme of mine might or might not have worked – one cannot tell. But, instead of having to go to all the bother of subterfuge, to which I always object, here we have a nice, clean-cut solution of the thing without any trouble at all.' He mused happily for a moment. 'I never thought,' he said, 'that the time would come when I would feel a gush of kindly feeling towards Ernie Finch; but, upon my Sam, laddie, if he were here now, I would embrace the fellow. Clasp him to my bosom, dash it!' He fell once more into a reverie. 'Amazing, old horse,' he proceeded, 'how things work out. Many a time I've been on the very point of paying that blighter Grindlay his money, merely to be rid of the annoyance of having him always popping up, but every time something seemed to stop me. I can't tell you what it was – a sort of feeling. Almost as if one had a guardian angel at one's elbow guiding one. My gosh, just think where I would have been if I had yielded to the impulse. It was Grindlay blowing in that turned the scale. By gad, Corky my boy, this is the happiest moment of my life.'

'It might be the happiest of mine,' I said, churlishly, 'if I thought I should ever see that one pound two and threepence again.'

'Now, laddie, laddie,' protested Ukridge, 'these are not the words of a friend. Don't mar a moment of unalloyed gladness. Don't you worry, you'll get your money back. A thousand-fold!'

'When?'

'One of these days,' said Ukridge, buoyantly. 'One of these days.'

Chapter 8

The Long Arm of Looney Coote

Given private means sufficiently large to pad them against the moulding buffets of Life, it is extraordinary how little men change in after years from the boys they once were. There was a youth in my house at school named Coote. J. G. Coote. And he was popularly known as Looney on account of the vain and foolish superstitions which seemed to rule his every action. Boys are hard-headed, practical persons, and they have small tolerance for the view-point of one who declines to join in a quiet smoke behind the gymnasium not through any moral scruples – which, to do him justice, he would have scorned – but purely on the ground that he had seen a magpie that morning. This was what J. G. Coote did, and it was the first occasion on which I remember him being addressed as Looney.

But, once given, the nickname stuck; and this in spite of the fact – seeing that we were caught half-way through the first cigarette and forcefully dealt with by a muscular head-master – that that magpie of his would appear to have known a thing or two. For five happy years, till we parted to go to our respective universities, I never called Coote anything but Looney; and it was as Looney that I greeted him when we happened upon each other one afternoon at Sandown, shortly after the conclusion of the three o'clock race.

'Did you do anything on that one?' I asked, after we had exchanged salutations.

'I went down,' replied Looney, in the subdued but not heart-broken manner of the plutocrat who can afford to do these things. 'I had a tenner on My Valet.'

'On My Valet!' I cried, aghast at this inexplicable patronage of an animal which, even in the preliminary saunter round the paddock, had shown symptoms of lethargy and fatigue, not to mention a disposition to trip over his feet. 'Whatever made you do that?'

'Yes, I suppose he never had a chance,' agreed Coote, 'but a week ago my man Spencer broke his leg, and I thought it might be an omen.'

And then I knew that, for all his moustache and added weight, he was still the old Looney of my boyhood.

'Is that the principle on which you always bet?' I inquired.

'Well, you'd be surprised how often it works. The day my aunt was shut up in the private asylum I collected five hundred quid by backing Crazy Jane for the Jubilee Cup. Have a cigarette?'

'Thanks.'

'Oh, my Lord!'

'Now what?'

'My pocket has been picked,' faltered Looney Coote, withdrawing a trembling hand. 'I had a note-case with nearly a hundred quid, and it's gone!'

The next moment I was astounded to observe a faint, resigned smile on the man's face.

'Well, that makes two,' he murmured, as if to himself.

'Two what?'

'Two misfortunes. These things always go in threes, you know. Whenever anything rotten happens, I simply brace myself up for the other two things. Well, there's only one more to come this time, thank goodness.'

'What was the first one?'

'I told you my man Spencer broke his leg.'

'I should have thought that would have ranked as one of Spencer's three misfortunes. How do you come in?'

'Why, my dear fellow, I've been having the devil of a time since he dropped out. The ass they sent me from the agency as a substitute is no good at all. Look at that!' He extended a shapely leg. 'Do you call that a crease?'

From the humble standpoint of my own bagginess, I should have called it an excellent crease, but he seemed thoroughly dissatisfied with it, so there was nothing to do but tell him to set his teeth and bear it like a man, and presently, the bell having rung for the three-thirty race, we parted.

'Oh, by the way,' said Looney, as he left me, 'are you going to be at the old Wrykinian dinner next week?'

'Yes, I'm coming. So is Ukridge.'

'Ukridge? Good Lord, I haven't seen old Ukridge for years.'

'Well, he will be there. And I expect he'll touch you for a temporary loan. That will make your third misfortune.'

Ukridge's decision to attend the annual dinner of the Old Boys of the school at which he and I had been – in a manner of speaking – educated had come as a surprise to me; for, though the meal was likely to be well-cooked and sustaining, the tickets cost half a sovereign apiece, and it was required of the celebrants that they wear evening-dress. And, while Ukridge sometimes possessed ten shillings which he had acquired by pawning a dress-suit, or a dress-suit which he had hired for ten shillings, it was unusual for him to have the two things together. Still, he was as good as his word, and on the night of the banquet turned up at my lodgings for a preliminary bracer faultlessly clad and ready for the feast.

Tactlessly, perhaps, I asked what bank he had been robbing.

'I thought you told me a week ago that money was tight,' I said.

'It was tighter,' said Ukridge, 'than these damned trousers. Never buy ready-made dress-clothes, Corky, my boy. They're always unsatisfactory. But all that's over now. I have turned the corner, old man. Last Saturday we cleaned up to an extra-ordinary extent at Sandown.'

'We?'

'The firm. I told you I had become a sleeping-partner in a bookie's business.'

'For Heaven's sake! You don't mean to say that it is really making money?'

'Making money? My dear old lad, how could it help making money? I told you from the first the thing was a gold-mine. Affluence stares me in the eyeball. The day before yesterday I bought half a dozen shirts. That'll show you!'

'How much have you made?'

'In some ways,' said Ukridge, sentimentally, 'I regret this prosperity. I mean to say, those old careless impecunious days were not so bad, Corky, old boy, eh? Life had a tang then. It was swift, vivid, interesting. And there's always the danger that one may allow oneself to grow slack and enervated with wealth. Still, it has its compensations. Yes, on the whole I am not sorry to have made my pile.'

'How much have you made?' I asked again, impressed by this time. The fact of Ukridge buying six shirts for himself instead of purloining mine suggested an almost Monte Cristo-like opulence.

'Fifteen quid,' said Ukridge. 'Fifteen golden sovereigns, my boy! And out of one week's racing! And you must remember that the thing is going on all the year round. Month by month, week by week, we shall expand, we shall unfold, we shall develop. It wouldn't be a bad scheme, old man, to drop a judicious word here and there among the lads at this dinner tonight, advising them to lodge their commissions with us. Isaac O'Brien is the name of the firm, 3 Blue Street, St James's. Telegraphic address "Ikobee, London", and our representative attends all the recognized meetings. But don't mention my connexion with the firm. I don't want it generally known, as it might impair my social standing. And now, laddie, if we don't want to be late for this binge, we had better be starting.'

Ukridge, as I have recorded elsewhere, had left school under something of a cloud. Not to put too fine a point on it, he had been expelled for breaking out at night to attend the local fair, and it was only after many years of cold exclusion that he had been admitted to the pure-minded membership of the Old Boys' Society.

Nevertheless, in the matter of patriotism he yielded to no one.

During our drive to the restaurant where the dinner was to be held he grew more and more sentimental about the dear old school, and by the time the meal was over and the speeches began he was in the mood when men shed tears and invite people, to avoid whom in calmer moments they would duck down side-streets, to go on long walking tours with them. He wandered from table to table with a large cigar in his mouth, now exchanging reminiscences, anon advising contemporaries who had won high positions in the Church to place their bets with Isaac O'Brien, of 3 Blue Street, St James's – a sound and trustworthy firm, telegraphic address 'Ikobee, London'.

The speeches at these dinners always opened with a long and statistical harangue from the President, who, furtively consulting his paper of notes, announced the various distinctions gained by Old Boys during the past year. On this occasion, accordingly, he began by mentioning that A. B. Bodger ('Good old Bodger!' – from Ukridge) had been awarded the Mutt-Spivis Gold Medal for Geological Research at Oxford University – that C. D. Codger had been appointed to the sub-junior deanery of Westchester Cathedral – ('That's the stuff, Codger, old horse!') – that as a reward for his services in connexion with the building of the new water works at Streslau, J. J. Swodger had received from the Government of Ruritania the Order of the Silver Trowel, third class (with crossed pickaxes).

'By the way,' said the President, concluding, 'before I finish there is one more thing I would like to say. An old boy, B. V. Lawlor, is standing for Parliament next week at Redbridge. If any of you would care to go down and lend him a hand, I know he would be glad of your help.'

He resumed his seat, and the leather-lunged toastmaster behind him emitted a raucous 'My Lord, Mr President, and gentlemen, pray silence for Mr H. K. Hodger, who will propose the health of "The Visitors".' H. K. Hodger rose with the purposeful expression only to be seen on the face of one who has been reminded by the remarks of the last speaker of the story of the two Irishmen; and the company, cosily replete, settled down to give him an indulgent attention.

Not so Ukridge. He was staring emotionally across the table at his old friend Lawlor. The seating arrangements at these dinners were usually designed to bring contemporaries together at the same table, and the future member for Redbridge was one of our platoon.

'Boko, old horse,' demanded Ukridge, 'is this true?'

A handsome but rather prominent nose had led his little playmates to bestow this affectionate sobriquet upon the coming M.P. It was one of those boyish handicaps which are never lived down, but I would not have thought of addressing B. V.

Lawlor in this fashion myself, for, though he was a man of my own age, the years had made him extremely dignified. Ukridge, however, was above any such weakness. He gave out the offensive word in a vinous bellow of such a calibre as to cause H. K. Hodger to trip over a 'begorra' and lose the drift of his story.

''Sh!' said the President, bending a reproving gaze at our table.

''Sh!' said B. V. Lawlor, contorting his smooth face.

'Yes, but is it?' persisted Ukridge.

'Of course it is,' whispered Lawlor. 'Be quiet!'

'Then, damme,' shouted Ukridge, 'rely on me, young Boko. I shall be at your side. I shall spare no efforts to pull you through. You can count on me to –'

'Really! Please! At that table down there,' said the President, rising, while H. K. Hodger, who had got as far as 'Then, faith and begob, it's me that'll be afther –' paused in a pained manner and plucked at the table-cloth.

Ukridge subsided. But his offer of assistance was no passing whim, to be lightly forgotten in the slumbers of the night. I was still in bed a few mornings later when he burst in, equipped for travel to the last button and carrying a seedy suit-case.

'Just off, laddie, just off!'

'Fine!' I said. 'Good-bye.'

'Corky, my boy,' boomed Ukridge, sitting creakingly on the bed and poisoning the air with his noisome tobacco, 'I feel happy this morning. Stimulated. And why? Because I am doing an altruistic action. We busy men of affairs, Corky, are too apt to exclude altruism from our lives. We are too prone to say 'What is there in it for me?' and, if there proves on investigation to be nothing in it for us, to give it the miss-in-balk. That is why this business makes me so confoundedly happy. At considerable expense and inconvenience I am going down to Redbridge today, and what is there in it for me? Nothing. Nothing, my boy, except the pure delight of helping an old schoolfellow over a tough spot. If I can do anything, however little, to bring young Boko in at the right end of the poll, that will be enough reward for me. I am going to do my bit, Corky, and it may be that my bit will turn out to be just the trifle that brings home the bacon. I shall go down there and talk –'

'I bet you will.'

'I don't know much about politics, it's true, but I can bone up enough to get by. Invective ought to meet the case, and I'm pretty good at invective. I know the sort of thing. You accuse the rival candidate of every low act under the sun, without giving him quite enough to start a libel action on. Now, what I want you to do, Corky, old horse –'

'Oh heavens!' I moaned at these familiar words.

'– is just to polish up this election song of mine. I sat up half the night writing it, but I can see it limps in spots. You can put it right in half an hour. Polish it up, laddie, and forward without fail to the Bull Hotel, Redbridge, this afternoon. It may just be the means of shoving Boko past the post by a nose.'

He clattered out hurriedly; and, sleep being now impossible, I picked up the sheet of paper he had left and read the verses.

They were well meant, but that let them out. Ukridge was no poet or he would never have attempted to rhyme 'Lawlor' with 'before us'.

A rather neat phrase happening to occur to me at the breakfast table, coincident with the reflection that possibly Ukridge was right and it did behove his old schoolfellows to rally round the candidate, I spent the morning turning out a new ballad. Having finished this by noon, I dispatched it to the Bull Hotel, and went off to lunch with something of that feeling of satisfaction which, as Ukridge had pointed out, does come to altruists. I was strolling down Piccadilly, enjoying an after-luncheon smoke, when I ran into Looney Coote.

On Looney's amiable face there was a mingled expression of chagrin and satisfaction.

'It's happened,' he said.

'What?'

'The third misfortune. I told you it would.'

'What's the trouble now? Has Spencer broken his other leg?'

'My car has been stolen.'

A decent sympathy would no doubt have become me, but from earliest years I had always found it difficult to resist the temptation to be airy and jocose when dealing with Looney Coote. The man was so indecently rich that he had no right to have troubles.

'Oh, well,' I said, 'you can easily get another. Fords cost practically nothing nowadays.'

'It wasn't a Ford,' bleated Looney, outraged. 'It was a brand-new Winchester-Murphy. I paid fifteen hundred pounds for it only a month ago, and now it's gone.'

'Where did you see it last?'

'I didn't see it last. My chauffeur brought it round to my rooms this morning, and, instead of staying with it as he should have done till I was ready, went off round the corner for a cup of coffee, so he says! And when he came back it had vanished.'

'The coffee?'

'The car, you ass. The car had disappeared. It had been stolen.'

'I suppose you have notified the police?'

'I'm on my way to Scotland Yard now. It just occurred to me. Have you any idea what the procedure is? It's the first time I've been mixed up with this sort of thing.'

'You give them the number of the car, and they send out word to police-stations all over the country to look out for it.'

'I see,' said Looney Coote, brightening. 'That sounds rather promising, what? I mean, it looks as if someone would be bound to spot it sooner or later.'

'Yes,' I said. 'Of course, the first thing a thief would do would be to take off the number-plate and substitute a false one.'

'Oh, Great Scott! Not really?'

'And after that he would paint the car a different colour.'

'Oh, I say!'

'Still, the police generally manage to find them in the end. Years hence they will come on it in an old barn with the tonneau stoved in and the engines taken out. Then they will hand it back to you and claim the reward. But, as a matter of fact, what you ought to be praying is that you may never get it back. Then the thing would be a real misfortune. If you get it back as good as new in the next couple of days, it won't be a misfortune at all, and you will have number three hanging over your head again, as before. And who knows what that third misfortune may be? In a way, you're tempting Providence by applying to Scotland Yard.'

'Yes,' said Looney Coote, doubtfully. 'All the same, I think I will, don't you know. I mean to say, after all, a fifteen-hundred-quid Winchester-Murphy *is* a fifteen-hundred-quid Winchester-Murphy, if you come right down to it, what?'

Showing that even in the most superstitious there may be grains of hard, practical common sense lurking somewhere.

It had not been my intention originally to take any part in the by-election in the Redbridge division beyond writing three verses of a hymn in praise of Boko Lawlor and sending him a congratulatory wire if he won. But two things combined to make me change my mind. The first was the fact that it occurred to me – always the keen young journalist – that there might be a couple of guineas of *Interesting Bits* money in it ('How a Modern Election is Fought: Humours of the Poll'); the second, that, ever since his departure Ukridge had been sending me a constant stream of telegrams so stimulating that eventually they lit the spark .

I append specimens:

Going strong. Made three speeches yesterday. Election song a sensation. Come on down. – UKRIDGE.

Boko locally regarded as walk-over. Made four speeches yesterday. Election song a breeze. Come on down. – UKRIDGE.

Victory in sight. Spoke practically all yesterday. Election song a riot. Children croon it in cots. Come on down. – UKRIDGE.

I leave it to any young author to say whether a man with one solitary political lyric to his credit could have resisted this. With the exception of a single music-hall song ('Mother, She's Pinching My Leg', tried out by Tim Sims, the Koy Komic, at the Peebles Hippodrome, and discarded, in response to a popular appeal, after one performance), no written words of mine had ever passed human lips. Naturally, it gave me a certain thrill to imagine the enlightened electorate of Redbridge – at any rate, the right-thinking portion of it – bellowing in its thousands those noble lines:

> No foreign foe's insidious hate
> Our country shall o'erwhelm
> So long as England's ship of state
> Has LAWLOR at the helm.

Whether I was technically correct in describing as guiding the ship of state a man who would probably spend his entire Parliamentary career in total silence, voting meekly as the Whip directed, I had not stopped to inquire. All I knew was that it sounded well, and I wanted to hear it. In addition to which, there was the opportunity, never likely to occur again, of seeing Ukridge make an ass of himself before a large audience.

I went to Redbridge.

The first thing I saw on leaving the station was a very large poster exhibiting Boko Lawlor's expressive features, bearing the legend:

LAWLOR

FOR

REDBRIDGE

This was all right, but immediately beside it, evidently placed there by the hand of an enemy, was a still larger caricature of this poster which stressed my old friend's prominent nose in a manner that seemed to me to go beyond the limits of a fair debate. To this was appended the words:

DO YOU

WANT

THIS

FOR A MEMBER?

To which, if I had been a hesitating voter of the constituency, I would certainly have replied 'No!' for there was something about that grossly elongated nose that convicted the man beyond hope of appeal of every undesirable quality a Member of Parliament can possess. You could see at a glance that here was one who, if elected, would do his underhand best to cut down the Navy, tax the poor man's food, and strike a series of blows at the very root of the home. And, as if this were not enough, a few yards farther on was a placard covering almost the entire side of a house, which said in simple, straightforward black letters a foot high:

DOWN WITH

BOKO

THE HUMAN GARGOYLE

How my poor old contemporary, after passing a week in the

constant society of these slurs on his personal appearance, could endure to look himself in the face in his shaving-mirror of a morning was more than I could see. I commented on this to Ukridge, who had met me at the station in a luxurious car.

'Oh, that's nothing,' said Ukridge, huskily. The first thing I had noticed about him was that his vocal cords had been putting in overtime since our last meeting. 'Just the usual give-and-take of an election. When we get round this next corner you'll see the poster we've got out to tickle up the other bloke. It's a pippin.'

I did, and it was indeed a pippin. After one glance at it as we rolled by, I could not but feel that the electors of Redbridge were in an uncommonly awkward position, having to choose between Boko, as exhibited in the street we had just passed, and this horror before me now. Mr Herbert Huxtable, the opposition candidate, seemed to run as generously to ears as his adversary did to nose, and the artist had not overlooked this feature. Indeed, except for a mean, narrow face with close-set eyes and a murderer's mouth, Mr Huxtable appeared to be all ears. They drooped and flapped about him like carpet-bags, and I averted my gaze, appalled.

'Do you mean to say you're *allowed* to do this sort of thing?' I asked, incredulously.

'My dear old horse, it's expected of you. It's a mere formality. The other side would feel awkward and disappointed if you didn't.'

'And how did they find out about Lawlor being called Boko?' I inquired, for the point had puzzled me. In a way, you might say that it was the only thing you could possibly call him, but the explanation hardly satisfied me.

'That,' admitted Ukridge, 'was largely my fault. I was a bit carried away the first time I addressed the multitude, and I happened to allude to the old chap by his nickname. Of course, the opposition took it up at once. Boko was a little sore about it for a while.'

'I can see how he might be.'

'But that's all over now,' said Ukridge, buoyantly. 'We're the greatest pals. He relies on me at every turn. Yesterday he admitted to me in so many words that if he gets in it'll be owing to my help as much as anything. The fact is, laddie, I've made rather a hit with the manyheaded. They seem to like to hear me speak.'

'Fond of a laugh, eh?'

'Now, laddie,' said Ukridge, reprovingly, 'this is not the right tone. You must curb that spirit of levity while you're down here. This is a dashed serious business, Corky, old man, and the sooner you realize it the better. If you have come here to gibe and to mock –'

'I came to hear my election song sung. When do they sing it?'

'Oh, practically all the time. Incessantly, you might say.'

'In their baths?'

'Most of the voters here don't take baths. You'll gather that when we reach Biscuit Row.'

'What's Biscuit Row?'

'It's the quarter of the town where the blokes live who work in Fitch and Weyman's biscuit factory, laddie. It's what you might call,' said Ukridge, importantly, 'the doubtful element of the place. All the rest of the town is nice and clean-cut, they're either solid for Boko or nuts on Huxtable – but these biscuit blokes are wobbly. That's why we have to canvass them so carefully.'

'Oh, you're going canvassing, are you?'

'*We* are,' corrected Ukridge.

'Not me!'

'Corky,' said Ukridge, firmly, 'pull yourself together. It was principally to assist me in canvassing these biscuit blighters that I got you down here. Where's your patriotism, laddie? Don't you want old Boko to get into Parliament, or what is it? We must strain every nerve. We must set our hands to the plough. The job you've got to tackle is the baby-kissing –'

'I won't kiss their infernal babies!'

'You will, old horse, unless you mean to spend the rest of your life cursing yourself vainly when it is too late that poor old Boko got pipped on the tape purely on account of your poltroonery. Consider, old man! Have some vision! Be an altruist! It may be that your efforts will prove the deciding factor in this desperately close-run race.'

'What do you mean, desperately close-run race? You said in your wire that it was a walk-over for Boko.'

'That was just to fool the telegraph-bloke, whom I suspect of being in the enemy camp. As a matter of fact, between ourselves, it's touch and go. A trifle either way will do the business now.'

'Why don't *you* kiss these beastly babies?'

'There's something about me that scares 'em, laddie. I've tried it once or twice, but only alienated several valuable voters by frightening their offspring into a nervous collapse. I think it's my glasses they don't like. But you – now, you,' said Ukridge, with revolting fulsomeness, 'are an ideal baby-kisser. The first time I ever saw you, I said: "There goes one of Nature's baby-kissers." Directly I started to canvass these people and realized what I was up against, I thought of you. "Corky's the man," I said to myself; "the fellow we want is old Corky. Good-looking. And not merely good-looking but *kind*-looking." They'll take to you, laddie. Yours is a face a baby can trust –'

'Now, listen!'

'And it won't last long. Just a couple of streets and we're through. So stiffen your backbone, laddie, and go at it like a man. Boko is going to entertain you with a magnificent banquet at his hotel tonight. I happen to know there will be champagne. Keep your mind fixed on that and the thing will seem easy.'

The whole question of canvassing is one which I would like some time to go into at length. I consider it to be an altogether abominable practice. An Englishman's home is his castle, and it seems to me intolerable that, just as you have got into shirt-sleeves and settled down to a soothing pipe, total strangers should be permitted to force their way in and bother you with their nauseous flattery and their impertinent curiosity as to which way you mean to vote. And, while I prefer not to speak at length of my experiences in Biscuit Row, I must say this much, that practically every resident of that dingy quarter appeared to see eye to eye with me in this matter. I have never encountered a body of men who were consistently less chummy. They looked at me with lowering brows, they answered my limping civilities with gruff monosyllables, they snatched their babies away from me and hid them, yelling, in distant parts of the house. Altogether a most discouraging experience, I should have said, and one which seemed to indicate that, as far as Biscuit Row was concerned, Boko Lawlor would score a blank at the poll.

Ukridge scoffed at this gloomy theory.

'My dear old horse,' he cried, exuberantly, as the door of the last house slammed behind us and I revealed to him the inferences I had drawn, 'you mustn't mind that. It's just their way. They treat everybody the same. Why, one of Huxtable's fellows got his hat smashed in at that very house we've just left. I consider the outlook highly promising, laddie.'

And so, to my surprise, did the candidate himself. When we had finished dinner that night and were talking over our cigars, while Ukridge slumbered noisily in an easy chair, Boko Lawlor spoke with a husky confidence of his prospects.

'And, curiously enough,' said Boko, endorsing what until then I had looked on as mere idle swank on Ukridge's part, 'the fellow who will have really helped me more than anybody else, if I get in, is old Ukridge. He borders, perhaps, a trifle too closely on the libellous in his speeches, but he certainly has the knack of talking to an audience. In the past week he has made himself quite a prominent figure in Redbridge. In fact, I'm bound to say it has made me a little nervous at times, this prominence of his. I know what an erratic fellow he is, and if he were to become the centre of some scandal it would mean defeat for a certainty.'

'How do you mean, scandal?'

'I sometimes conjure up a dreadful vision,' said Boko Lawlor, with a slight shudder, 'of one of his creditors suddenly rising in the audience and denouncing him for not having paid for a pair of trousers or something.'

He cast an apprehensive eye at the sleeping figure.

'You're all right if he keeps on wearing that suit,' I said, soothingly, 'because it happens to be one he sneaked from me. I have been wondering why it was so familiar.'

'Well, anyhow,' said Boko, with determined optimism, 'I suppose, if anything like that was going to happen, it would have happened before. He has been addressing meetings all the week, and nothing has occurred. I'm going to let him open the ball at our last rally tomorrow night. He has a way of warming up the audience. You'll come to that, of course?'

'If I am to see Ukridge warming up an audience, nothing shall keep me away.'

'I'll see that you get a seat on the platform. It will be the biggest affair we have had. The polling takes place on the next day, and this will be our last chance of swaying the doubters.'

'I didn't know doubters ever came to these meetings. I thought the audience was always solid for the speakers.'

'It may be so in some constituencies,' said Boko, moodily, 'but it certainly isn't at Redbridge.'

The monster meeting in support of Boko Lawlor's candidature was held at that popular eyesore, the Associated Mechanics' Hall. As I sat among the elect on the platform, waiting for the proceedings to commence, there came up to me a mixed scent of dust, clothes, orange-peel, chalk, wood, plaster, pomade, and Associated Mechanics – the whole forming a mixture which, I began to see, was likely to prove too rich for me. I changed my seat in order to bring myself next to a small but promising-looking door, through which it would be possible, if necessary, to withdraw without being noticed.

The principle on which chairmen at these meetings are selected is perhaps too familiar to require recording here at length, but in case some of my readers are not acquainted with the workings of political machines, I may say that no one under the age of eighty-five is eligible and the preference is given to those with adenoids. For Boko Lawlor the authorities had extended themselves and picked a champion of his class. In addition to adenoids, the Right Hon. the Marquess of Cricklewood had – or seemed to have – a potato of the maximum size and hotness in his mouth, and he had learned his elocution in one of those correspondence schools which teach it by mail. I caught his first sentence – that he would only detain us a moment – but for fifteen minutes after that he baffled me completely. That he was still speaking I could tell by the way his Adam's apple wiggled, but what he was saying I could not even guess. And presently, the door at my side offering its silent invitation, I slid softly through and closed it behind me.

Except for the fact that I was now out of sight of the chairman, I did not seem to have bettered my position greatly. The scenic effects of the hall had not been alluring, but there was nothing much more enlivening to look at here. I found myself in a stone-flagged corridor with walls of an unhealthy green, ending in a flight of stairs. I was just about to proceed towards these in a casual spirit of exploration, when footsteps made themselves heard, and in another moment a helmet loomed into view, followed by a red face, a blue uniform, and large, stout boots – making in all one constable, who proceeded along the corridor towards me with a measured step as if pacing a beat. I thought his face looked stern and disapproving, and attributed it to the fact that I had just lighted a cigarette – presumably in a place where smoking was not encouraged. I dropped the cigarette and placed a guilty heel on it – an action which I regretted the next moment, when the constable himself produced one from the recesses of his tunic and asked me for a match.

'Not allowed to smoke on duty,' he said, affably, 'but there's no harm in a puff.'

I saw now that what I had taken for a stern and disapproving look was merely the official mask. I agreed that no possible harm could come of a puff.

'Meeting started?' inquired the officer, jerking his head towards the door.

'Yes. The chairman was making a few remarks when I came out.'

'Ah! Better give it time to warm up,' he said, cryptically. And there was a restful silence for some minutes, while the scent of a cigarette of small price competed with the other odours of the corridor.

Presently, however, the stillness was interrupted. From the unseen hall came the faint clapping of hands, and then a burst of melody. I started. It was impossible to distinguish the words, but surely there was no mistaking that virile rhythm:

> Tum tumty tumty tumty tum,
>   Tum tumty tumty tum,
> Tum tumty tumty tumty tum,
>   Tum TUMTY tumty tum.

It was! It must be! I glowed all over with modest pride.

'That's mine,' I said, with attempted nonchalance.

'Ur?' queried the constable, who had fallen into a reverie.

'That thing they're singing. Mine. My election song.'

It seemed to me that the officer regarded me strangely. It may have been admiration, but it looked more like disappointment and disfavour.

'You on Lawlor's side?' he demanded, heavily.

'Yes. I wrote his election song. They're singing it now.'

'I'm opposed to him *in toto* and root and branch,' said the constable, emphatically, 'I don't like 'is views – subversive, that's what I call 'em. Subversive.'

There seemed nothing to say to this. This divergence of opinion was unfortunate, but there it was. After all, there was no reason why political differences should have to interfere with what had all the appearance of being the dawning of a beautiful friendship. Pass over it lightly, that was the tactful course. I endeavoured to steer the conversation gently back to less debatable grounds.

'This is my first visit to Redbridge,' I said, chattily.

'Ur?' said the constable, but I could see that he was not interested. He finished his cigarette with three rapid puffs and stamped it out. And as he did so a strange, purposeful tenseness seemed to come over him. His boiled-fish eyes seemed to say that the time of dalliance was now ended and constabulary duty was to be done. 'Is that the way to the platform, mister?' he asked, indicating my door with a jerk of the helmet.

I cannot say why it was, but at this moment a sudden foreboding swept over me.

'Why do you want to go on the platform?' I asked, apprehensively.

There was no doubt about the disfavour with which he regarded me now. So frigid was his glance that I backed against the door in some alarm.

'Never you mind,' he said, severely, 'why I want to go on that platform. If you really want to know,' he continued, with that slight inconsistency which marks great minds, 'I'm goin' there to arrest a feller.'

It was perhaps a little uncomplimentary to Ukridge that I

should so instantly have leaped to the certainty that, if anybody on a platform on which he sat was in danger of arrest, he must be the man. There were at least twenty other earnest supporters of Boko grouped behind the chairman beyond that door, but it never even occurred to me as a possibility that it could be one of these on whom the hand of the law proposed to descend. And a moment later my instinct was proved to be unerring. The singing had ceased, and a stentorian voice had begun to fill all space. It spoke, was interrupted by a roar of laughter, and began to speak again.

'That's 'im,' said the constable, briefly.

'There must be some mistake,' I said. 'That is my friend, Mr Ukridge.'

'I don't know 'is name and I don't care about 'is name,' said the constable sternly. 'But if 'e's the big feller with glasses that's stayin' at the Bull, that's the man I'm after. He may be a 'ighly 'umorous and diverting orator,' said the constable, bitterly, as another happy burst of laughter greeted what was presumably a further sally at the expense of the side which enjoyed his support, 'but, be that as it may, 'e's got to come along with me to the station and explain how 'e 'appens to be in possession of a stolen car that there's been an inquiry sent out from 'ead-quarters about.'

My heart turned to water. A light had flashed upon me.

'Car?' I quavered.

'Car,' said the constable.

'Was it a gentleman named Coote who lodged the complaint about his car being stolen? Because –'

'I don't –'

'Because, if so, there has been a mistake. Mr Ukridge is a personal friend of Mr Coote, and –'

'I don't know whose name it is's car's been stolen,' said the constable, elliptically. 'All I know is, there's been an inquiry sent out, and this feller's got it.'

At this point something hard dug into the small of my back as I pressed against the door. I stole a hand round behind me, and my fingers closed upon a key. The policeman was stooping to retrieve a dropped note book. I turned the key softly and pocketed it.

'If you would kindly not object to standing back a bit and giving a feller a chance to get at that door,' said the policeman, straightening himself. He conducted experiments with the handle. ''Ere, it's locked!'

'Is it?' I said 'Is it?'

''Ow did you get out through this door if it's locked?'

'It wasn't locked when I came through.'

He eyed me with dull suspicion for a moment, then knocked imperatively with a large red knuckle.

'Shush! Shush!' came a scandalized whisper through the keyhole.

'Never you mind about "Shush! Shush!"' said the constable, with asperity. 'You open this door, that's what you do.' And he substituted for the knuckle a leg-of-mutton-like fist. The sound of his banging boomed through the corridor like distant thunder.

'Really, you know,' I protested, 'you're disturbing the meeting.'

'I *want* to disturb the meeting,' replied this strong but not silent man, casting a cold look over his shoulder. And the next instant, to prove that he was as ready with deeds as with words, he backed a foot or two, lifted a huge and weighty foot, and kicked.

For all ordinary purposes the builder of the Associated Mechanics' Hall had done his work adequately, but he had never suspected that an emergency might arise which would bring his doors into competition with a policeman's foot. Any lesser maltreatment the lock might have withstood, but against this it was powerless. With a sharp sound like the cry of one registering a formal protest the door gave way. It swung back, showing a vista of startled faces beyond. Whether or not the noise had reached the audience in the body of the hall I did not know, but it had certainly impressed the little group on the platform. I had a swift glimpse of forms hurrying to the centre of the disturbance, of the chairman gaping like a surprised sheep, of Ukridge glowering; and then the constable blocked out my view as he marched forward over the debris.

A moment later there was no doubt as to whether the audience was interested. A confused uproar broke out in every corner of the hall, and, hurrying on to the platform, I perceived that the hand of the Law had fallen. It was grasping Ukridge's shoulder in a weighty grip in the sight of all men.

There was just one instant before the tumult reached its height in which it was possible for the constable to speak with a chance of making himself heard. He seized his opportunity adroitly. He threw back his head and bellowed as if he were giving evidence before a deaf magistrate.

''E's – stolen – a – mo – tor – car! I'm a-r-resting – 'im – for – 'avin' sto – len – a – norter-mo*bile!*' he vociferated in accents audible to all. And then, with the sudden swiftness of one practised in the art of spiriting felons away from the midst of their friends, he was gone, and Ukridge with him.

There followed a long moment of bewildered amazement. Nothing like this had ever happened before at political meetings at Redbridge, and the audience seemed doubtful how to act. The first person to whom intelligence returned was a grim-looking little man in the third row, who had forced himself into prominence during the chairman's speech with some determined heckling. He bounded out of his chair and stood on it.

'Men of Redbridge!' he shouted.

'Siddown!' roared the audience automatically.

'Men of Redbridge,' repeated the little man, in a voice out of all proportion to his inches, 'are you going to trust – do you mean to support – is it your intention to place your affairs in the hands of one who employs *criminals* –'

'Siddown!' recommended many voices, but there were many others that shouted ''Ear, 'Ear!'

'— who employs *criminals* to speak on his platform? Men of Redbridge, I –'

Here someone grasped the little man's collar and brought him to the floor. Somebody else hit the collar-grasper over the head with an umbrella. A third party broke the umbrella and smote its owner on the nose. And after that the action may be said to have become general. Everybody seemed to be fighting everybody else, and at the back of the hall a group of serious thinkers, in whom I seemed to recognize the denizens of Biscuit Row, had begun to dismember the chairs and throw them at random. It was when the first rush was made for the platform that the meeting definitely broke up. The chairman headed the stampede for my little door, moving well for a man of his years, and he was closely followed by the rest of the elect. I came somewhere mid-way in the procession, outstripped by the leaders, but well up in the field. The last I saw of the monster meeting in aid of Boko Lawlor's candidature was Boko's drawn and agonized face as he barked his shin on an overturned table in his efforts to reach the exit in three strides.

The next morning dawned bright and fair, and the sun, as we speeded back to London, smiled graciously in through the windows of our third-class compartment. But it awoke no answering smile on Ukridge's face. He sat in his corner scowling ponderously out at the green countryside. He seemed in no way thankful that his prison-life was over, and he gave me no formal thanks for the swiftness and intelligence with which I had obtained his release.

A five-shilling telegram to Looney Coote had been the means of effecting this. Shortly after breakfast Ukridge had come to my hotel, a free man, with the information that Looney had wired the police of Redbridge directions to unbar the prison cell. But liberty he appeared to consider a small thing compared with his wrongs, and now he sat in the train, thinking, thinking, thinking.

I was not surprised when his first act on reaching Paddington was to climb into a cab and request the driver to convey him immediately to Looney Coote's address.

Personally, though I was considerate enough not to say so, I was pro-Coote. If Ukridge wished to go about sneaking his friends' cars without a word of explanation, it seemed to me that he did so at his own risk. I could not see how Looney Coote could be expected to know by some form of telepathy that his vanished Winchester-Murphy had fallen into the hands of an old school-fellow. But Ukridge, to judge by his stony stare and tightened lips, not to mention the fact that his collar had jumped off its stud and he had made no attempt to adjust it, thought differently. He sat in the cab, brooding silently, and when we reached our destination and were shown into Looney's luxurious sitting-room, he gave one long, deep sigh, like that of a fighter who hears the gong go for round one.

Looney fluttered out of the adjoining room in pyjamas and a flowered dressing-gown. He was evidently a late riser.

'Oh, here you are!' he said, pleased. 'I say, old man, I'm awfully glad it's all right.'

'All right!' An overwrought snort escaped Ukridge. His bosom swelled beneath his mackintosh. 'All right!'

'I'm frightfully sorry there was any trouble.'

Ukridge struggled for utterance.

'Do you know I spent the night on a beastly plank bed,' he said, huskily.

'No, really? I say!'

'Do you know that this morning I was washed by the authorities?'

'I say, no!'

'And you say it's all right!'

He had plainly reached the point where he proposed to deliver a lengthy address of a nature calculated to cause alarm and despondency in Looney Coote, for he raised a clenched fist, shook it passionately, and swallowed once or twice. But before he could embark on what would certainly have been an oration worth listening to, his host anticipated him.

'I don't see that it was my fault,' bleated Looney Coote, voicing my own sentiments.

'You don't see that it was your fault!' stuttered Ukridge.

'Listen, old man,' I urged pacifically. 'I didn't like to say so before, because you didn't seem in the mood for it, but what else could the poor chap have done? You took his car without a word of explanation –'

'What?'

'– and naturally he thought it had been stolen and had word sent out to the police-stations to look out for whoever had got it. As a matter of fact, it was I who advised him to.'

Ukridge was staring bleakly at Looney.

'Without a word of explanation!' he echoed. 'What about my letter, the long and carefully-written letter I sent you explaining the whole thing?'

'Letter?'

'Yes!'

'I got no letter,' said Looney Coote.

Ukridge laughed malevolently.

'You're going to pretend it went wrong in the post, eh? Thin, very thin. I am certain that letter was posted. I remember placing it in my pocket for that purpose. It is not there now, and I have been wearing this suit ever since I left London. See. These are all the contents of my –'

His voice trailed off as he gazed at the envelope in his hand. There was a long silence. Ukridge's jaw dropped slowly.

'Now, how the deuce did that happen?' he murmured.

I am bound to say that Looney Coote in this difficult moment displayed a nice magnanimity which I could never have shown. He merely nodded sympathetically.

'I'm always doing that sort of thing myself,' he said. 'Never can remember to post letters. Well, now that that's all explained, have a drink, old man, and let's forget about it.'

The gleam in Ukridge's eye showed that the invitation was a welcome one, but the battered relics of his conscience kept him from abandoning the subject under discussion as his host urged.

'But upon my Sam, Looney, old horse,' he stammered, 'I – well, dash it, I don't know what to say. I mean –'

Looney Coote was fumbling in the sideboard for the materials for a friendly carouse.

'Don't say another word, old man, not another word,' he pleaded. 'It's the sort of thing that might have happened to anyone. And, as a matter of fact, the whole affair has done me a bit of good. Dashed lucky it has turned out for me. You see, it came as a sort of omen. There was an absolute outsider running in the third race at Kempton Park the day after the car went called Stolen Goods, and somehow it seemed to me that the thing had been sent for a purpose. I crammed on thirty quid at twenty-five to one. The people round about laughed when they saw me back this poor, broken-down-looking moke, and, dash it, the animal simply romped home! I collected a parcel!'

We clamoured our congratulations on this happy ending. Ukridge was especially exuberant.

'Yes,' said Looney Coote, 'I won seven hundred and fifty-quid. Just like that! I put it on with that new fellow you were telling me about at the O.W. dinner, old man – that chap Isaac

O'Brien. It sent him absolutely broke and he's had to go out of business. He's only paid me six hundred quid so far, but says he has some sort of a sleeping partner or something who may be able to raise the balance.'

Chapter 9

The Exit of Battling Billson

The Theatre Royal, Llunindnno, is in the middle of the principal thoroughfare of that repellent town, and immediately opposite its grubby main entrance there is a lamp-post. Under this lamp-post, as I approached, a man was standing. He was a large man, and his air was that of one who has recently passed through some trying experience. There was dust on his person, and he had lost his hat. At the sound of my footsteps he turned, and the rays of the lamp revealed the familiar features of my old friend Stanley Featherstonehaugh Ukridge.

'Great Scott!' I ejaculated. 'What are you doing here?'

There was no possibility of hallucination. It was the man himself in the flesh. And what Ukridge, a free agent, could be doing in Llunindnno was more that I could imagine. Situated, as its name implies, in Wales, it is a dark, dingy, dishevelled spot, inhabited by tough and sinister men with suspicious eyes and three-day beards; and to me, after a mere forty minutes' sojourn in the place, it was incredible that anyone should be there except on compulsion.

Ukridge gaped at me incredulously.

'Corky, old horse!' he said, 'this is, upon my Sam, without exception the most amazing event in the world's history. The last bloke I expected to see.'

'Same here. Is anything the matter?' I asked, eyeing his bedraggled appearance.

'Matter? I should say something was the matter!' snorted Ukridge, astonishment giving way to righteous indignation. 'They chucked me out!'

'Chucked you out? Who? Where from?'

'This infernal theatre, laddie. After taking my good money, dash it! At least, I got it on my face, but that has nothing to do with the principle of the thing. Corky, my boy, don't you ever go about this world seeking for justice, because there's no such thing under the broad vault of heaven. I had just gone out for a breather after the first act, and when I came back I found some fiend in human shape had pinched my seat. And just because I tried to lift the fellow out by the ears, a dozen hired assassins swooped down and shot me out. Me, I'll trouble you! The injured party! Upon my Sam,' he said, heatedly, with a longing look at the closed door, 'I've a dashed good mind to –'

'I shouldn't,' I said, soothingly. 'After all, what does it matter? It's just one of those things that are bound to happen from time to time. The man of affairs passes them off with a light laugh.'

'Yes, but –'

'Come and have a drink.'

The suggestion made him waver. The light of battle died down in his eyes. He stood for a moment in thought.

'You wouldn't bung a brick through the window?' he queried, doubtfully.

'No, no!'

'Perhaps you're right.'

He linked his arm in mine and we crossed the road to where the lights of a public-house shone like heartening beacons. The crisis was over.

'Corky,' said Ukridge, warily laying down his mug of beer on the counter a few moments later, lest emotion should cause him to spill any of its contents, 'I can't get over, I simply cannot get over the astounding fact of your being in this blighted town.'

I explained my position. My presence in Llunindnno was due to the fact that the paper which occasionally made use of my services as a special writer had sent me to compose a fuller and more scholarly report than its local correspondent seemed capable of concocting of the activities of one Evan Jones, the latest of those revivalists who periodically convulse the emotions of the Welsh mining population. His last and biggest meeting was to take place next morning at eleven o'clock.

'But what are you doing here?' I asked.

'What am *I* doing here?' said Ukridge. 'Who me? Why, where else would you expect me to be? Haven't you heard?'

'Heard what?'

'Haven't you seen the posters?'

'What posters? I only arrived an hour ago.'

'My dear old horse! Then naturally you aren't abreast of local affairs.' He drained his mug, breathed contentedly, and led me out into the street. 'Look!'

He was pointing at a poster, boldly lettered in red and black, which decorated the side-wall of the Bon Ton Millinery Emporium. The street-lighting system of Llunindnno is defective, but I was able to read what it said:

ODDFELLOWS' HALL
Special Ten-Round Contest
LLOYD THOMAS
(Llunindnno)
vs.
BATTLING BILLSON
(Bermondsey)

'Comes off tomorrow night,' said Ukridge. 'And I don't mind telling you, laddie, that I expect to make a colossal fortune.'

'Are you still managing the Battler?' I said surprised at this dogged perseverance. 'I should have thought that after your last two experiences you would have had about enough of it.'

'Oh, he means business this time! I've been talking to him like a father.'

'How much does he get?'

'Twenty quid.'

'Twenty quid? Well, where does the colossal fortune come in? Your share will only be a tenner.'

'No, my boy. You haven't got on to my devilish shrewdness. I'm not in on the purse at all this time. I'm the management.'

'The management?'

'Well, part of it. You remember Isaac O'Brien, the bookie I was partner with till that chump Looney Coote smashed the business? Izzy Previn is his real name. We've gone shares in this thing. Izzy came down a week ago, hired the hall, and looked after the advertising and so on; and I arrived with good old Billson this afternoon. We're giving him twenty quid, and the other fellow's getting another twenty; and all the rest of the cash Izzy and I split on a fifty-fifty basis. Affluence, laddie!

That's what it means. Affluence beyond the dreams of a Monte Cristo. Owing to this Jones fellow the place is crowded, and every sportsman for miles around will be there tomorrow at five bob a head, cheaper seats two-and-six, and standing-room one shilling. Add lemonade and fried fish privileges, and you have a proposition almost without parallel in the annals of commerce. I couldn't be more on velvet if they gave me a sack and a shovel and let me loose in the Mint.'

I congratulated him in suitable terms.

'How is the Battler?' I asked.

'Trained to an ounce. Come and see him tomorrow morning.'

'I can't come in the morning. I've got to go to this Jones meeting.'

'Oh, yes. Well make it early in the afternoon, then. Don't come later than three, because he will be resting. We're at Number Seven, Caerleon Street. Ask for the Cap and Feathers public-house and turn sharp to the left.'

I was in a curiously uplifted mood on the following afternoon as I set out to pay my respects to Mr Billson. This was the first time I had had occasion to attend one of these revival meetings, and the effect it had had on me was to make me feel as if I had been imbibing large quantities of champagne to the accompaniment of a very loud orchestra. Even before the revivalist rose to speak, the proceedings had had an effervescent quality singularly unsettling to the sober mind, for the vast gathering had begun to sing hymns directly they took their seats; and while the opinion I had formed of the inhabitants of Llunindnno was not high, there was no denying their vocal powers. There is something about a Welsh voice when raised in song that no other voice seems to possess – a creepy, heart-searching quality that gets right into a man's inner consciousness and stirs it up with a pole. And on top of this had come Evan Jones's address.

It did not take me long to understand why this man had gone through the countryside like a flame. He had magnetism, intense earnestness, and the voice of a prophet crying in the wilderness. His fiery eyes seemed to single out each individual in the hall, and every time he paused sighings and wailings went up like the smoke of a furnace. And then, after speaking for what I discovered with amazement on consulting my watch was considerably over an hour, he stopped. And I blinked like an aroused somnambulist, shook myself to make sure I was still there, and came away. And now, as I walked in search of the Cap and Feathers, I was, as I say, oddly exhilarated: and I was strolling along in a sort of trance when a sudden uproar jerked me from my thoughts. I looked about me, and saw the sign of the Cap and Feathers suspended over a building across the street.

It was a dubious-looking hostelry in a dubious neighbourhood: and the sounds proceeding from its interior were not reassuring to a peace-loving pedestrian. There was a good deal of shouting going on and much smashing of glass; and, as I stood there, the door flew open and a familiar figure emerged rather hastily. A moment later there appeared in the doorway a woman.

She was a small woman, but she carried the largest and most intimidating mop I had ever seen. It dripped dirty water as she brandished it; and the man, glancing apprehensively over his shoulder, proceeded rapidly on his way.

'Hallo, Mr Billson!' I said, as he shot by me.

It was not, perhaps, the best-chosen moment for endeavouring to engage him in light conversation. He showed no disposition whatever to linger. He vanished round the corner, and the woman, with a few winged words, gave her mop a victorious flourish and re-entered the public-house. I walked on, and a little later a huge figure stepped cautiously out of an alleyway and fell into step at my side.

'Didn't recognize you, mister,' said Mr Billson, apologetically.

'You seemed in rather a hurry,' I agreed.

' 'R!' said Mr Billson, and a thoughtful silence descended upon him for a space.

'Who,' I asked, tactlessly, perhaps, 'was your lady friend?'

Mr Billson looked a trifle sheepish. Unnecessarily, in my opinion. Even heroes may legitimately quail before a mop wielded by an angry woman.

'She come out of a back room,' he said, with embarrassment. 'Started makin' a fuss when she saw what I'd done. So I come away. You can't dot a woman,' argued Mr Billson, chivalrously.

'Certainly not,' I agreed. 'But what was the trouble?'

'I been doin' good,' said Mr Billson, virtuously.

'Doing good?'

'Spillin' their beers.'

'Whose beers?'

'All of their beers. I went in and there was a lot of sinful fellers drinkin' beers. So I spilled 'em. All of 'em. Walked round and spilled all of them beers, one after the other. Not 'arf surprised them pore sinners wasn't,' said Mr Billson, with what sounded to me not unlike a worldly chuckle.

'I can readily imagine it.'

'Huh?'

'I say I bet they were.'

''R!' said Mr Billson. He frowned. 'Beer,' he proceeded, with cold austerity, 'ain't right. Sinful, that's what beer is. It stingeth like a serpent and biteth like a ruddy adder.'

My mouth watered a little. Beer like that was what I had been scouring the country for for years. I thought it was imprudent, however, to say so. For some reason which I could not fathom, my companion, once as fond of his half-pint as the next man, seemed to have conceived a puritanical hostility to the beverage. I decided to change the subject.

'I'm looking forward to seeing you fight tonight,' I said.

He eyed me woodenly.

'Me?'

'Yes. At the Oddfellows' Hall, you know.'

He shook his head.

'I ain't fighting at no Oddfellows' Hall,' he replied. 'Not at no Oddfellows' Hall nor nowhere else I'm not fighting, not tonight nor no night.' He pondered stolidly, and then, as if coming to the conclusion that his last sentence could be improved by the addition of a negative, added 'No!'

And having said this, he suddenly stopped and stiffened like a pointing dog; and, looking up to see what interesting object by the wayside had attracted his notice, I perceived that we were standing beneath another public-house sign, that of the Blue Boar. Its windows were hospitably open, and through them came a musical clinking of glasses. Mr Billson licked his lips with a quiet relish.

' 'Scuse me, mister,' he said, and left me abruptly.

My one thought now was to reach Ukridge as quickly as possible, in order to acquaint him with these sinister developments. For I was startled. More, I was alarmed and uneasy. In one of the star performers at a special ten-round contest, scheduled to take place that evening, Mr Billson's attitude seemed to me peculiar, not to say disquieting. So, even though a sudden crash and uproar from the interior of the Blue Boar called invitingly to me to linger, I hurried on, and neither stopped, looked, nor listened until I stood on the steps of Number Seven Caerleon Street. And eventually, after my prolonged ringing and knocking had finally induced a female of advanced years to come up and open the door, I found Ukridge lying on a horse-hair sofa in the far corner of the sitting-room.

I unloaded my grave news. It was wasting time to try to break it gently.

'I've just seen Billson,' I said, 'and he seems to be in rather a strange mood. In fact, I'm sorry to say, old man, he rather gave me the impression –'

'That he wasn't going to fight tonight?' said Ukridge, with a strange calm. 'Quite correct. He isn't. He's just been in here to tell me so. What I like about the man is his consideration for all concerned. *He* doesn't want to upset anybody's arrangements.'

'But what's the trouble? Is he kicking about only getting twenty pounds?'

'No. He thinks fighting's sinful!'

'What?'

'Nothing more nor less, Corky, my boy. Like chumps, we took our eyes off him for half a second this morning, and he sneaked off to that revival meeting. Went out shortly after a light and wholesome breakfast for what he called a bit of a mooch round, and came in half an hour ago a changed man, Full of loving-kindness, curse him. Nasty shifty gleam in his eye. Told us he thought fighting sinful and it was all off, and then buzzed out to spread the Word.'

I was shaken to the core. Wilberforce Billson, the peerless but temperamental Battler, had never been an ideal pugilist to manage, but hitherto he had drawn the line at anything like this. Other little problems which he might have brought up for his manager to solve might have been overcome by patience and tact; but not this one. The psychology of Mr Billson was as an open book to me. He possessed one of those single-track minds, capable of accommodating but one idea at a time, and he had the tenacity of the simple soul. Argument would leave him unshaken. On that bone-like head Reason would beat in vain. And, these things being so, I was at a loss to account for Ukridge's extraordinary calm. His fortitude in the hour of ruin amazed me.

His next remark, however, offered an explanation.

'We're putting on a substitute,' he said.

I was relieved.

'Oh, you've got a substitute? That's a bit of luck. Where did you find him?'

'As a matter of fact, laddie, I've decided to go on myself.'

'What! You!'

'Only way out, my boy. No other solution.'

I stared at the man. Years of the closest acquaintance with S. F. Ukridge had rendered me almost surprise-proof at anything he might do, but this was too much.

'Do you mean to tell me that you seriously intend to go out there tonight and appear in the ring?' I cried.

'Perfectly straightforward business-like proposition, old man,' said Ukridge, stoutly. 'I'm in excellent shape. I sparred with Billson every day while he was training.'

'Yes, but –'

'The fact is, laddie, you don't realize my potentialities. Recently, it's true, I've allowed myself to become slack and what you might call enervated, but, damme, when I was on that trip in that tramp-steamer, scarcely a week used to go by without my having a good earnest scrap with somebody. Nothing barred,' said Ukridge, musing lovingly on the care-free past, 'except biting and bottles.'

'Yes, but hang it – a professional pugilist!'

'Well, to be absolutely accurate, laddie,' said Ukridge, suddenly dropping the heroic manner and becoming confidential, 'the thing's going to be fixed. Izzy Previn has seen the bloke Thomas's manager, and has arranged a gentleman's agreement. The manager, a Class A blood-sucker, insists on us giving his man another twenty pounds after the fight, but that can't be helped. In return, the Thomas bloke consents to play light for three rounds, at the end of which period, laddie, he will tap me on the side of the head and I shall go down and out, a popular loser. What's more, I'm allowed to hit him hard – once – just so long as it isn't on the nose. So you see, a little tact, a little diplomacy, and the whole thing fixed up as satisfactorily as anyone could wish.'

'But suppose the audience demands its money back when they find they're going to see a substitute?'

'My dear old horse,' protested Ukridge, 'surely you don't imagine that a man with a business head like mine overlooked that? Naturally, I'm going to fight as Battling Billson. Nobody knows him in this town. I'm a good big chap, just as much a heavy-weight as he is. No, laddie, pick how you will, you can't pick a flaw in this.'

'Why mayn't you hit him on the nose?'

'I don't know. People have these strange whims. And now, Corky, my boy, I think you had better leave me. I ought to relax.'

The Oddfellows' Hall was certainly filling up nicely when I arrived that night. Indeed, it seemed as though Llunindnno's devotees of sport would cram it to the roof. I took my place in the line before the pay-window, and, having completed the business end of the transaction, went in and inquired my way to the dressing-rooms. And presently, after wandering through divers passages, I came upon Ukridge, clad for the ring and swathed in his familiar yellow mackintosh.

'You're going to have a wonderful house,' I said. 'The populace is rolling up in shoals.'

He received the information with a strange lack of enthusiasm. I looked at him in concern, and was disquieted by his forlorn appearance. That face, which had beamed so triumphantly at our last meeting, was pale and set. Those eyes, which normally shone with the flame of an unquenchable optimism, seemed dull and careworn. And even as I looked at him he seemed to rouse himself from a stupor and, reaching out for his shirt, which hung on a near-by peg, proceeded to pull it over his head.

'What's the matter?' I asked.

His head popped out of the shirt, and he eyed me wanly.

'I'm off,' he announced, briefly.

'Off? How do you mean, off?' I tried to soothe what I took to be an eleventh-hour attack of stage-fright. 'You'll be all right.'

Ukridge laughed hollowly.

'Once the gong goes, you'll forget the crowd.'

'It isn't the crowd,' said Ukridge, in a pale voice, climbing into his trousers. 'Corky, old man,' he went on, earnestly, 'if ever you feel your angry passions rising to the point where you want to swat a stranger in a public place, restrain yourself. There's nothing in it. This bloke Thomas was in here a moment ago with his manager to settle the final details. He's the fellow I had the trouble with at the theatre last night!'

'The man you pulled out of the seat by his ears?' I gasped.

Ukridge nodded.

'Recognized me at once, confound him, and it was all his manager, a thoroughly decent cove whom I liked, could do to prevent him getting at me there and then.'

'Good Lord!' I said, aghast at this grim development, yet thinking how thoroughly characteristic it was of Ukridge, when he had a whole townful of people to quarrel with, to pick the one professional pugilist.

At this moment, when Ukridge was lacing his left shoe, the door opened and a man came in.

The new-comer was stout, dark, and beady-eyed, and from his manner of easy comradeship and the fact that when he spoke he supplemented words with the language of the waving palm, I deduced that this must be Mr Izzy Previn, recently trading as Isaac O'Brien. He was cheeriness itself.

'Vell,' he said, with ill-timed exuberance, 'how'th the boy?'

The boy cast a sour look at him.

'The house,' proceeded Mr Previn, with an almost lyrical enthusiasm, 'is absolutely full. Crammed, jammed, and packed. They're hanging from the roof by their eyelids. It'th goin' to be a knock-out.'

The expression, considering the circumstances, could hardly have been less happily chosen. Ukridge winced painfully, then spoke in no uncertain voice.

'I'm not going to fight!'

Mr Previn's exuberance fell from him like a garment. His cigar dropped from his mouth, and his beady eyes glittered with sudden consternation.

'What do you mean?'

'Rather an unfortunate thing has happened,' I explained. 'It seems that this man Thomas is a fellow Ukridge had trouble with at the theatre last night.'

'What do you mean, Ukridge?' broke in Mr Previn. 'This is Battling Billson.'

'I've told Corky all about it,' said Ukridge over his shoulder as he laced his right shoe. 'Old pal of mine.'

'Oh!' said Mr Previn, relieved. 'Of course, if Mr Corky is a friend of yours and quite understands that all this is quite private among ourselves and don't want talking about outside, all right. But what were you thayin'? I can't make head or tail of it. How do you mean, you're not goin' to fight? Of course you're goin' to fight.'

'Thomas was in here just now,' I said. 'Ukridge and he had a row at the theatre last night, and naturally Ukridge is afraid he will go back on the agreement.'

'Nonthense,' said Mr Previn, and his manner was that of one soothing a refractory child. '*He* won't go back on the agreement. He promised he'd play light and he will play light. Gave me his word as a gentleman.'

'He isn't a gentleman,' Ukridge pointed out, moodily.

'But lithen!'

'I'm going to get out of here as quick as I dashed well can!'

'Conthider!' pleaded Mr Previn, clawing great chunks out of the air.

Ukridge began to button his collar.

'Reflect!' moaned Mr Previn. 'There's that lovely audience all sitting out there, jammed like thardines, waiting for the thing to start. Do you expect me to go and tell 'em there ain't goin' to be no fight? I'm thurprised at you,' said Mr Previn, trying an appeal to his pride. 'Where's your manly spirit? A big, husky feller like you, that's done all sorts of scrappin' in your time –'

'Not,' Ukridge pointed out coldly, 'with any damned professional pugilists who've got a grievance against me.'

'*He* won't hurt you.'

'He won't get the chance.'

'You'll be safe and cosy in that ring with him as if you was playing ball with your little thister.'

Ukridge said he hadn't got a little sister.

'But think!' implored Mr Previn, flapping like a seal. 'Think of the money! Do you realize we'll have to return it all, every penny of it?'

A spasm of pain passed over Ukridge's face, but he continued buttoning his collar.

'And not only that,' said Mr Previn, 'but, if you ask me, they'll be so mad when they hear there ain't goin' to be no fight, they'll lynch me.'

Ukridge seemed to regard this possibility with calm.

'And you, too,' added Mr Previn.

Ukridge started. It was a plausible theory, and one that had not occurred to him before. He paused irresolutely. And at this moment a man came hurrying in.

'What's the matter?' he demanded, fussily. 'Thomas has been in the ring for five minutes. Isn't your man ready?'

'In one half tick,' said Mr Previn. He turned meaningly to Ukridge. 'That's right, ain't it? You'll be ready in half a tick?'

Ukridge nodded wanly. In silence he shed shirt, trousers, shoes, and collar, parting from them as if they were old friends whom he never expected to see again. One wistful glance he cast at his mackintosh, lying forlornly across a chair; and then, with more than a suggestion of a funeral procession, we started down the corridor that led to the main hall. The hum of many voices came to us; there was a sudden blaze of light, and we were there.

I must say for the sport-loving citizens of Llunindnno that they appeared to be fair-minded men. Stranger in their midst though he was, they gave Ukridge an excellent reception as he climbed into the ring; and for a moment, such is the tonic effect of applause on a large scale, his depression seemed to lift. A faint, gratified smile played about his drawn mouth, and I think it would have developed into a bashful grin, had he not at this instant caught sight of the redoubtable Mr Thomas towering massively across the way. I saw him blink, as one who, thinking absently of this and that, walks suddenly into a lamp-post; and his look of unhappiness returned.

My heart bled for him. If the offer of my little savings in the bank could have transported him there and then to the safety of his London lodgings, I would have made it unreservedly. Mr Previn had disappeared, leaving me standing at the ring-side, and as nobody seemed to object I remained there, thus getting an excellent view of the mass of bone and sinew that made up Lloyd Thomas. And there was certainly plenty of him to see.

Mr Thomas was, I should imagine, one of those men who do not look their most formidable in mufti – for otherwise I could not conceive how even the fact that he had stolen his seat could have led Ukridge to lay the hand of violence upon him. In the exiguous costume of the ring he looked a person from whom the sensible man would suffer almost any affront with meekness. He was about six feet in height, and wherever a man could bulge with muscle he bulged. For a moment my anxiety for Ukridge was tinged with a wistful regret that I should never see this sinewy citizen in action with Mr Billson. It would, I mused, have been a battle worth coming even to Llunindnno to see.

The referee, meanwhile, had been introducing the principals in the curt, impressive fashion of referees. He now retired, and with a strange foreboding note a gong sounded on the farther side of the ring. The seconds scuttled under the ropes. The man Thomas, struggling – it seemed to me – with powerful emotions, came ponderously out of his corner.

In these reminiscences of a vivid and varied career, it is as a profound thinker that I have for the most part had occasion to portray Stanley Featherstonehaugh Ukridge. I was now to be reminded that he also had it in him to be a doer. Even as Mr Thomas shuffled towards him, his left fist shot out and thudded against the other's ribs. In short, in a delicate and difficult situation, Ukridge was comporting himself with an adequacy that surprised me. However great might have been his reluctance to embark on this contest, once in he was doing well.

And then, half-way through the first round, the truth dawned upon me. Injured though Mr Thomas had been, the gentleman's agreement still held. The word of a Thomas was as good as his bond. Poignant though his dislike of Ukridge might be, nevertheless, having pledged himself to mildness and self-restraint for the first three rounds, he intended to abide by the contract. Probably, in the interval between his visit to Ukridge's dressing-room and his appearance in the ring, his manager had been talking earnestly to him. At any rate, whether it was managerial authority or his own sheer nobility of character that influenced him, the fact remains that he treated Ukridge with a quite remarkable forbearance, and the latter reached his corner at the end of round one practically intact.

And it was this that undid him. No sooner had the gong sounded for round two than out he pranced from his corner, thoroughly above himself. He bounded at Mr Thomas like a Dervish.

I could read his thoughts as if he had spoken them. Nothing could be clearer than that he had altogether failed to grasp the true position of affairs. Instead of recognizing his adversary's forbearance for what it was and being decently grateful for it, he was filled with a sinful pride. Here, he told himself, was a man who had a solid grievance against him – and, dash it, the fellow couldn't hurt him a bit. What the whole thing boiled down to, he felt, was that he, Ukridge, was better than he had suspected, a man to be reckoned with, and one who could show a distinguished gathering of patrons of sport something worth looking at. The consequence was that, where any sensible person would have grasped the situation at once and endeavoured to show his appreciation by toying with Mr Thomas in gingerly fashion, whispering soothing compliments into his ear during the clinches, and generally trying to lay the foundations of a beautiful friendship against the moment when the gentleman's agreement should lapse, Ukridge committed the one unforgivable act. There was a brief moment of fiddling and feinting in the centre of the ring, then a sharp smacking sound, a startled yelp, and Mr Thomas, with gradually reddening eye, leaning against the ropes and muttering to himself in Welsh.

Ukridge had hit him on the nose.

Once more I must pay a tribute to the fair-mindedness of the

sportsmen of Llunindnno. The stricken man was one of them –
possibly Llunindnno's favourite son – yet nothing could have
exceeded the heartiness with which they greeted the visitor's
achievement. A shout went up as if Ukridge had done each
individual present a personal favour. It continued as he advanced buoyantly upon his antagonist, and – to show how entirely
Llunindnno audiences render themselves impartial and free
from any personal bias – it became redoubled as Mr Thomas,
swinging a fist like a ham, knocked Ukridge flat on his back.
Whatever happened, so long as it was sufficiently violent, seemed to be all right with that broad-minded audience.

Ukridge heaved himself laboriously to one knee. His sensibilities had been ruffled by this unexpected blow, about fifteen
times as hard as the others he had received since the beginning
of the affray, but he was a man of mettle and determination.
However humbly he might quail before a threatening landlady,
or however nimbly he might glide down a side-street at the sight
of an approaching creditor, there was nothing wrong with his
fighting heart when it came to a straight issue between man and
man, untinged by the financial element. He struggled painfully
to his feet, while Mr Thomas, now definitely abandoning the
gentleman's agreement, hovered about him with ready fists, only
restrained by the fact that one of Ukridge's gloves still touched
the floor.

It was at this tensest of moments that a voice spoke in my ear.

' 'Alf a mo', mister!'

A hand pushed me gently aside. Something large obscured the
lights. And Wilberforce Billson, squeezing under the ropes,
clambered into the ring.

For the purposes of the historian it was a good thing that for
the first few moments after this astounding occurrence a dazed
silence held the audience in its grip. Otherwise, it might have
been difficult to probe motives and explain underlying causes. I
think the spectators were either too surprised to shout, or else
they entertained for a few brief seconds the idea that Mr Billson
was the forerunner of a posse of plain-clothes police about to
raid the place. At any rate, for a space they were silent, and he
was enabled to say his say.

'Fightin',' bellowed Mr Billson, 'ain't right!'

There was an uneasy rustle in the audience. The voice of the referee came thinly, saying, 'Here! Hi!'

'Sinful,' explained Mr Billson, in a voice like a fog-horn.

His oration was interrupted by Mr Thomas, who was endeavouring to get round him and attack Ukridge. The Battler pushed him gently back.

'Gents,' he roared, 'I, too, have been a man of voylence! I 'ave struck men in anger. 'R, yes! But I 'ave seen the light. Oh, my brothers –'

The rest of his remarks were lost. With a startling suddenness the frozen silence melted. In every part of the hall indignant seatholders were rising to state their views.

But it is doubtful whether, even if he had been granted a continuance of their attention, Mr Billson would have spoken to much greater length; for at this moment Lloyd Thomas, who had been gnawing at the strings of his gloves with the air of a man who is able to stand just so much and whose limit has been exceeded, now suddenly shed these obstacles to the freer expression of self, and advancing bare-handed, smote Mr Billson violently on the jaw.

Mr Billson turned. He was pained, one could see that, but more spiritually than physically. For a moment he seemed uncertain how to proceed. Then he turned the other cheek.

The fermenting Mr Thomas smote that, too.

There was no vacillation or uncertainty now about Wilberforce Billson. He plainly considered that he had done all that could reasonably be expected of any pacifist. A man has only two cheeks. He flung up a mast-like arm, to block a third blow, countered with an accuracy and spirit which sent his aggressor reeling to the ropes; and then, swiftly removing his coat, went into action with the unregenerate zeal that had made him the petted hero of a hundred water-fronts. And I, tenderly scooping Ukridge up as he dropped from the ring, hurried him away along the corridor to his dressing-room. I would have given much to remain and witness a mix-up which, if the police did not interfere, promised to be the battle of the ages, but the claims of friendship are paramount.

Ten minutes later, however, when Ukridge, washed, clothed, and restored as near to the normal as a man may be who has received the full weight of a Lloyd Thomas on a vital spot, was reaching for his mackintosh, there filtered through the intervening doors and passageways a sudden roar so compelling that my sporting spirit declined to ignore it.

'Back in a minute, old man,' I said.

And, urged by that ever-swelling roar, I cantered back to the hall.

In the interval during which I had been ministering to my stricken friend a certain decorum seemed to have been restored to the proceedings. The conflict had lost its first riotous abandon. Upholders of the decencies of debate had induced Mr Thomas to resume his gloves, and a pair had also been thrust upon the Battler. Moreover, it was apparent that the etiquette of the tourney now governed the conflict, for rounds had been introduced, and one had just finished as I came in view of the ring. Mr Billson was leaning back in a chair in one corner undergoing treatment by his seconds, and in the opposite corner loomed Mr Thomas; and one sight of the two men was enough to tell me what had caused that sudden tremendous outburst of enthusiasm among the patriots of Llunindnno. In the last stages of the round which had just concluded the native son must have forged ahead in no uncertain manner. Perhaps some chance blow had found its way through the Battler's guard, laying him open and defenceless to the final attack. For his attitude, as he sagged in his corner, was that of one whose moments are numbered. His eyes were closed, his mouth hung open, and exhaustion was writ large upon him. Mr Thomas, on the contrary, leaned forward with hands on knees, wearing an impatient look, as if this formality of a rest between rounds irked his imperious spirit.

The gong sounded and he sprang from his seat.

'Laddie!' breathed an anguished voice, and a hand clutched my arm.

I was dimly aware of Ukridge standing beside me. I shook him off. This was no moment for conversation. My whole attention was concentrated on what was happening in the ring.

'I say, laddie?'

Matters in there had reached that tense stage when audiences lose their self-control – when strong men stand on seats and weak men cry 'Siddown!' The air was full of that electrical thrill that precedes the knock-out.

And the next moment it came. But it was not Lloyd Thomas who delivered it. From some mysterious reservoir of vitality Wilberforce Billson, the pride of Bermondsey, who an instant before had been reeling under his antagonist's blows like a stricken hulk before a hurricane, produced that one last punch that wins battles. Up it came, whizzing straight to its mark, a stupendous, miraculous uppercut which lurched forward to complete his task. It was the last word. Anything milder Llunin-dnno's favourite son might have borne with fortitude, for his was a teak-like frame impervious to most things short of dynamite; but this was final. It left no avenue for argument or evasion. Lloyd Thomas spun round once in a complete circle, dropped his hands, and sank slowly to the ground.

There was one wild shout from the audience, and then a solemn hush fell. And in the hush Ukridge's voice spoke once more in my ear.

'I say, laddie, that blighter Previn has bolted with every penny of the receipts!'

The little sitting-room of Number Seven Caerleon Street was very quiet and gave the impression of being dark. This was because there is so much of Ukridge and he takes Fate's blows so hardly that when anything goes wrong his gloom seems to fill a room like a fog. For some minutes after our return from the Oddfellows' Hall a gruesome silence had prevailed. Ukridge had exhausted his vocabulary on the subject of Mr Previn; and as for me, the disaster seemed so tremendous as to render words of sympathy a mere mockery.

'And there's another thing I've just remembered,' said Ukridge, hollowly, stirring on his sofa.

'What's that?' I inquired, in a bedside voice.

'The bloke Thomas. He was to have got another twenty pounds.'

'He'll hardly claim it, surely?'

'He'll claim it all right,' said Ukridge, moodily. 'Except, by Jove,' he went on, a sudden note of optimism in his voice, 'that he doesn't know where I am. I was forgetting that. Lucky we legged it away from the hall before he could grab me.'

'You don't think that Previn, when he was making the arrangements with Thomas's manager, may have mentioned where you were staying?'

'Not likely. Why should he? What reason would he have?'

'Gentleman to see you, sir,' crooned the aged female at the door.

The gentleman walked in. It was the man who had come to the dressing-room to announce that Thomas was in the ring; and though on that occasion we had not been formally introduced I did not need Ukridge's faint groan to tell me who he was.

'Mr Previn?' he said. He was a brisk man, direct in manner and speech.

'He's not here,' said Ukridge.

'You'll do. You're his partner. I've come for that twenty pounds.'

There was a painful silence.

'It's gone,' said Ukridge.

'What's gone?'

'The money, dash it. And Previn, too. He's bolted.'

A hard look came into the other's eyes. Dim as the light was, it was strong enough to show his expression, and that expression was not an agreeable one.

'That won't do,' he said, in a metallic voice.

'Now, my dear old horse –'

'It's no good trying anything like that on me. I want my money, or I'm going to call a policeman. Now, then!'

'But, laddie, be reasonable.'

'Made a mistake in not getting it in advance. But now'll do. Out with it!'

'But I keep telling you Previn's bolted!'

'He's certainly bolted,' I put in, trying to be helpful.

'That's right, mister,' said a voice at the door. 'I met 'im sneakin' away.'

It was Wilberforce Billson. He stood in the doorway diffidently, as one not sure of his welcome. His whole being was apologetic. He had a nasty bruise on his left cheek and one of his eyes was closed, but he bore no other signs of his recent conflict.

Ukridge was gazing upon him with bulging eyes.

'You *met* him!' he moaned. 'You actually met him?'

' 'R,' said Mr Billson. 'When I was comin' to the 'all. I seen 'im puttin' all that money into a liddle bag, and then 'e 'urried off.'

'Good lord!' I cried. 'Didn't you suspect what he was up to?'

' 'R,' agreed Mr Billson. 'I always knew 'e was a wrong 'un.'

'Then why, you poor swollen-headed fish,' bellowed Ukridge, exploding, 'why on earth didn't you stop him?'

'I never thought of that,' admitted Mr Billson, apologetically.

Ukridge laughed a hideous laugh.

'I just pushed 'im in the face,' proceeded Mr Billson, 'and took the liddle bag away from 'im.'

He placed on the table a small weather-worn suitcase that jingled musically as he moved it; then, with the air of one who dismisses some triviality from his mind, moved to the door.

' 'Scuse me, gents,' said Battling Billson, deprecatingly. 'Can't stop. I've got to go and spread the light.'

Chapter 10

Ukridge Rounds a Nasty Corner

The late Sir Rupert Lakenheath, K.C.M.G., C.B., M.V.O., was one of those men at whom their countries point with pride. Until his retirement on a pension in the year 1906, he had been Governor of various insanitary outposts of the British Empire situated around the equator, and as such had won respect and esteem from all. A kindly editor of my acquaintance secured for me the job of assisting the widow of this great administrator to prepare his memoirs for publication; and on a certain summer afternoon I had just finished arraying myself suitably for my first call on her at her residence in Thurloe Square, South Kensington, when there was a knock at the door, and Bowles, my landlord, entered, bearing gifts.

These consisted of a bottle with a staring label and a large cardboard hat-box. I gazed at them blankly, for they held no message for me.

Bowles, in his ambassadorial manner, condescended to explain.

'Mr Ukridge,' he said, with the ring of paternal affection in his voice which always crept into it when speaking of that menace to civilization, 'called a moment ago, sir, and desired me to hand you these.'

Having now approached the table on which he had placed the objects, I was enabled to solve the mystery of the bottle. It was one of those fat, bulging bottles, and it bore across its diaphragm in red letters the single word 'PEPPO'. Beneath this, in black letters, ran the legend, 'It Bucks You Up'. I had not seen Ukridge for more than two weeks, but at our last meeting, I remembered, he had spoken of some foul patent medicine of which he had somehow secured the agency. This, apparently, was it.

'But what's in the hat-box?' I asked.

'I could not say, sir,' replied Bowles.

At this point the hat-box, which had hitherto not spoken, uttered a crisp, sailorly oath, and followed it up by singing the opening bars of 'Annie Laurie'. It then relapsed into its former moody silence.

A few doses of Peppo would, no doubt, have enabled me to endure this remarkable happening with fortitude and phlegm. Not having taken that specific, the thing had a devastating effect upon my nervous centres. I bounded back and upset a chair, while Bowles, his dignity laid aside, leaped silently towards the ceiling. It was the first time I had ever seen him lay off the mask, and even in that trying moment I could not help being gratified by the spectacle. It gave me one of those thrills that come once in a lifetime.

'For Gord's sake!' ejaculated Bowles.

'Have a nut,' observed the hat-box, hospitably. 'Have a nut.'

Bowles's panic subsided.

'It's a bird, sir. A parrot!'

'What the deuce does Ukridge mean,' I cried, becoming the outraged householder, 'by cluttering up my rooms with his beastly parrots? I'd like that man to know –'

The mention of Ukridge's name seemed to act on Bowles like a soothing draught. He recovered his poise.

'I have no doubt, sir,' he said, a touch of coldness in his voice that rebuked my outburst, 'that Mr Ukridge has good reasons for depositing the bird in our custody. I fancy he must wish you to take charge of it for him.'

'He may wish it –' I was beginning, when my eye fell on the clock. If I did not want to alienate my employer by keeping her waiting, I must be on my way immediately.

'Put that hat-box in the other room, Bowles,' I said. 'And I suppose you had better give the bird something to eat.'

'Very good, sir. You may leave the matter in my hands with complete confidence.'

The drawing-room into which I was shown on arriving at Thurloe Square was filled with many mementoes of the late Sir Rupert's gubernatorial career. In addition the room contained a small and bewilderingly pretty girl in a blue dress, who smiled upon me pleasantly.

'My aunt will be down in a moment,' she said, and for a few moments we exchanged commonplaces. Then the door opened and Lady Lakenheath appeared.

The widow of the Administrator was tall, angular, and thin, with a sun-tanned face of a cast so determined as to make it seem a tenable theory that in the years previous to 1906 she had done at least her share of the administrating. Her whole appearance was that of a woman designed by Nature to instil law and order into the bosoms of boisterous cannibal kings. She surveyed me with an appraising glance, and then, as if reconciled to the fact that, poor specimen though I might be, I was probably as good as anything else that could be got for the money, received me into the fold by pressing the bell and ordering tea.

Tea had arrived, and I was trying to combine bright dialogue with the difficult feat of balancing my cup on the smallest saucer I had ever seen, when my hostess, happening to glance out of the window into the street below, uttered something midway between a sigh and a click of the tongue.

'Oh, dear! That extraordinary man again!'

The girl in the blue dress, who had declined tea and was sewing in a distant corner, bent a little closer over her work.

'Millie!' said the administratess, plaintively, as if desiring sympathy in her trouble.

'Yes, Aunt Elizabeth?'

'That man is calling again!'

There was a short but perceptible pause. A delicate pink appeared in the girl's cheeks.

'Yes, Aunt Elizabeth?' she said.

'Mr Ukridge,' announced the maid at the door.

It seemed to me that if this sort of thing was to continue, if existence was to become a mere series of shocks and surprises, Peppo would have to be installed as an essential factor in my life. I stared speechlessly at Ukridge as he breezed in with the unmistakable air of sunny confidence which a man shows on familiar ground. Even if I had not had Lady Lakenheath's words as evidence, his manner would have been enough to tell me that he was a frequent visitor in her drawing-room; and how he had come to be on calling terms with a lady so pre-eminently respectable it was beyond me to imagine. I awoke from my stupor to find that we were being introduced, and that Ukridge, for some reason clear, no doubt, to his own tortuous mind but inexplicable to me, was treating me as a complete stranger. He nodded courteously but distantly, and I, falling in with his unspoken wishes, nodded back. Plainly relieved, he turned to Lady Lakenheath and plunged forthwith into the talk of intimacy.

'I've got good news for you,' he said. 'News about Leonard.'

The alteration in our hostess's manner at these words was remarkable. Her somewhat forbidding manner softened in an instant to quite a tremulous fluttering. Gone was the hauteur which had caused her but a moment back to allude to him as 'that extraordinary man'. She pressed tea upon him, and scones.

'Oh, Mr Ukridge!' she cried.

'I don't want to rouse false hopes and all that sort of thing laddie – I mean, Lady Lakenheath, but, upon my Sam, I really believe I am on the track. I have been making the most assiduous inquiries.'

'How very kind of you!'

'No, no,' said Ukridge, modestly.

'I have been so worried,' said Lady Lakenheath, 'that I have scarcely been able to rest.'

'Too bad!'

'Last night I had a return of my wretched malaria.'

At these words, as if he had been given a cue, Ukridge reached under his chair and produced from his hat, like some conjurer, a bottle that was own brother to the one he had left in my rooms. Even from where I sat I could read those magic words of cheer on its flaunting label.

'Then I've got the very stuff for you,' he boomed. 'This is what you want. Glowing reports on all sides. Two doses, and cripples fling away their crutches and join the Beauty Chorus.'

'I am scarcely a cripple, Mr Ukridge,' said Lady Lakenheath, with a return of her earlier bleakness.

'No, no! Good heavens, no! But you can't go wrong by taking Peppo.'

'Peppo?' said Lady Lakenheath, doubtfully.

'It bucks you up.'

'You think it might do me good?' asked the sufferer, wavering. There was a glitter in her eye that betrayed the hypochondriac, the woman who will try anything once.

'Can't fail.'

'Well, it is most kind and thoughtful of you to have brought it. What with worrying over Leonard –'

'I know, I know,' murmured Ukridge, in a positively bedside manner.

'It seems so strange,' said Lady Lakenheath, 'that, after I had advertised in all the papers, someone did not find him.'

'Perhaps someone did find him!' said Ukridge, darkly.

'You think he must have been stolen?'

'I am convinced of it. A beautiful parrot like Leonard, able to talk in six languages –'

'And sing,' murmured Lady Lakenheath.

'– *and* sing,' added Ukridge, 'is worth a lot of money. But don't you worry, old – er – don't you worry. If the investigations which I am conducting now are successful, you will have Leonard back safe and sound tomorrow.'

'Tomorrow?'

'Absolutely tomorrow. Now tell me all about your malaria.'

I felt that the time had come for me to leave. It was not merely that the conversation had taken a purely medical turn and that I was practically excluded from it; what was really driving me away was the imperative necessity of getting out in the open somewhere and thinking. My brain was whirling. The world seemed to have become suddenly full of significant and disturbing parrots. I seized my hat and rose. My hostess was able to take only an absent-minded interest in my departure. The last thing I saw as the door closed was Ukridge's look of big-hearted tenderness as he leaned forward so as not to miss a syllable of his companion's clinical revelations. He was not actually patting Lady Lakenheath's hand and telling her to be a brave little woman, but short of that he appeared to be doing everything a man could do to show her that, rugged though his exterior might be, his heart was in the right place and aching for her troubles.

I walked back to my rooms. I walked slowly and pensively, bumping into lamp-posts and pedestrians. It was a relief, when

I finally reached Ebury Street, to find Ukridge smoking on my sofa. I was resolved that before he left he should explain what this was all about, if I had to wrench the truth from him.

'Hallo, laddie!' he said. 'Upon my Sam, Corky, old horse, did you ever in your puff hear of anything so astounding as our meeting like that? Hope you didn't mind my pretending not to know you. The fact is my position in that house – What the dickens were you doing there, by the way?'

'I'm helping Lady Lakenheath prepare her husband's memoirs.'

'Of course, yes. I remember hearing her say she was going to rope in someone. But what a dashed extraordinary thing it should be you! However, where was I? Oh, yes. My position in the house, Corky, is so delicate that I simply didn't dare risk entering into any entangling alliances. What I mean to say is, if we had rushed into each other's arms, and you had been established in the old lady's eyes as a friend of mine, and then one of these days you had happened to make a bloomer of some kind – as you well might, laddie – and got heaved into the street on your left ear – well, you see where I would be. I should be involved in your downfall. And I solemnly assure you, laddie, that my whole existence is staked on keeping in with that female. I *must* get her consent!'

'Her what?'

'Her consent. To the marriage.'

'The marriage?'

Ukridge blew a cloud of smoke, and gazed through it sentimentally at the ceiling.

'Isn't she a perfect angel?' he breathed, softly.

'Do you mean Lady Lakenheath?' I asked, bewildered.

'Fool! No, Millie.'

'Millie? The girl in blue?'

Ukridge sighed dreamily.

'She was wearing that blue dress when I first met her, Corky. And a hat with thingummies. It was on the Underground. I gave her my seat, and, as I hung over her, suspended by a strap, I fell in love absolutely in a flash. I give you my honest word, laddie, I fell in love with her for all eternity between Sloane Square and South Kensington stations. She got out at South Kensington. So did I. I followed her to the house, rang the bell, got the maid to show me in, and, once I was in, put up a yarn about being misdirected and coming to the wrong address and all that sort of thing. I think they thought I was looney or trying to sell life insurance or something, but I didn't mind that. A few days later I called, and after that I hung about, keeping an eye on their movements, met 'em everywhere they went, and bowed and passed a word and generally made my presence felt, and – well, to cut a long story short, old horse, we're engaged. I happened to find out that Millie was in the habit of taking the dog for a run in Kensington Gardens every morning at eleven, and after that things began to move. It took a bit of doing, of course, getting up so early, but I was on the spot every day and we talked and bunged sticks for the dog, and – well, as I say, we're engaged. She is the most amazing, wonderful girl, laddie, that you ever encountered in your life.'

I had listened to this recital dumbly. The thing was too cataclysmal for my mind. It overwhelmed me.

'But –' I began.

'But,' said Ukridge, 'the news has yet to be broken to the old lady, and I am striving with every nerve in my body, with every fibre of my brain, old horse, to get in right with her. That is why I brought her that Peppo. Not much, you may say, but every little helps. Shows zeal. Nothing like zeal. But, of course, what I'm really relying on is the parrot. That's my ace of trumps.'

I passed a hand over my corrugated forehead.

'The parrot!' I said, feebly. 'Explain about the parrot.' Ukridge eyed me with honest astonishment.

'Do you mean to tell me you haven't got on to that? A man of your intelligence! Corky, you amaze me. Why, I pinched it, of course. Or, rather, Millie and I pinched it together. Millie – a girl in a million, laddie! – put the bird in a string-bag one night when her aunt was dining out and lowered it to me out of the drawing-room window. And I've been keeping it in the background till the moment was ripe for the spectacular return. Wouldn't have done to take it back at once. Bad strategy. Wiser to hold it in reserve for a few days and show zeal and work up the interest. Millie and I are building on the old lady's being so supremely bucked at having the bird restored to her that there will be nothing she won't be willing to do for me.'

'But what do you want to dump the thing in my rooms for?' I demanded, reminded of my grievance. 'I never got such a shock as when that damned hat-box began to back-chat at me.'

'I'm sorry, old man, but it had to be. I could never tell that the old lady might not take it into her head to come round to my rooms about something. I'd thrown out – mistakenly, I realize now – an occasional suggestion about tea there some afternoon. So I had to park the bird with you. I'll take it away tomorrow.'

'You'll take it away tonight!'

'Not tonight, old man,' pleaded Ukridge. 'First thing to-morrow. You won't find it any trouble. Just throw it a word or two every now and then and give it a bit of bread dipped in tea or something, and you won't have to worry about it at all. And I'll be round by noon at the latest to take it away. May Heaven reward you, laddie, for the way you have stood by me this day!'

For a man like myself, who finds at least eight hours of sleep essential if that schoolgirl complexion is to be preserved, it was unfortunate that Leonard the parrot should have proved to be a bird of high-strung temperament, easily upset. The experiences which he had undergone since leaving home had, I was to discover, jarred his nervous system. He was reasonably tranquil during the hours preceding bedtime, and had started his beauty-sleep before I myself turned in; but at two in the morning something in the nature of a nightmare must have attacked him, for I was wrenched from slumber by the sounds of a hoarse soliloquy in what I took to be some native dialect. This lasted without a break till two-fifteen, when he made a noise like a steam-riveter for some moments; after which, apparently sooth-ed, he fell asleep again. I dropped off at about three, and at three-thirty was awakened by the strains of a deep-sea chanty. From then on our periods of sleep never seemed to coincide. It was a wearing night, and before I went out after breakfast, I left imperative instructions with Bowles for Ukridge, on arrival, to be informed that, if anything went wrong with his plans for removing my guest that day, the mortality statistics among parrots would take an up-curve. Returning to my rooms in the evening, I was pleased to see that this manifesto had been taken to heart. The hat-box was gone, and about six o'clock Ukridge appeared, so beaming and effervescent that I understood what had happened before he spoke. 'Corky, my boy,' he said, vehemently, 'this is the maddest, merriest day of all the glad New Year, and you can quote me as saying so!'

'Lady Lakenheath has given her consent?'

'Not merely given it, but bestowed it blithely, jubilantly.'

'It beats me,' I said.

'What beats you?' demanded Ukridge, sensitive to the jarring note.

'Well, I don't want to cast any aspersions, but I should have thought the first thing she would have done would be to make searching inquiries about your financial position.'

'My financial position? What's wrong with my financial position? I've got considerably over fifty quid in the bank, and I'm on the eve of making an enormous fortune out of this Peppo stuff.'

'And that satisfied Lady Lakenheath?' I said, incredulously.

Ukridge hesitated for a moment.

'Well, to be absolutely frank, laddie,' he admitted, 'I have an idea that she rather supposes that in the matter of financing the venture my aunt will rally round and keep things going till I am on my feet.'

'Your aunt! But your aunt has finally and definitely disowned you.'

'Yes, to be perfectly accurate, she has. But the old lady doesn't know that. In fact, I rather made a point of keeping it from her. You see, I found it necessary, as things turned out, to play my aunt as my ace of trumps.'

'You told me the parrot was your ace of trumps.'

'I know I did. But these things slip up at the last moment. She seethed with gratitude about the bird, but when I seized the opportunity to ask her for her blessing I was shocked to see that she put her ears back and jibbed. Got that nasty steely look in her eyes and began to talk about clandestine meetings and things being kept from her. It was an occasion for the swiftest thinking, laddie. I got an inspiration. I played up my aunt. It worked like magic. It seems the old lady has long been an admirer of her novels, and has always wanted to meet her. She went down and out for the full count the moment I introduced my aunt into the conversation, and I have had no trouble with her since.'

'Have you thought what is going to happen when they do meet? I can't see your aunt delivering a striking testimonial to your merits.'

'That's all right. The fact of the matter is, luck has stood by me in the most amazing way all through. It happens that my aunt is out of town. She's down at her cottage in Sussex finishing a novel, and on Saturday she sails for America on a lecturing tour.'

'How did you find that out?'

'Another bit of luck. I ran into her new secretary, a bloke named Wassick, at the Savage smoker last Saturday. There's no chance of their meeting. When my aunt's finishing a novel, she won't read letters or telegrams, so it's no good the old lady trying to get a communication through to her. It's Wednesday now, she sails on Saturday, she will be away six months – why, damme, by the time she hears of the thing I shall be an old married man.'

It had been arranged between my employer and myself during the preliminary negotiations that I should give up my afternoons to the memoirs and that the most convenient plan would be for me to present myself at Thurloe Square daily at three o'clock. I had just settled myself on the following day in the ground-floor study when the girl Millie came in, carrying papers.

'My aunt asked me to give you these,' she said. 'They are Uncle Rupert's letters home for the year 1889.'

I looked at her with interest and something bordering on awe. This was the girl who had actually committed herself to the appalling task of going through life as Mrs Stanley Featherstone-haugh Ukridge – and, what is more, seemed to like the prospect. Of such stuff are heroines made.

'Thank you,' I said, putting the papers on the desk. 'By the way, may I – I hope you will – What I mean is, Ukridge told me all about it. I hope you will be very happy.'

Her face lit up. She really was the most delightful girl to look at I had ever met. I could not blame Ukridge for falling in love with her.

'Thank you very much,' she said. She sat in the huge arm-chair, looking very small. 'Stanley has been telling me what friends you and he are. He is devoted to you.'

'Great chap!' I said, heartily. I would have said anything which I thought would please her. She exercised a spell, this girl. 'We were at school together.'

'I know. He is always talking about it.' She looked at me with round eyes exactly like a Persian kitten's. 'I suppose you will be his best man?' She bubbled with happy laughter. 'At one time I was awfully afraid there wouldn't be any need for a best man. Do you think it was very wrong of us to steal Aunt Elizabeth's parrot?'

'Wrong?' I said, stoutly. 'Not a bit of it. What an idea!'

'She was terribly worried,' argued the girl.

'Best thing in the world,' I assured her. 'Too much peace of mind leads to premature old age.'

'All the same, I have never felt so wicked and ashamed of myself. And I know Stanley felt just like that, too.'

'I bet he did!' I agreed, effusively. Such was the magic of this Dresden china child that even her preposterous suggestion that Ukridge possessed a conscience could not shake me.

'He's so wonderful and chivalrous and considerate.'

'The very words I should have used myself!'

'Why to show you what a beautiful nature he has, he's gone out now with my aunt to help her do her shopping.'

'You don't say so!'

'Just to try to make it up to her, you see, for the anxiety we caused her.'

'It's noble! That's what it is. Absolutely noble!'

'And if there's one thing in the world he loathes it is carrying parcels.'

'The man,' I exclaimed, with fanatical enthusiasm, 'is a per-fect Sir Galahad!'

'Isn't he! Why, only the other day –'

She was interrupted. Outside, the front door slammed. There came a pounding of large feet in the passage. The door of the study flew open and Sir Galahad himself charged in, his arms full of parcels.

'Corky!' he began. Then, perceiving his future wife, who had risen from the chair in alarm, he gazed at her with a wild pity in his eyes, as one who has bad news to spring. 'Millie, old girl,' he said, feverishly, 'we're in the soup!'

The girl clutched the table.

'Oh, Stanley, darling!'

'There is just one hope. It occurred to me as I was –'

'You don't mean that Aunt Elizabeth has changed her mind?'

'She hasn't yet, But,' said Ukridge, grimly, 'she's pretty soon going to, unless we move with the utmost dispatch.'

'But what has happened?'

Ukridge shed the parcels. The action seemed to make him calmer.

'We had just come out of Harrod's,' he said, 'and I was about to leg it home with these parcels, when she sprang it on me! Right out of the blue sky!'

'What, Stanley, dear? Sprang what?'

'This ghastly thing. This frightful news that she proposes to attend the dinner of the Pen and Ink Club on Friday night. I saw her talking to a pug-nosed female we met in the fruit, vegetable, birds, and pet dogs department, but I never guessed what they were talking about. She was inviting the old lady to that infernal dinner!'

'But, Stanley, why shouldn't Aunt Elizabeth go to the Pen and Ink Club dinner?'

'Because my aunt is coming up to town on Friday specially to speak at that dinner, and your aunt is going to make a point of introducing herself and having a long chat about me.'

We gazed at one another silently. There was no disguising the gravity of the news. Like the coming together of two uncongenial chemicals, this meeting of aunt with aunt must inevitably produce an explosion. And in that explosion would perish the hopes and dreams of two loving hearts.

'Oh, Stanley! What can we do?'

If the question had been directed at me, I should have been hard put to it to answer; but Ukridge, that man of resource, though he might be down, was never out.

'There is just one scheme. It occurred to me as I was sprinting along the Brompton Road. Laddie,' he proceeded, laying a heavy hand on my shoulder, 'it involves your cooperation.'

'Oh, how splendid!' cried Millie.

It was not quite the comment I would have made myself. She proceeded to explain.

'Mr Corcoran is so clever. I'm sure, if it's anything that can be done, he will do it.'

This ruled me out as a potential resister. Ukridge I might have been able to withstand, but so potently had this girl's spell worked upon me that in her hands I was as wax.

Ukridge sat down on the desk, and spoke with a tenseness befitting the occasion.

'It's rummy in this life, laddie,' he began in moralizing vein, 'how the rottenest times a fellow goes through may often do him a bit of good in the end. I don't suppose I have enjoyed any period of my existence less than those months I spent at my aunt's house in Wimbledon. But mark the sequel, old horse! It was while going through that ghastly experience that I gained a knowledge of her habits which is going to save us now. You remember Dora Mason?'

'Who is Dora Mason?' inquired Millie, quickly.

'A plain, elderly sort of female who used to be my aunt's secretary,' replied Ukridge, with equal promptness.

Personally I remembered Miss Mason as a rather unusually pretty and attractive girl, but I felt that it would be injudicious to say so. I contented myself with making a mental note to the effect that Ukridge, whatever his drawbacks as a husband, had at any rate that ready tact which is so helpful in the home.

'Miss Mason,' he proceeded, speaking, I thought, in a manner a shade more careful and measured, 'used to talk to me about her job from time to time. I was sorry for the poor old thing, you understand, because hers was a grey life, and I made rather a point of trying to cheer her up now and then.'

'How like you, dear!'

It was not I who spoke – it was Millie. She regarded her betrothed with shining and admiring eyes, and I could see that she was thinking that my description of him as a modern Galahad was altogether too tame.

'And one of the things she told me,' continued Ukridge, 'was that my aunt, though she's always speaking at these bally dinners, can't say a word unless she has her speech written for her and memorizes it. Miss Mason swore solemnly to me that she had written every word my aunt had spoken in public in the last two years. You begin to get on to the scheme, laddie? The long and the short of it is that we must get hold of that speech she's going to deliver at the Pen and Ink Club binge. We must intercept it, old horse, before it can reach her. We shall thus spike her guns. Collar that speech, Corky, old man, before she can get her hooks on it, and you can take it from me that she'll find she has a headache on Friday night and can't appear.'

There stole over me that sickening conviction that comes to those in peril that I was for it.

'But it may be too late,' I faltered, with a last feeble effort at self-preservation. 'She may have the speech already.'

'Not a chance. I know what she's like when she's finishing one of these beastly books. No distractions of any sort are permitted. Wassick, the secretary bloke, will have had instructions to send the thing to her by registered post to arrive Friday morning, so that she can study it in the train. Now, listen carefully, laddie, for I have thought this thing out to the last detail. My aunt is at her cottage at Market Deeping, in Sussex. I don't know how the trains go, but there's sure to be one that'll get me to Market Deeping tonight. Directly I arrive I shall send a wire to Wassick – signed "Ukridge",' said the schemer. 'I have a perfect right to sign telegrams "Ukridge",' he added, virtuously, 'in which I tell him to hand the speech over to a gentleman who will call for it as arrangements have been made for him to take it down to the cottage. All you have to do is to call at my aunt's house, see Wassick – a splendid fellow, and just the sort of chump who won't suspect a thing – get the manuscript, and biff off. Once round the corner, you dump it in the nearest garbage-box, and all is well.'

'Isn't he wonderful, Mr Corcoran?' cried Millie.

'I can rely on you, Corky? You will not let me down over your end of the business?'

'You *will* do this for us, Mr Corcoran, won't you?' pleaded Millie.

I gave one look at her. Her Persian kitten eyes beamed into mine – gaily, trustfully, confidently. I gulped.

'All right,' I said, huskily.

A leaden premonition of impending doom weighed me down next morning as I got into the cab which was to take me to Heath House, Wimbledon Common. I tried to correct this shuddering panic, by telling myself that it was simply due to my recollection of what I had suffered at my previous visit to the place, but it refused to leave me. A black devil of apprehension sat on my shoulder all the way, and as I rang the front-door bell it seemed to me that this imp emitted a chuckle more sinister than any that had gone before. And suddenly as I waited there I understood.

No wonder the imp had chuckled! Like a flash I perceived where the fatal flaw in this enterprise lay. It was just like Ukridge, poor impetuous, woollen-headed ass, not to have spotted it; but that I myself should have overlooked it was bitter indeed. The simple fact which had escaped our joint attention was this – that, as I had visited the house before, the butler would recognize me. I might succeed in purloining the speech, but it would be reported to the Woman Up Top that the mysterious visitor who had called for the manuscript was none other than the loathly Mr Corcoran of hideous memory – and what would happen then? Prosecution! Jail? Social ruin?

I was on the very point of retreating down the steps when the door was flung open, and there swept over me the most exquisite relief I have ever known.

It was a new butler who stood before me.

'Well?'

He did not actually speak the word, but he had a pair of those expressive, beetling eyebrows, and they said it for him. A most forbidding man, fully as grim and austere as his predecessor.

'I wish to see Mr Wassick,' I said, firmly.

The butler's manner betrayed no cordiality, but he evidently saw that I was not to be trifled with. He led the way down that familiar hall, and presently I was in the drawing-room, being inspected once more by the six Pekingese, who, as on that other occasion, left their baskets, smelt me, registered disappointment, and made for their baskets again.

'What name shall I say, sir?'

I was not to be had like that.

'Mr Wassick is expecting me,' I replied, coldly.

'Very good, sir.'

I strolled buoyantly about the room, inspecting this object and that. I hummed lightly. I spoke kindly to the Pekes.

'Hallo, you Pekes!' I said.

I sauntered over to the mantelpiece, over which was a mirror. I was gazing at myself and thinking that it was not such a bad sort of face – not handsome, perhaps, but with a sort of something about it – when of a sudden the mirror reflected something else.

That something was the figure of that popular novelist and well-known after-dinner speaker, Miss Julia Ukridge. 'Good-morning,' she said.

It is curious how often the gods who make sport of us poor humans defeat their own ends by overdoing the thing. Any contretemps less awful than this, however slightly less awful, would undoubtedly have left me as limp as a sheet of carbon paper, rattled and stammering, in prime condition to be made sport of. But as it was I found myself strangely cool. I had a subconscious feeling that there would be a reaction later, and that the next time I looked in a mirror I should find my hair strangely whitened, but for the moment I was unnaturally composed, and my brain buzzed like a circular-saw in an ice-box.

'How do you do?' I heard myself say. My voice seemed to come from a long distance, but it was steady and even pleasing in timbre.

'You wished to see me, Mr Corcoran?'

'Yes.'

'Then why,' inquired Miss Ukridge, softly, 'did you ask for my secretary?'

There was that same acid sub-tinkle in her voice which had been there at our previous battle in the same ring. But that odd alertness stood by me well.

'I understood that you were out of town,' I said.

'Who told you that?'

'They were saying so at the Savage Club the other night.' This seemed to hold her.

'Why did you wish to see me?' she asked, baffled by my ready intelligence.

'I hoped to get a few facts concerning your proposed lecture tour in America.'

'How did you know that I was about to lecture in America?' I raised my eyebrows. This was childish.

'They were saying so at the Savage Club,' I replied. Baffled again.

'I had an idea, Mr Corcoran,' she said, with a nasty gleam in her blue eyes, 'that you might be the person alluded to in my nephew Stanley's telegram.'

'Telegram?'

'Yes. I altered my plans and returned to London last night instead of waiting till this evening, and I had scarcely arrived when a telegram came, signed Ukridge, from the village where I had been staying. It instructed my secretary to hand over to a gentleman who would call this morning the draft of the speech which I am to deliver at the dinner of the Pen and Ink Club. I assume the thing to have been some obscure practical joke on the part of my nephew, Stanley. And I also assumed, Mr Corcoran, that you must be the gentleman alluded to.'

I could parry this sort of stuff all day.

'What an odd idea!' I said.

'You think it odd? Then why did you tell my butler that my secretary was expecting you?'

It was the worst one yet, but I blocked it.

'The man must have misunderstood me. He seemed,' I added loftily, 'an unintelligent sort of fellow.'

Our eyes met in silent conflict for a brief instant, but all was well. Julia Ukridge was a civilized woman, and this handicapped her in the contest. For people may say what they like about the artificialities of modern civilization and hold its hypocrisies up to scorn, but there is no denying that it has one outstanding merit. Whatever its defects, civilization prevents a gently-bred lady of high standing in the literary world from calling a man a liar and punching him on the nose, however convinced she may be that he deserves it. Miss Ukridge's hands twitched, her lips tightened, and her eyes gleamed bluely – but she restrained herself. She shrugged her shoulders.

'What do you wish to know about my lecture tour?' she said.
It was the white flag.

Ukridge and I had arranged to dine together at the Regent Grill Room that night and celebrate the happy ending of his troubles. I was first at the tryst, and my heart bled for my poor friend as I noted the care-free way in which he ambled up the aisle to our table. I broke the bad news as gently as I could, and the man sagged like a filleted fish. It was not a cheery meal. I extended myself as host, plying him with rich foods and spirited young wines, but he would not be comforted. The only remark he contributed to the conversation, outside of scattered monosyllables, occurred as the waiter retired with the cigar-box.

'What's the time, Corky, old man?'

I looked at my watch.

'Just on half-past nine.'

'About now,' said Ukridge, dully, 'my aunt is starting to give the old lady an earful!'

Lady Lakenheath was never, even at the best of times, what I should call a sparkling woman, but it seemed to me, as I sat with her at tea on the following afternoon, that her manner was more sombre than usual. She had all the earmarks of a woman who has had disturbing news. She looked, in fact, exactly like a woman who has been told by the aunt of the man who is endeavouring to marry into her respectable family the true character of that individual.

It was not easy in the circumstances to keep the ball rolling on the subject of the 'Mgomo-'Mgomos, but I was struggling bravely, when the last thing happened which I should have predicted.

'Mr Ukridge,' announced the maid.

That Ukridge should be here at all was astounding: but that he should bustle in, as he did, with that same air of being the household pet which had marked his demeanour at our first meeting in this drawing-room, soared into the very empyrean of the inexplicable. So acutely was I affected by the spectacle of this man, whom I had left on the previous night a broken hulk, behaving with the ebullience of an honoured member of the family, that I did what I had been on the verge of doing every time I had partaken of Lady Lakenheath's hospitality – upset my tea.

'I wonder,' said Ukridge, plunging into speech with the same old breezy abruptness, 'if this stuff would be any good, Aunt Elizabeth.'

I had got my cup balanced again as he started speaking, but at the sound of this affectionate address over it went again. Only a juggler of long experience could have manipulated Lady Lakenheath's miniature cups and saucers successfully under the stress of emotions such as I was experiencing.

'What is it, Stanley?' asked Lady Lakenheath, with a flicker of interest.

They were bending their heads over a bottle which Ukridge had pulled out of his pocket.

'It's some new stuff, Aunt Elizabeth. Just put on the market. Said to be excellent for parrots. Might be worth trying.'

'It is exceedingly thoughtful of you, Stanley, to have brought it,' said Lady Lakenheath, warmly. 'And I shall certainly try the effect of a dose if Leonard has another seizure. Fortunately, he seems almost himself again this afternoon.'

'Splendid!'

'My parrot,' said Lady Lakenheath, including me in the conversation, 'had a most peculiar attack last night. I cannot account for it. His health has always been so particularly good. I was dressing for dinner at the time, and so was not present at the outset of the seizure, but my niece, who was an eye-witness of what occurred, tells me he behaved in a most unusual way. Quite suddenly, it appears, he started to sing very excitedly; then, after a while, he stopped in the middle of a bar and appeared to be suffering. My niece, who is a most warm-hearted girl, was naturally exceedingly alarmed. She ran to fetch me, and when I came down poor Leonard was leaning against the side of his cage in an attitude of complete exhaustion, and all he would say was, "Have a nut!" He repeated this several times in a low voice, and then closed his eyes and tumbled off his perch. I was up half the night with him, but now he seems mercifully to have turned the corner. This afternoon he is almost his old bright self again, and has been talking in Swahili, always a sign that he is feeling cheerful.'

I murmured my condolences and congratulations.

'It was particularly unfortunate,' observed Ukridge, sympathetically, 'that the thing should have happened last night, because it prevented Aunt Elizabeth going to the Pen and Ink Club dinner.'

'What!' Fortunately I had set down my cup by this time.

'Yes,' said Lady Lakenheath, regretfully. 'And I had been so looking forward to meeting Stanley's aunt there. Miss Julia Ukridge, the novelist. I have been an admirer of hers for many years. But, with Leonard in this terrible state, naturally I could not stir from the house. His claims were paramount. I shall have to wait till Miss Ukridge returns from America.'

'Next April,' murmured Ukridge, softly.

'I think, if you will excuse me now, Mr Corcoran, I will just run up and see how Leonard is.'

The door closed.

'Laddie,' said Ukridge, solemnly, 'doesn't this just show —'

I gazed at him accusingly.

'Did you poison that parrot?'

'Me? Poison the parrot? Of course I didn't poison the parrot. The whole thing was due to an act of mistaken kindness carried out in a spirit of the purest altruism. And, as I was saying, doesn't it just show that no little act of kindness, however trivial, is ever wasted in the great scheme of things? One might have supposed that when I brought the old lady that bottle of Peppo the thing would have begun and ended there with a few conventional words of thanks. But mark, laddie, how all things work together for good. Millie, who, between ourselves, is absolutely a girl in a million, happened to think the bird was looking a bit off colour last night, and with a kindly anxiety to do him a bit of good, gave him a slice of bread soaked in Peppo. Thought it might brace him up. Now, what they put in that stuff, old man, I don't know, but the fact remains that the bird almost instantly became perfectly pie-eyed. You have heard the old lady's account of the affair, but, believe me, she doesn't know one half of it. Millie informs me that Leonard's behaviour had to be seen to be believed. When the old lady came down he was practically in a drunken stupor, and all today he has been suffering from a shocking head. If he's really sitting up and taking notice again, it simply means that he has worked off one of the finest hang-overs of the age. Let this be a lesson to you, laddie, never to let a day go by without its act of kindness. What's the time, old horse?'

'Getting on for five.'

Ukridge seemed to muse for a moment, and a happy smile irradiated his face.

'About now,' he said, complacently, 'my aunt is out in the Channel somewhere. And I see by the morning paper that there is a nasty gale blowing up from the south-east!'

More About Penguins

Penguinews, which appears every month, contains details of all the new books issued by Penguins as they are published. From time to time it is supplemented by *Penguins in Print*, which is a complete list of all available books published by Penguins. (There are well over three thousand of these.)

A specimen copy of *Penguinews* will be sent to you free on request, and you can become a subscriber for the price of the postage. For a year's issues (including the complete lists) please send 3op if you live in the United Kingdom, or 6op if you live elsewhere. Just write to Dept EP, Penguin Books Ltd, Harmondsworth, Middlesex, enclosing a cheque or postal order, and your name will be added to the mailing list.

Note: *Penguinews* and *Penguins in Print* are not available in the U.S.A. or Canada

The Complete Golf Gamesmanship

Stephen Potter

Gamesmanship, which improved everybody's chances
and nobody's golf, appeared shortly after the Second
World War, though too late to stop it. After a decent interval
it was followed in 1968 by *The Complete Golf Gamesmanship*.
In 1970 Tony Jacklin won the American Open.
In 1971 Britain won the Walker Cup for the second
time in fifty years of driving and putting.
There may be no connection; or there may not.
To play safe (if no better) every golfer will do well to
buy this book.
There may be absolutely nothing in it; or again there
may not.
Certainly, whatever Stephen Potter has failed to do for
grip, stance, swing or stroke, he was and remains the
first to offer hope, with his match-winning system of
gambits, ploys and hampers (and the judicious use of
dogs), to the high-handicap rabbit.

P. G. Wodehouse in Penguins

'Mr Wodehouse's idyllic world can never stale. He will continue to release future generations from captivity that may be more irksome than our own. He has made a world for us to live in and delight in' –
Evelyn Waugh in a B.B.C. broadcast

The following titles by P. G. Wodehouse are available in Penguins:

* *Available in the U.S.A.*
Remaining titles not for sale in the USA.